PURE
SILK

SUSAN JOHNSON

KENSINGTON PUBLISHING CORP.
http://www.kensingtonbooks.com

BRAVA BOOKS are published by

Kensington Publishing Corp.
119 West 40th Street
New York, NY 10018

All Kensington Titles, Imprints, and Distributed Lines are available at special quantity discounts for bulk purchases for sales promotions, premiums, fund-raising, and educational or institutional use. Special book excerpts or customized printings can also be created to fit specific needs. For details, write or phone the office of the Kensington special sales manager: Kensington Publishing Corp., 119 West 40th Street, New York, NY, 10018, attn: Special Sales Department, Phone: 1-800-221-2647.

Brava Books and the B logo Reg. U.S. Pat. & TM Off.

ISBN-13: 978-1-57566-810-9
ISBN-10: 1-57566-810-6

First trade paperback printing: January 2004
First mass market printing: July 2011

10 9 8 7 6 5 4 3 2 1

Printed in the United States of America

Chapter

1

November 1868
Northern Japan

The sound of a horseman riding fast brought her sitting upright in her bed. The brazier fire was burning low, the air so chill, Tama pulled the silk quilt up to her chin as she listened to the pounding hoofbeats draw near. Reports of the battle between her father's army and imperial forces had begun filtering in that morning: the Lord of Otari had been defeated; the northern forces were in retreat; the Mikado's general had been killed; the imperial army was vanquished; victory lay with the north—no, the south. The rumors were so wildly divergent, it had been impossible to glean the truth.

The outer gate was creaking open. With the war raging, only her father's men would be allowed entrance at this time of night. Was her father back? Please, God, let it be him! Leaping up, she snatched a heavy quilted robe lying on the chest near her bed, slid her arms through the sleeves and ran.

Lanterns illuminated her swift passage through the corridors of Otari castle, the cries of retainers, a horse's high-pitched squeal, the creaking of the gate as it closed once again, echoing upward from the courtyard to her ears. Home to the Lords of Otari since time immemorial, the castle fortress was one of the most magnificent of princely homes, exquisitely painted screens, gold filigree work, carved pillars and lintels, lacquer work medallions flashing by as Tama raced through the halls and galleries leading to the courtyard.

At the sight of her servants standing heads bowed at the entrance portal, fear gripped her heart. Dashing past them, she came to an abrupt halt at the edge of the porch, a scream caught in her throat.

Her father's bodyguard was sprawled on the snow, still as death, the grooms standing at a respectful distance, uncertain what to do.

Quickly descending the short flight of stairs, she knelt beside Shosho, his life draining away in crimson rivulets already congealing on the snow. One arm was nearly severed at the shoulder, his body so lacerated by shrapnel and sword cuts it was a miracle he'd stayed alive long enough to reach the castle. Wakamatsu, where the northern forces had taken their stand, was ten *ri* distant.

As though sensing her presence, his eyes fluttered open and he struggled to rise. But his powerful body no longer responded to his brain's commands. Tears came to his eyes.

"We'll get the doctor," Tama murmured. "You'll soon be well again," she lied.

"Not this time," he whispered, a grimace of pain flickering over his features. "I bring—sad news, my lady." He gasped for air. "Wakamatsu fell."

"Is my—is he—" She couldn't bring herself to mouth the fatal words. "Tell me," she whispered.

"You are—now . . . the head of—Otari."

She went numb, momentarily paralyzed by inexpressible loss, aware of neither the cold nor the blood soaking through her robe, the servants' sobs and cries unheard. Her father was dead, their cause defeated, the castle at Wakamatsu, under siege for two weeks, had fallen. It was over. The clans of the northern alliance would be hunted down and exterminated—to the last living child.

"He's gone, my lady," her chamberlain murmured. Had protocol allowed, he would have taken her in his arms and offered her comfort.

Roused from her grief, she glanced up at Togai and nodded. Reaching out, she gently closed Shosho's eyes. He'd been faithful to the end, executing her father's last command by sheer force of will. "Go to heaven and smile again," she whispered to the young man who had always made her laugh, who had taught her the way of the sword without scoffing or teasing. "He must have a proper burial before we go," she said, slowly rising, suddenly realizing she was barefoot in the snow. Taking note of her bloodstained robe, she was reminded how little time they had before their enemies arrived. "No one of Otari is safe. Patrols could reach us within hours." Her voice was without emotion, her entire focus on what she must do. "Tell the staff to take what they wish from the castle before it's set afire."

After Shosho's burial, everyone packed what they could carry and with her own hands Tama put torch to the fortress to keep it from falling into enemy hands. Standing well away in the distant reaches of the garden, she and her staff watched the flames begin to destroy the castle, each leaping, crackling spiral of fire eating away at the towering structure that had been their home. Otari princes had lived on this land since the first emperor sat on his throne at Nara. And soon, the grand fortress would be gone. "I'm sorry, Father," she whispered, tears streaming down her face. "I'm so sorry," she repeated, at a loss to express the magnitude of her anguish. "I wish you could have come home," she softly murmured, wishing as a child might that everything could be as it once was.

As though in response to her wistful yearning, a huge section of the great curved third-story roof suddenly collapsed in an explosion that shook the ground. Wrenched back to reality, she reminded herself that she was a princess of the blood who understood what was expected of her. Wiping away her tears, she turned to her servants huddled around her and said with a determination that startled even herself, "I intend to bring Prince Komei home. We'll clear our name and rebuild the castle." She had wanted to offer her retainers hope, but as the words tumbled out, she found her spirits lifting. Why shouldn't Komei return? Why shouldn't they regain their titles and lands? Political pardons were not without conspicuous precedence in Japan.

"Will the young prince return?" Togai gravely asked, aware of the reasons Komei had left Japan.

"Under the circumstances, he must." The words

seemed to bolster her resolve; a new firmness resonated in her voice.

"And what of the *eta* woman?" Her maid's sneer was obvious.

"The prince's *wife* will return as well," Tama crisply replied. "The world is changing." There had long been talk in the more enlightened political circles of erasing the strict caste system in Japan. Even the outcasts such as Miyo would be accepted into society. Maybe her father had been fighting among other things for just such a cause—unlike the southern clans who wanted to maintain the conservative status quo. "I'll send word to you once we return," Tama said, offering the servants a confident smile, feeling suddenly as though anything were possible. Even escape. "Now go," she urged. "Scatter like the birds and leave a hundred trails for our enemies to follow. Until we meet again," she said with more hope than certainty, "may the Goddess of Mercy protect and comfort you."

But hope, however slight, was a blessing in the wretched sorrow of this night, and she desperately wanted to believe she was being shown the way.

She would travel to Edo, book passage to Paris and bring her brother home.

Had he not said as though prescient on the night he'd left, "If you ever need me . . ."?

Disguised as a peasant boy, Tama journeyed south, avoiding well-traveled roads with their checkpoints and guard posts, keeping company with pilgrims on their way to local shrines when possible, securing an occasional ride on a farmer's oxcart, above all—keeping to the shadow world.

The snows of the north gradually gave way to a parched brown landscape, the crowds of travelers and dust raised by the northwest winds increasing as she neared Edo.

The shogun had retired to his estates to study Chinese poetry she heard as she moved south, the man for whom her father had died enjoying a comfortable retirement. Anger and resentment further fueled her sense of purpose. It wasn't fair that Yoshinobu was allowed to live a princely life when her father was dead, his estates confiscated and the Otari clan labeled traitor.

Adauchi—vendetta—was powerful motive in Japan.

Perhaps, someday, she would cancel Yoshnobu's debt to her father.

As she arrived in the city, thoughts of retribution gave way to the practicalities of surreptitiously finding a ship to take her to France. Government spies would be everywhere; spies spied on spies in the capital. Every bureaucratic post was filled by two men so they could watch each other, distrust and suspicion the natural consequence of autocratic rule. But in a city of a million souls, perhaps one small peasant boy might escape detection.

Making her way to the Yoshiwara, the fabled pleasure quarter most likely to offer both anonymity and an obliging sea captain, she stood outside the entrance as evening fell, gazing at the colorful scene through a gray mist of rain. In such a place, one could lose oneself. In such a place, anything and anyone was for sale. In fact, *she* might have been for sale here had she been captured by the Mikado's soldiers and allowed to live.

But she wasn't caught yet.

Dressed roughly, her face half hidden in a muffler, her long hair tied up, shielded from the rain and closer inspection by a broad-brimmed straw hat, she slipped through the torch-lit Great Gate without notice. Moving down the central Naka-no-Cho avenue lined with the leafless cherry trees of winter, she kept well in the center of the throng. And the streets were crowded despite the rain, rickshaw men vying with each other to grab departing guests or deposit those arriving to take part in the pleasures offered by the brothels, restaurants, fancy shops, high fashion and Kabuki theaters. Hawkers wandered the streets lined with lanterned food stalls, their gaily printed awnings bright as those on the many snack sellers' carts. The air was filled with the twang of the three-stringed samisen and voices raised in song drifted out into the night from the brothels.

The Yoshiwara was even more popular since the emperor had moved the capital to Edo and foreigners had been allowed to do business in the city. And those *ketto*—hairy barbarians—were just what she needed right now. With luck and enough Mexican silver, the currency of commerce in the East, she would buy passage from Edo tonight.

As she progressed down the street, her heart was beating like a drum. Beyond the fear of capture, it was unheard of for a highborn lady to enter this district. On the other hand, sea captains were prime customers for the exotic wares the Yoshiwara dispensed, and she intended to find a bearded foreigner to take her away from her enemies.

A familiar face suddenly loomed into her line of vision and murmuring a quick prayer of gratitude, she eased out of the stream of humanity flowing down the busy thoroughfare. Taking shelter under an awning, she surveyed a red-lacquered palanquin and the burly seaman leaning against it, smoking his pipe. He was unmistakable—a giant of a man with carrot red hair and a matching beard she'd first seen at Niigata last summer. As first mate, he'd accompanied his captain to a meeting with her father and herself where the Lord of Otari had purchased five thousand repeating rifles and twenty cannon.

With their business concluded, her father had asked Captain Drummond if he was concerned about slipping back past the Mikado's naval blockade.

He'd run guns for the Confederacy through a Yankee blockade so tight you could hear the Yankee sailors sneeze, Captain Drummond had said with a smile. The Mikado's navy was child's play.

Such confidence would serve her well.

And no doubt, a gunrunner would be willing to overlook the fact that she was in flight from the authorities.

The red palanquin rested on the flags before a sumptuous Green House, the sailor seemingly immune to the rain, lounging against the porch railing smoking and exchanging witticisms with other

foreigners who passed by, his booming laughter
making her forget for a moment her utter peril.
Her father's retainers would wait for him like that,
enjoying their pipes and laughing while he visited
the teahouses. How long ago it all seemed. How
impossibly long ago. She shut her eyes briefly, half
hoping when she opened them she would be
home with a brazier fire burning, the scent of incense in the air, her father smiling at her as he listened to her read his favorite poems.

    She opened her eyes to another loud burst of
laughter, the chill night air in sharp contrast to her
dreams, the bawdy Yoshiwara so far removed from
the refinements of her home her eyes filled with
tears. But a daimyo's daughter didn't cry, nor did
she allow herself to be bowed by heartache. Drawing in a sustaining breath, she touched the fortune
in pearls out of sight beneath the plain blue
padded jacket, clutched her pack closer and debated how best to conceal herself within the American's palanquin.

Chapter

2

The moment Tama saw Red Beard ascend the stairs to the Green House and disappear inside, she moved toward the palanquin, forcing herself to walk slowly—as though she were out for a stroll. But once she reached the litter, she shot a glance at the bearers, saw that they were still enthralled by a performing acrobat and quickly jumped inside.

As she slid over the silk cushions, her wet clothes and muddied sandals stained the pale fabric—the smudges a sudden stark reminder of how much her world had changed. Only days ago, a servant would have shielded her from the rain with a parasol and lifted her sandals from her feet as she entered the palanquin; when she alighted, her sandals would have been replaced before her feet touched the ground. An anomaly now in a world speeding toward revolution, her servants' jealously guarded prerogatives as obsolete as muzzle loaders.

A thundering shout erupted from inside the

brothel, Red Beard's voice raised in impatient demand and Tama's reflections on the past gave way to more immediate perils. Quickly unwrapping her short sword from her pack, she shifted to one side of the door so she wouldn't be visible when it opened, gripped the hilt of her weapon, and waited.

A short time later, the wafting scent of perfume struck Tama's senses only seconds before a geisha's exquisitely coiffed head intruded into the palanquin. At the sight of Tama, she hesitated, her eyes flaring wide. "Get in," Tama hissed, her short sword raised in threat.

Displaying no emotion, the courtesan obeyed, seating herself in the small space with a fluid grace and composure only years of training could instill.

Quickly sliding the door shut, Tama frowned. "Where's Drummond?" She'd caught a bird of paradise when she'd been expecting the captain.

"I have no idea."

"His first mate came for you," Tama murmured, slipping her knife blade under the courtesan's throat. "So you know."

As the bearers lifted the palanquin, Sunskoku steadied herself against the sudden movement, not wishing to mar the perfection of her much-admired swanlike neck. And while the captain was charming for a barbarian outsider, she'd not reached her exalted position in the first ranks of *tayu* courtesans without understanding the subtleties of survival. "He waits for me at his residence," she offered, wincing slightly as the bearer's rhythmic step altered for a moment and the sharp blade nearly drew blood. "Please." She indicated the dagger with a slight motion of her fingers. "I have no intention of disclosing your presence."

Tama eased her blade away. "I'll kill you if you do," she warned.

"I have no intention of moving." Sunskoku calmly scrutinized her captor. The chief of the secret police whom she served would want to know of this peasant seeking Hugh-sama—just as he wished to know any information about the captain's activities. An arms dealer was, by definition, of questionable allegiance. "Hugh-sama's not expecting you, I assume," Sunskoku remarked, hoping to draw this little would-be ninja into conversation. "If he was, you would have knocked on his door."

"I mean him no harm."

Sunskoku smiled faintly. "He'd make short work of you if you did—even with your *wakizashi*."

Tama's gaze narrowed. "He could try."

"Such bravado from a peasant who's not even allowed to carry a *wakizashi*," Sunskoku noted, lightly teasing.

"The world's changing," Tama curtly noted.

Apparently, this young female with a cultured northern accent thought she was a match for Hugh-sama—an expert in Bushido. Although she might have other than martial plans in mind, Sunskoku reflected. "If you think to tempt the captain's vices," she casually observed, "he prefers women to boys." Although even in the dim light of the interior lantern, it was clear this was no boy.

"How fortunate for me."

"You mustn't know him or you wouldn't say that." Sunskoku smiled again, a practiced warm smile, as though they were old friends. This young woman of rank, disguised as she was, gave rise to keen speculation—especially with her accent and the recent fighting in the north, particularly in light of the captain's business interests.

"Why don't I leave his amorous activities to you."

"How fortunate for *me*," Sunskoku purred, parroting Tama's words. "He's so much larger than the ordinary man—if you know what I mean," she added with an arch smile. "And so very accomplished in giving pleasure." Her brows rose faintly. "One hardly expects such subtlety from a barbarian."

Color warmed Tama's cheeks.

"You poor boy, I've embarrassed you, haven't I?"

"Not in the least," Tama lied, glancing out the window, preferring not to discuss the captain's sexual expertise.

"Certainly, you're not too young for sex. As I recall," Sunskoku murmured, "village customs are—shall we say—crude in the extreme. You can't possibly be a—"

"Why have we entered the Kurobiki?" Tama abruptly interposed, taking note of the street into which they passed with sudden alarm.

"Hugh-sama resides here."

Tama was surprised the American had been allowed entry to the area reserved for daimyos and samurai. "He must be well connected." She tried to speak mildly, but her pulse had quickened. Only her enemies lived in this district now, the city estates of the defeated clans having been confiscated by the imperial army.

"Of course. He's a useful ally. The captain's friends who profit from his endeavors are from the highest echelons of the new government."

So he'd been dealing with both sides in the war. Not a comforting thought when she was about to put her life in his hands. *Dare she trust him?* Tama wondered. Or to what extent could she trust him? Might he turn her in for a reward? Should she offer him more? Or should she jump from the palanquin and flee while she still had the chance? Gauging the distance to the door, she was already planning her escape route when the bearers suddenly stopped before a torch-lit gate. The door opened a second later and Red Beard's bulk effectively blocked any escape. "The captain be waitin' fer you," Paddy McDougal growled. He didn't approve of Hugh's cure for discontent.

The captain had been drunk for nearly a fortnight—as he was every November. Not that he didn't have reason. Four years ago this month, his plantation had been seized by a carpetbagger, his wife had run off with a Yankee colonel and his ship had been broadsided and nearly sunk off Wilmington, North Carolina. Although Hugh had been unaware of the disastrous changes in his life until after Appomattox. By that time, the new owner of Indigo Hill had filed title to Hugh's plantation, and Lucinda was ensconced in a splendid mansion in Boston, enjoying a luxurious life compliments of her wealthy new husband.

Paddy had been with Hugh when he'd barged into his ex-wife's house on Beacon Hill demanding an explanation, and he'd been with him when they'd been thrown out into the street by ten burly stevedores who called themselves footmen.

"He's with me," Sunskoku calmly said to Paddy's sudden scowl as Tama followed her. "Hugh-sama won't mind."

She was right about that. Hugh didn't care about damned near anything now except that his bourbon didn't run out. "Suit yerself." Paddy nodded toward the gate. "He be waitin' inside."

Chapter
3

When the two women were ushered into his bedchamber, Hugh neither moved nor acknowledged their presence. Shrugging at his master's lack of response, the servant departed, sliding the door shut behind him, leaving the ladies waiting in the chill room, the scent of whiskey pungent in their nostrils.

The captain stood at an open window, his robe and hair ruffled by the brisk breeze blowing up from Edo Bay, his gaze narrowed against the wind. Restless, discontent, half drunk—or perhaps not drunk enough yet to still his mindless resentment—he wondered what he was doing so far from home. Not that he actually had a home anymore, he bitterly recalled. Or a reason not to get drunker.

The bay bordered by shadowy, pine-clad hills, the moon shining through a misty haze, the lights of the city spread out in a twinkling carpet offered an idyllic view. But weeks of drinking and a corrosive, all-inclusive sense of aggrievement curtailed his finer sensibilities and nature's beauty went unappreciated. Sullen memory looped through his brain in chafing frustration, all past and present grievances melding into a caustic moody umbrage that overlooked fine vistas and silvery moons.

If only his cargo had come down to Osaka in time, he would have been on the open seas by now, he bitterly reflected. If the war in the northern fiefs hadn't been so protracted, and the new administration less wrought with turmoil, his annual descent into alcoholic stupor would have transpired at sea in the solitude of his cabin, not in this damnable alien place. But silk merchants and war and political machinations had hindered his best laid plans, and here he was in a damnably foul mood.

In fact, he was no longer sure he wanted a woman tonight.

In his current temper, he wasn't sure he could be trusted with one.

Ordinarily, Sunskoku would have knelt and bowed her head to the floor until her client bade her rise, but the foreigners didn't seem to care—so she remained standing, her small hands hidden in her kimono sleeves, her expression a benign mask.

Too long a princely daimyo's daughter, unacquainted with either deference or humility, Tama chaffed at her servility. She surveyed the simple bedchamber and the captain's broad-shouldered form, took note of the chrysanthemum design—newly prohibited to all but the emperor's family—prominent on the back of the captain's robe, and

wondered whether he didn't know or didn't care
that he was in breach of imperial edict.

The courtesan beside her gave every appearance of infinite patience and if her own rather
pressing issues weren't so urgent, Tama might
have appreciated the geisha's cultivated manners.
However, *her* life was in peril. She politely cleared
her throat. To no effect. Noisily shifting her stance,
she coughed lightly.

Sunskoku turned her head, signaling silence
with a sharp glance.

Not sure whether to take offense or recognize a
superior judgment, Tama chose instead to take
charge. "Captain Drummond!" she said, speaking
in a resounding tone that even a man in his cups
couldn't ignore. "I need to discuss a business matter with you! If you would give me five minutes of
your time!"

At the crisp, clear Queen's English, Hugh
swung around, perhaps not above fantasizing after
weeks of considerable bourbon that Lucinda's
southern drawl had sharpened during her years in
Boston. Instead of the much imagined blonde,
blue-eyed prettiness of his ex-wife, however, he
met the dark, direct gaze of the Lord of Otari's
daughter. Even drunk, even in lantern light, even
in her ridiculous beggar's disguise he immediately
recognized the beautiful princess he'd met in Niigata last summer.

How the hell had she found him?

More to the point—what in bloody hell did
Lady Otari want, as if he didn't know. News of the
northern alliance's defeat was common knowledge.

"Did you hear me?" A small heated intensity colored Tama's voice. "This matter is of some importance."

"I heard. Give me a minute." He half lifted his hand as though asking her forbearance, when in fact, he was considering the advantages of turning her in. A fugitive of her distinction would realize enormous gratitude from the new government. In his case, that gratitude would no doubt take the form of highly lucrative contracts. The modernization of the Japanese army and navy was being accomplished with all speed.

He had no personal ties to Lady Otari. Why should he be concerned with her plight? The feudal lords of Japan had been fighting each other since the dawn of time. She wasn't his problem.

But a modicum of conscience still operated beneath the harsh cynicism he'd co-opted since the Civil War and he recalled the visits he'd had with the principled, highly educated Lord of Otari with fondness. Prince Otari had been more enlightened than most westerners, his hospitality gracious, their discussions of Japan's future spirited. "Damn," he softly swore, silently cursing the gentlemanly honor he'd not been able to completely jettison. He supposed he could at least listen to what she had to say. "If you could return later, Sunskoku," he said, smiling at the geisha who had been amusing him of late, "I'd appreciate it. Business first, I'm afraid. I'll have Paddy escort you back."

"There's no need for an escort, Hugh-sama. I'm perfectly safe." Sunskoku bowed low so the beauty of her nape was properly displayed.

"You're sure?" Hugh's courtesy was automatic, his mind already racing with worst case scenarios apropos of the young lady in peasant mufti leaving puddles on his floor.

"Absolutely sure." It wouldn't be prudent to point out that as Hiroaki's protégée she was above the law. His name alone was enough to put the most deadly assassin to flight.

Hugh smiled again. "My apologies for bringing you out in such dismal weather."

The courtesan waved away his apology. "I'm always at your service, Hugh-sama." She offered him a seductive glance. "Will I see you soon?" A test question that would indicate his visitor's importance.

Hugh shot a glance at Tama. "Of course," he said, a moment too late. "Why don't I send you a note."

That brief falter was problematic, but Sunskoku's smile was faultless in its warmth. "In that case, I'll look forward to hearing from you." Turning in a soft swish of silk, she exited the room.

The flagrant danger posed by Lady Otari was sobering Hugh more effectively than a gun to his head. Which cogent thought caused him to move to his bed and retrieve his revolver from under his pillow. Tucking the navy Colt into his trouser waistband, he motioned toward an outside door. "Might I suggest a stroll under the pergola." He spoke quietly in English, the language least likely to be understood by his servants. "You'll enjoy the view of the bay." Shrugging out of his robe as he approached her, he draped the quilted dressing gown over her shoulders. "You're wet," he said, smiling to allay her wariness. "It's cold out." He indicated her pack with a nod of his head. "Let me take that so you can slip your arms into the sleeves."

Quickly backing away, she shook her head.

He raised his hands, palms out. "I'm here to help, my lady. Your swords are safe. The servants aren't allowed to pilfer when they're in the pay of the court." At her startled look, he smiled. "Westerners are spied on by the government too. This is a country of equal opportunity observation. So put down your weapons and we'll find somewhere congenial to discuss"—his brows rose infinitesimally—"the present state of the world."

Indecision spiked through her senses. Dare she leave her weapons? Was this a ruse? Would the captain give her over to her enemies once she was unarmed? He was very large and close, much stronger than she, his bare, muscled chest only inches away, the heat of his body a discernable warmth as he towered over her. Moving back a step as though that small distance would equalize their great differences, she lifted her gaze.

"I'm not your enemy," he said softly.

"How do I know? You sell to both sides."

"That's business." Although, he wasn't entirely sure what this was. The role of knight errant was novel for him.

Could she afford to cavil? It wasn't as though she could return to the Yoshiwara in search of another foreign captain. Courtesans were well-known informers as was everyone associated with the floating world. The *yakuza*—criminal syndicates—that ran the houses of prostitution were tolerated by the authorities as long as they didn't

overstep their bounds. Which, in effect, meant a
degree of cooperation was necessary between the
government and the yakuza. So she had very few
options remaining. Correction—none, she sensibly decided. "Perhaps a discussion on the state of
the world would be in order," she said, her dark
eyes grave. "Your world, I expect, is a good deal
better than mine," she added, setting her silk-
wrapped swords on a nearby chest.

"And I intend it keep it that way," Hugh murmured, waving her toward the door. "After you, my
lady."

Although he wore only trousers, he seemed immune to the cold as he led them away from the
house, indifferent as well to the coarse gravel path
beneath his bare feet. Had the liquor he'd con-
sumed dulled his senses, Tama wondered, or was
he trained, like the Tendai monks, to withstand
pain and discomfort? Wrapped in the warmth of
his quilted robe, Tama followed him, grateful for
his gallantry whatever the state of his perceptions.

Stopping at last under a pergola overlooking the
bay, he didn't immediately speak, his hand resting
on one of the old gnarled wisteria vines that en-
twined the structure, his gaze on the bay below.
How exactly did one resolve honor, principle and
pragmatism? Or more pertinently, how did one
avoid gambling against overwhelming odds? If he
decided to take on Lady Otari's dilemma, he'd be
effectively disregarding every survival instinct he'd
subscribed to for years.

"I realize I'm imposing on you," Tama said quietly.

The understatement of the century or perhaps

the millennium, he glumly reflected, but he turned at her words and contemplated the woman seeking his assistance. Dwarfed by his robe, the skirts were puddled on the flagstones at her feet and if anyone looked as though they needed help against the might of the imperial government, she definitely did.

What the hell, he decided, cavalier disregard for what was proper and fitting practically his mantra of late. He should be able to hide one small woman for a few days. "Tell me what I can do for you," he said.

"Are you sober enough to understand?"

His brows flew up, amusement flickering in his eyes. "Not for weeks, I'm afraid, although your appearance certainly has had a sobering effect."

She had the grace to smile. "This is hardly the time for excessive scruples, I suppose."

He grinned. "I wouldn't think so. Unless you have other options—which I suspect you don't. Why don't you ask me what you've come here to ask."

His bluntness was off-putting, although she couldn't blame him. He, better than most, understood the hazards involved. "I need passage to France to bring my brother home. I'll pay you handsomely."

"Very well."

Instant danger signals bombarded her senses. Why was he so agreeable? "You have no questions?" She watched him closely. "No misgivings?"

He shrugged away the multitude and diverse caveats, most of which involved his head being separated from his body. "None that concern you," he said simply. "My cargo should be loaded soon or so I'm promised daily by the honorable merchant houses in Osaka," he added, a faint cynicism to his tone. "Not that time means much here, but once the silk is actually on board, I sail for London. To set you ashore at Calais shouldn't be a problem."

"You have no fear of the authorities?"

This would be an opportune time to change his mind, he thought, and for a fleeting moment he wondered why he was being chivalrous. Old habits died hard, he supposed, or maybe he was too easily tempted by exotic beauty. Perhaps, at base, he wasn't chivalrous at all. "I expect you to conceal yourself as well as you obviously have since Waka-matsu," he said gruffly, suppressing an unconscionable lust that would only complicate an already seriously complicated matter. "If you remain hidden, the authorities shouldn't be an issue. Although, just to be safe, I'll take you to a more secure location in the morning. If we were to travel tonight, every sentry point on the Tokaido road would report us to the authorities."

She understood the merits of losing oneself in a crowd—as she understood he was helping her with reluctance. "The house of Otari is in your debt." Her gaze was solemn. "We are grateful."

If someone had asked him why he was doing something so stupid he wouldn't have had an answer. After losing his plantation, his wife, and damned near his ship to a war he hadn't started, he no longer believed in causes. He only profited from them. "Under the circumstances, I'll require a substantial sum to take you out of the country," he said coolly, not wanting her gratitude. Wanting instead, a simple business arrangement that would allow them both to survive.

She heard the sudden chill in his voice and wondered once again whether he could be trusted. But she needed to reach her brother and, at the moment, Captain Drummond was her only means to that end. "Name your price and I'll pay it," she said.

Chapter

4

When O-metsuke, Chief Inspector, Hiroaki entered the anteroom to his office an hour later, his expression was forbidding. As the supreme inspector of the government, he reported directly to the senior officials who advised the Mikado. He was well aware of his consequence. "I trust this information is important," he said coldly. "You've taken me from my pleasures."

A fact Sunskoku was well aware of since he spent most evenings with his mistress. And if Hiroaki hadn't purchased her contract from the Green House, she might have mentioned *her* inconvenience in having to wait so long. "I believe you'll find it of interest," she said instead, offering him a serene smile as she raised her head from a bow. He'd promised her freedom in two years if she served him well and for that she could be tractable. "Does the name Otari mean anything to you?"

"Don't toy with me," he snapped, but he immedi-

ately waved her into his office, ordering his bodyguards to stay outside.

Walking through his office, he entered his private chambers, carefully shutting the door before
turning to Sunskoku who had once again pros-
trated herself as was required for a man of Hiroaki's station. "You have something to tell me?"
His voice was gruff and he didn't bid her rise from
her knees as he might have if he chose to be gracious.

It was obvious he was trying to curtail his excitement. Did the old fool think she couldn't see it in
his eyes? Did he think she'd survived the Yoshiwara on her beauty alone? But her voice was sub-
dued when she spoke, her gaze half lifted in
deference to his rank. "I've seen Princess Otari,
Your Excellency."

His gaze went shuttered as though he'd realized
his lapse. "Where? When?"

A shame the chief couldn't still the slight trem-
ble in his voice. "At Captain Drummond's house
earlier in the evening," she calmly replied, careful
not to mention she'd accompanied the princess
there. "Lady Otari was in the garden with Drummond when I arrived. I was sent away, but naturally
returned to overhear their conversation. The servants you've placed there are not sufficiently bilin-
gual to be really useful, I'm afraid."

"When I want your advice, I'll ask for it," he
muttered. "Go on."

"The princess asked Captain Drummond to
take her to France. He agreed," Sunskoku replied
succinctly.

"Are they still at his home?"

"As far as I know."

"That will be all." He dismissed her with a curt nod.

"The captain is armed, as are his crew." Her warning was meant to ingratiate.

Hiroaki smiled tightly. "I'm aware of the stupid barbarians' customs, but *o-niwaban,* one in the garden, as we call the ninja, are never seen until it's too late."

The Mikado's assassins might be expert at their craft, but the captain's men were a motley crew of mercenaries who weren't above a murder or two themselves. Not that Sunskoku was inclined to offer further counsel. Hiroaki had made it clear he didn't want her advice. "I'll bid you good night, then, O-metsuke." *And much good fortune against the captain's repeating rifles,* she mused cynically.

Already moving toward the door, Hiroaki didn't reply and a moment later Sunskoku was alone, only the echo of running footsteps resonating in her ears. Rising from her knees, Sunskoku glanced around the stark room from which such evil emanated and congratulated herself for performing her part so well. As the sole support of her family, she knew her duty, just as she knew why poor families sold their daughters into the floating world. But her twenty-year contract might be shortened if she pleased the Mikado's chief inspector. Which meant dismissing issues of good and evil and walking from this room without a backward glance.

But then, never looking back had become her way of life.

Chapter
5

Dressed in a wool shirt and chamois trousers, Hugh sat with his back against the wall, his boot-clad feet stretched out in a sprawl to deter anyone who might be disposed to enter by the hall door. His revolvers were strapped to his hips, his rifle on the floor beside him, his senses on full alert—or relatively so after a fortnight of drinking. Actually, he could use a drink now. But he wouldn't because he didn't trust Sunskoku; he didn't trust his servants. He didn't trust anyone in this city but his men who like he, were armed and waiting.

The princess slept soundly on the futon he'd rolled out for her, her breathing so light it was barely audible even in the quiet of his room. She'd not argued when he'd suggested she try to sleep. A sensible woman. Although she had to have considerable intelligence to survive so long with the hunt for her at full cry. Perhaps she had the advantage of being small enough to hide anywhere, he reflected, gazing at her slender form scarcely visible beneath the bulky silk quilts. Unlike Lucinda, he thought incongruously—as though it mattered who was taller or shorter, larger or smaller. When really nothing mattered except they survive the night and get the hell out of there at first light. The Tokaido came to life at dawn, the crowds of farmers and merchants thronging the road sufficient to allow even a foreigner and his servant to go unnoticed.

The captain planned on taking the princess to the small teahouse where he'd spent a month last year waiting for one of his ships to dock. It was off the beaten path, well outside the venues common to westerners, and the owner had a fondness for him. He half smiled in the darkness at the memories of those lazy spring days with Oen and her staff. Perhaps he'd have time to tarry briefly before his silk arrived in Osaka. While Sunskoku's sexual talents were masterful—even inspiring on occasion—there was something to be said for naivete. And Oen had a simple sweetness that charmed.

Perhaps the sudden appearance of the princess had been opportune, the perfect antidote for his useless dwelling on the past. He was wide awake, more so than he'd been in days, his senses alive, hot-blooded energy coursing through his veins. Sex and battle had that effect on him—a restless excitement stirring him to action.

And at the moment, battle was imminent, unless he missed his guess. A shame the princess was off-limits. She was damned convenient. Glancing at her, he felt himself harden in defiance of practicalities and good sense. Reminding himself that taking advantage of a lady in distress was reprehensible, not to mention a violation of his friendship with her father, he forcibly repressed his lust.

But her exquisite beauty was tantalizing. He remembered first seeing her last summer in her pale green kimono, her dark hair tied back loosely like a young maid, and thinking how tempting she was. And tonight, even in peasant garb, the delicacy of her face and form lured the senses.

She'd not been afraid of asking for what she wanted last summer, either, taking part in the arms negotiations with mastery and aplomb—just as she had spoken up tonight. She'd not exactly ordered him to listen to her, but damned near. *Would she be as demanding in bed?* he mused, his erection swelling at the tantalizing thought. Would she take charge, as she had tonight? Or would she play the submissive role expected of Japanese females? He swore softly, images of the princess in his bed damnably provoking.

"I brung more reason to swear, Boss." Paddy stepped into the room. "The servants just run off."

Nothing like approaching death to clear the mind, Hugh thought grimly, coming to his feet in a surge of lean muscle. "The men are in place?" His voice was crisp.

"Yup. The geisha set you up, sure as hell."

"Or one of the staff. Not that it matters. Shoot first, ask questions later. And no heroics." Hugh jabbed his finger at Paddy. "Understood? We have the advantage with our Spencer rifles. No one has to get hurt."

"Unless they overrun us."

"We'll have to see that they don't."

"Gotcha, Boss." Paddy nodded toward the bed. "You gonna wake her?"

The captain shook his head. "She'll get in the way. I'll guard her door. You take your post at the end of the veranda." He didn't seriously question their ability to defend themselves. Rifles against swords weren't even close. "Once this is over, we'll find a safer venue. Oen's teahouse should work. You and the men make for the ship."

"You'll join us in a couple of days?"

Again, the captain shook his head. "Not till the cargo is loaded and you're ready to weigh anchor. Let me know." Hugh suddenly lifted his hand, the faint sound of soft footfalls striking the ground an indication the perimeter fence was being breached. Quickly moving to the door opening onto the veranda, he stationed himself on the verge of the porch, motioning Paddy to his left. From his post, Paddy passed the command to shoot on sight to the next man and he to the next and so the warning traveled around the line of defenders circling the house.

As the first shadowy form came into view, Hugh fired, the rattle of gunfire suddenly exploding in a steady, clamorous din as wave after screaming wave of Hiroaki's men swarmed the residence. The attackers didn't turn and run this time, but kept coming despite their casualties, apparently highly motivated—more likely in fear of reprisals should their mission fail. Which meant someone knew the princess was here, Hugh realized, keeping his finger hard on the trigger, spraying a deadly fire into the sword-wielding intruders. It wasn't as though assaults on westerners were rare; he'd seen his share of them. Resentment against foreigners ran high. But in the past, if faced with withering fire, the samurai fled to fight another day. These men didn't.

Tama's high-pitched scream spun him around. "Paddy!" he shouted, sprinting toward the bedroom door. "Cover me!" Tossing his rifle aside, he dove through the opening, rolling up into a crouch, revolvers raised. But the princess didn't need saving. She was standing over the body of her attacker. Even in the shadowed room it was apparent the man was dead—sliced through from shoulder to opposite hip with the deadly *kesa-giri* blow.

"He came through the roof!" She pointed upward, the noise of gunfire overwhelming her voice.

"Nice work!" He would have said more—like *how the hell did you do that?*—if the screams of their attackers hadn't indicated a renewed assault. Slipping his revolvers back in their holsters, he grabbed her hand and waved Paddy off. "I'm taking her to safety!" he yelled.

"I can defend myself!" Tama protested, digging in her heels.

Maybe against one man, but not the horde outside. "That's great," he muttered, dragging her across the tatami mats.

"Let go!"

He felt the air move past his ear as she hoisted her sword and, swivelling around, he swung his hand downward in a blur, chopping her *katana,* long sword, from her grasp. "Stupid bitch," he growled, scooping her up into his arms and striding toward the hallway. "Don't give me any fucking trouble."

How dare he strike her, she fumed, going rigid in his arms. How dare he touch her without permission!

At least she couldn't stab him now, he thought, her stiff silence preferable to being sliced open by her wicked blade. And despite her affront he needed to get her to safety. She was the attackers' target, no mistake. They'd even known what room she was in.

Traversing the corridor at a near run, he entered the parlor, walked directly to the *tokonoma*, the household shrine, and set her on her feet. "Don't move," he commanded gruffly. "Don't even think about it." Reaching out, he pulled away the embroidered screen on the rear wall of the niche, jerked the back panel aside and motioned her forward with a snap of his fingers.

"What if I refuse?" Her mouth firmed into a stubborn line.

"Don't be stupid. They've come for you."

"Then I need my weapons."

"I've plenty." His gaze flicked downward to the bandoleers crossed over his chest, the *wakizashi* short sword stuck through his belt, his revolvers riding his hips. "Do me a favor, lady, get the hell in there," he rapped out, taking a step backward to give her clearance.

"Do I have a choice?"

"Not if you want to live."

She stepped up onto the shallow dais, her eyes flashing. "I'm doing this under duress," she muttered testily.

"Lady, we're all under duress in case you haven't noticed," he snarled. "Move it."

Following her through the opening a second later, he slid the panel closed, descended a short range of steps after her and entered a large chamber he'd had excavated beneath his house in the event some disgruntled buyer took issue with him. The arms business was by nature one of fleeting alliances.

"This is totally unnecessary," Tama fulminated, her cheeks flushed with anger. "I'm well trained; I can defend myself."

"Not against fifty ninja." He threw her an irritable glance as he locked the door. "You're not that good."

"Surely you and your men could do *your* share."

Suppressing the inclination to call the princess any number of vulgar epithets that came to mind, he counted to ten before turning around. "We can hold our own," he brusquely said. "Here or anywhere." He and his men had fought their way through four years of Civil War and four years more on the pirate-ridden China Sea. He didn't have to explain their bravery or courage to any spoiled blue-blood princess.

"I'd feel better if I were armed."

"It's not necessary. We're safe here."

"Such assurance, Captain." Her tone was snide.

He smiled tightly. "That's me. Mr. Assured."

Her brows rose and she surveyed him with a mocking glance. "Is it possible you're afraid of an armed woman?"

He gave her an acid look. "Look, lady, I'm saving your ass, you're not saving mine. If you don't want passage to France, be my guest—go upstairs and give hell to the mob of ninja trying to kill us.

Otherwise, sit down," he growled, waving her to a chair, "and shut the fuck up. Some of my men might be wounded because of you. I'm not in a good mood."

Tama wasn't certain of some of the captain's words, her English tutor having been an Anglican missionary, but she was fully aware the captain's temper had reached a point where he meant what he said. If she chose to leave, he'd let her. And much as she hated to acknowledge his accuracy when he was so annoyingly surly—he *was* right. She couldn't meet her attackers alone. "Forgive me," she said, avoiding outright capitulation with an unspecified apology. "I was tactless."

"Damn right you were."

"As were you." It was difficult to yield completely when her life had been that of an idolized princess.

"I apologize." Then he smiled the smile that had charmed countless women in countless countries because the sound of gunfire had been steadily diminishing the past few minutes, which meant they'd be leaving soon. And he didn't relish traveling with an angry female.

"Thank you," she said with an imperious lift of her chin.

"You're welcome." His grin was boyish and smoothly affable. "I was out of line, Princess. Sorry."

The flashing warmth of his smile was practiced, captivating and always successful in disarming wrathful women. And the princess was no more immune than the scores of women before her.

The captain and his men *had* been instrumental

in saving her from her attackers, she suddenly thought, feeling a newfound charity toward her benefactor, thinking perhaps she'd viewed him too harshly. "I *am* grateful for your help," she murmured, actually experiencing a modicum of guilt over her conduct. "I wouldn't want you to think I wasn't."

"Don't mention it. My pleasure." But his attention was attuned to the heavy tread approaching. "My first mate's on his way," he said, lifting his chin upward toward the sound. "The attackers must have fled. They'll be back, though, so pack up your swords. I'll carry them." He understood the bond between a swordsman and his weapon, but they'd be traveling fast. He didn't want her burdened.

"I'm capable of carrying my own swords. I always have—then again," she quickly interposed, taking note of his faint scowl, "if you wish to." Apparently, the captain's authority wasn't open to question. "May I ask where we're going?"

"To a teahouse I know. We'll be safe there until my ship sails."

"Provided we reach it undetected." She gave him a considering look. "You're very tall *and* a foreigner."

"A foreigner traveling with his servant," he pointedly noted. "Not such an unusual sight. Just don't argue with me in public."

"Yes, Captain."

Her sudden demureness was unexpected; his gaze narrowed.

"I understand the hazards. You'll find me completely amenable."

She shouldn't have smiled. It incited sudden, unethical, wholly inappropriate desires, particularly when she'd said, "completely amenable" in that breathy little whisper. "I'm glad to hear it." He tried to keep his voice neutral and didn't quite succeed.

It was her turn to register doubt, his soft innuendo overtly sensual.

"I didn't mean to suggest—"

"Nor I." But his heated gaze belied his words and her breathing had changed.

"This is wholly—"

"—impractical."

"I was going to say unwelcome."

He should have apologized, but he recognized female arousal whether she chose to acknowledge it or not. "Were you?" he said instead, as though he didn't believe her.

She should have protested, voiced her disapproval, but his dark eyes were mesmerizing, his beauty striking at close range, and if she'd been able to ignore her initial response to his sexually charged insinuation, she no longer could. "Please," she breathed. "I beg of you . . ."

Was she asking or rebuffing him—her words as ambiguous as the tremulousness in her gaze. "We're alone," he murmured, gently touching her cheek, her skittishness perversely exciting. "No one will come in."

"Don't," she whispered.

She didn't mean it, of course, the word barely audible. "We've plenty of time . . ." Slipping his finger under her chin, he lifted her face, her half-parted lips blatant invitation.

Paddy's sharp rap on the door shattered the hush.

"I can tell him to leave . . ." His head dipped so their eyes were level.

His dark hair had swung forward when he'd lowered his head and the temptation to touch it made her fingers tingle.

"Tell me what you want," he murmured.

A second passed, two before she rallied her traitorous senses. "I don't want this," she said, taking a step back.

Hugh's gaze went shuttered, his hand dropped away. "As soon as your swords are packed, we leave," he said briskly, and turned to unlatch the door.

"I appreciate your understanding."

He shot her a cool glance. "Five minutes and we leave, with or without you."

Before she could register anger the door swung open.

"Two of them buggers got away," Paddy announced, disapproval in every churlish syllable. "They'll be comin' back with reinforcements."

"Take the men and go. No horses; they'll attract too much attention this time of night. We'll be right behind you." Hugh nodded at Tama. "Ready?"

"Of course," she replied crisply and slipped past the men, grateful for having been saved from a terrible near-blunder. What had happened between the captain and herself was a moment of hysteria . . . understandable under the circumstances. Anyone would have felt sympathy for a man who rendered such valuable service. But it certainly wouldn't happen again.

When Hugh reached his bedroom after some last minute instructions to Paddy, Tama had rolled up her two swords in a length of silk and secured them. She handed them over to Hugh with a businesslike nod. "I'm ready whenever you are."

"Stay close behind me," the captain ordered, adding her pack to his, tossing in a few additional rounds of ammunition. "And try to keep up."

"That won't be a problem."

Everything in his life was a fucking problem now, thanks to her, Hugh thought irritably. Throwing his pack on his back, he cast a quick glance around the room, not wishing to leave any evidence of the princess. But all she had was the clothes on her back and her swords—both accounted for. With a faint bow, he waved her out the door.

The ninja reinforcements arrived hard on their heels, Hiroaki himself in charge. But the chief inspector kept his distance until it was evident the dwelling was deserted; heroism was for witless men. Once his lieutenant signaled an all clear, Hiroaki entered the residence with his bodyguards and impatiently waited for some useful clues to be unearthed. But his men tore the house apart to no purpose. Hugh's home was bereft of personal items outside his numerous bourbon bottles. Other than the fact that the captain drank to excess, there was nothing to give the slightest indication of the style of man who had lived there or of his possible destination.

As it became increasingly evident the princess had eluded them, Hiroaki's frustration was taken out on anyone not sensible enough to get out of his way. "Heads will roll," he raged, stomping through the house. "Incompetent fools! I practically gave you the princess! All you had to do was bring her in!" Capturing the Princess of Otari would have meant not only far-reaching fame for him, but an important promotion, maybe even a place on the Mikado's senior council. Damn the stupidity of the troops he was forced to rely on! They would pay dearly for their ineptness, he fumed, kicking aside a dead ninja who lay in his path. He should have been discussing his new position with the court council by now.

Ordering his men to line up in the courtyard, his voice held the cold finality of death. Scanning the assembled ninja, their heads bowed, many planning their death poems, Hiroaki had just raised his arm to point out his first victim, when one of his bodyguards ran into the courtyard.

"A sentry on Lord Nogu's estate at the base of the hill saw a tall foreigner pass down the lane behind the gardens!" he cried. "The westerner was with a peasant boy!"

"When?" Hiroaki snapped.

"Not more than twenty minutes ago!"

"I trust you dolts are capable of following a trail," the chief inspector snarled, surveying his men with an icy gaze. "I want Drummond's vessel found. I want him found. I want his men found. I want the princess back in Edo within the day. Now, get out of my sight," he curtly ordered. "And don't come back without the princess and the foreign scum.

Chapter

6

Conscious their trackers would be professionals, Hugh avoided the obvious egress points from the city—the river, the waterfront, the routes leading to the Tokaido, hoping to gain a lead on their pursuers. Once beyond the city, he knew some of the lesser known paths and byways thanks to various excursions he'd taken with his crew, many of whom were native to Asia, familiar with Japan and able to move freely in the country.

In contrast, Tama's knowledge of the south was limited. Her father had lived in Edo on alternate years as required by law—although the shogun had recently dismissed the requirement. But unlike other families of feudal lords who had remained permanent hostages in the capital, the Prince of Otari had ignored the centuries-old edict and his wife and children had stayed in the north.

Consequently, Tama viewed the captain's circuitous route through meandering lanes and dark alleys with admiration and not a little curiosity. For a man only recently allowed to do business in the capital, he was extremely familiar with the underbelly of Edo. But she knew better than to question him. The paths they traveled were so narrow, their shoulders brushed against the bordering houses from time to time. The sound of a voice would filter through the paper-thin walls with ease.

Not that twisted routes and utter silence were of much value with the captain's huge boot prints giving them away, she thought, hoping they were well ahead of their pursuers.

Hugh cursed the rain, knowing their trail was blatant. Although, that was the least of his worries after being seen by the sentry in the Kurobiki district. Not to mention the princess wasn't going to be able to keep up all night as he'd intended, regardless that he'd shortened his stride. She was having to run even to maintain his slowed pace.

The teahouse hours away was going to be out of the question. Altering his plans as they moved through the outlying districts, he decided to try to reach the Buddhist temple at Sano. If they could stay ahead of their trackers, they could disappear into the grotto beneath the Amida—sacred ground beyond the powers of the government to defile. At least in theory.

Traveling the Tokaido was no longer an option. If they'd been seen, as he suspected, the road south would be awash with agents and police. He could only hope the unsullied record of delay at the merchant houses of Osaka continued unabated because it looked as though he and the princess might be guests of the reverend abbot for some time.

Three hours later, Hugh literally dragged Tama up the last hundred yards of rain-washed stone leading to the Temple of the Shin-Shiu sect. He would have picked her up and carried her a mile back, but wasn't certain she would have allowed such license. And this near to their goal, he didn't want any unnecessary controversy.

"We're almost there," he murmured, dipping his head to make sure she heard.

"They won't—let us . . . in," she gasped. The heavy wooden gate was closed, and monastery or not, it was rare to allow entrance after dark.

"There's a smaller gate to the left—under that pine. I have a key. I'm a generous donor," he said in response to her astonished expression. "More importantly, my donations take the form of the latest weapons." Considering how many political dissenters had been banished to monasteries, it wasn't unusual for monks to be of a militant nature. "This temple lent their aid to the losing side in the war," he added, leading her toward the small gate. "We should be safe."

If she'd been able to catch her breath she would have offered the captain her heartfelt gratitude.

Unlocking the studded wooden gate, he pushed it open and lifted her over the foot-high threshold. Setting her down, he slipped his pack from his shoulders and let it drop to the ground. "I'll be back soon," he murmured. "Wait here."

As if she could have moved, she thought, nodding agreement, her legs collapsing beneath her as though at last she had leave to give in to weakness. The ground was cold, but she didn't notice, sweating from their headlong pace. She shut her eyes . . . just for a minute . . .

When Hugh returned from concealing what he could of their tracks, he found her sprawled on the grass, fast asleep. Standing over her small form, he gazed at her with the look of a stranger. *Why me?* he thought grimly. Why was *he* burdened with the responsibility for her safety? Why not some other of the hundreds of captains in Edo last night? Reluctant from the beginning to take on the role of savior, he wondered if he could just leave her with the abbot. She was relatively safe now. Hadn't he done enough by taking her out of Edo? How much more was he expected to do?

But no easy answers were forthcoming, no simple solution offered itself, and for a graceless moment he questioned whether he was being punished for his sins. But that would only be possible, he decided a moment later, if he actually believed in God.

No, this was no more than the fickle hand of fate. He happened to be in the vicinity—and voila.

Bad luck, bad karma.

And now he was screwed.

But it was play or pay in this unforgiving world and exhaling softly, he bent to pick up his pack. Slipping the strap over his shoulder, he stooped to lift Tama's slight weight into his arms. At least she'd cut short his drinking, he acknowledged, if there were a bright side to this race for survival. Cradling her in his arms, he hoped like hell she didn't wake up and scream.

But she didn't so much as pause in her breathing.

Instead, she nestled against his chest with a small contented sigh.

He was shocked to find himself reacting to her sleepy acquiescence. You'd think he'd be too exhausted to even think about sex. Forcibly tamping down his initial reaction—and his second through tenth as well—he told himself to behave. He wasn't an animal, or at least not all of the time, he noted cynically. Although, too many years of war made it impossible to claim more than a conditional membership in the brotherhood of virtuous men. But regardless of his shortcomings, the princess didn't need to be the object of his carnal impulses. She needed a protector—and not that kind. The right kind.

Cursing the fact that he'd ever met Sunskoku and by default the Princess of Otari, he moved toward the small lantern-lit pavilion on the hill.

Chapter

7

A servant opened the door as Hugh approached, the abbot coming forward to greet him as he entered the small dwelling.

"I've come to beg asylum, Reverend Abbot," Hugh murmured, bowing his head to the man who wore monk's robes with the air of a prince. "Assassins are on our trail."

"Our gates are closed to the outside world, as you know."

"They may seek entrance in the name of the imperial government."

Lord Yabe, who had once been the shogun's favorite cousin, smiled. "We live by a higher law, Hugh-san. They will not be admitted. You and your woman are safe."

"She's not mine. I've become involved by accident and I'd—"

"Masao will take her." The abbot lifted his hand to beckon his servant forward. "Come, Hugh-san. Have tea with me and tell me of this involvement that brings assassins to our quiet sanctuary."

Once Tama was transferred to the sturdy arms of the young servant and carried away, Hugh followed the former governor of Edo to a small four-and-a-half tatami mat room, the traditional size for the tea ceremony. Taking off his boots, he sat opposite the abbot, grateful for the warmth of a brazier. The men spoke of trivialities as the water boiled and the tea brewed, and only after their first contemplative sips of the scented beverage did the conversation turn to serious matters.

"I'm afraid I may have brought war to your door. The Princess of Otari is outlawed, as you may have heard."

"Ah." The abbot drank another sip of tea before looking up again. "With the Princess of Otari here, we'll have more than a few assassins to contend with."

"I was hoping we could conceal ourselves in the grotto beneath the Amida and put them off our scent."

"Of course."

"Perhaps you can plead ignorance and they'll go on their way."

"Or we can help them along." The abbot was of middle age, but fit and trim, his strong sword arm testament to the fact that he spent more time in the dojo than in prayer.

"I'm hoping it won't come to that. The Princess would prefer leaving the country undetected."

"I understand. We will be discreet."

"I also need a message delivered to my vessel in Osaka."

"A simple task, Hugh-san."

"I'm afraid we might be here for some time before my cargo is on board."

"Don't trouble yourself, my friend. You are welcome for any length of time. Tell me now, how did the princess happen to come to you?"

Hugh explained as much as he knew, giving the abbot a brief account of the attack on his house in Edo as well. "She's hoping to reach her brother in Paris. I offered her passage on the *Southern Belle*."

"Not without misgivings, I gather." The ex-commander of the shogun's army appraised his guest.

Hugh shrugged. "Can you blame me? She presents enormous risks."

The abbot smiled. "But you were charitable, nonetheless."

"Hardly. She's paying me a fortune."

"You fail to perceive your own kindness, Hugh-san. You've brought her here tonight at much peril."

"Perhaps I like a challenge," Hugh murmured sardonically.

"Or perhaps your heart opened to someone in need."

"You give me too much credit, *Wajo*. The princess is very beautiful and vulnerable. I may be far from charitable."

"You westerners mistake lust for perversity when it's no more than a common impulse. If the princess is trained in Bushido as you say, she faces the world with strength and courage. She may find *you* vulnerable."

Hugh set his tea bowl down. "No," he said firmly, the thought incredible. "She won't."

"Disbelief can change to belief in the span of a heartbeat," the abbot replied calmly.

"Like you've embraced monkhood, you mean."

Lord Yabe's mouth curved into a wry smile. "If peace were to come to our land, who knows, I too might retreat from the affairs of man and find solace with Amida."

"You let me know when that happens," Hugh remarked, grinning, "and I'll look into becoming vulnerable. In the meantime, I hope your guards are alert. If the trackers find us, the troops they bring up will attack in strength."

"We're ready," the abbot affirmed, his tone mild. A thousand highly trained warriors comprised the monastery's first line of defense. Their reserves numbered four thousand more. "Your bath will be ready now. Rest, Hugh-san, and we'll speak again in the morning."

"Thank you for your hospitality. The way I feel right now, I may sleep through an attack."

"Please do. We have no need of your assistance. The weapons you've given us are enough to vanquish the Mikado's entire army." The abbot's eyes twinkled above the rim of his tea bowl. "My youngest samurai enjoy the Gatling guns most. I fear they're like children with a new toy. Rest well, Hugh-san. No one will scale our walls tonight."

Chapter

8

On his passage to the grotto, fatigue suddenly overcame Hugh in a wave. Perhaps his weeks of drinking had finally taken their toll or maybe the warmth of the brazier had been too much after not having slept for so long.

The bathhouse was steamy and warm, the hot water heavenly after their long, cold journey. The tray of food left for him beside his bed was superb. Lord Yabe, monk though he might be now, kept a distinguished kitchen.

Hugh was surprised to find himself housed in the same room as the princess, but fell onto his mattress beside hers without undue contemplation. The grotto was small. Perhaps the abbot was beyond issues of desire and temptation. It didn't matter in any case; Hugh was asleep in seconds.

The secret chamber had been built by a pious noble of the Heian era who would retreat from the world on occasion to meditate and pray. In his search for nirvana, however, he preferred worldly comforts, and the small apartment beneath the

temple of Amida was rich with ornament executed
in the finest of materials—coffered ceilings in gold
leaf, exquisite screens painted by the great artists of
his time, colorful lacquerware chests and tables fit
for a potentate, all the architectural detail and
carved friezes picked out in shimmering gilt, mar-
quetry and niello work. When Hugh had first seen
the rooms two years ago, he'd been dazzled and
amused and remembered hoping the Amida didn't
take points off for ostentation when considering
which souls to guide in the true path to salvation.

But no luxury was so blissful as the soft silk mattress and quilts in which he was cocooned. For the
comforts of this bed, his weary soul might have
given serious thought to reciting "I call on thee
Amida Buddha," the salvation-by-faith-alone phrase
that made Amida Buddhism so popular. The pleasure of uninterrupted sleep was indeed paradise.

Sometime later, deep in slumber, swathed and
muffled in her quilt, Tama rolled in a languorous
flow from her futon to the one beside hers. Meeting the solid warmth of the captain's body, she un-
consciously pressed closer to the blissful heat.

In a dream state detached from substance and
reality, Hugh felt the small form drift into his back,
curve along the contours of his spine, melt into his
body. Shifting minutely, he sought to heighten the
pleasure.

His dreams were of the princess, her image
floating whimsically in and out of his imagina-
tion—as she looked last summer, elegant and refined, a princess in silken garb . . . or as she had
appeared tonight, wet and muddied, her delicate

beauty fresh scrubbed and pure despite her drab attire. And she would smile in his dreams from time to time and laugh.

He stirred in his sleep, wanting to reach that elusive smile.

And she purred in response, a hushed, breathy sound.

After years of playing at love, his senses were attuned to dulcet murmurs, his receptors alert to female longing. He came awake. Lying utterly still, his nostrils flared at the scent of a woman, and a smile slowly curved the corners of his mouth. Perhaps paradise was being offered to him in this hermitage at Amida's feet. Perhaps he was being rewarded for his kindness.

Under normal circumstances he would have known what to do. He would have rolled over, wakened her with a kiss and taken what Buddha offered. Under any other circumstances he wouldn't have hesitated.

So why was he now?

There was no one here to stop him. No one to hear. No one who even cared if he did what he wanted to do to her. And surely, when a woman purred in that flagrantly voluptuous way, ethical issues of morality ceased to exist. Right? "Damn right," he muttered inadvertently.

Her hand came up in response to his utterance and she gently stroked his shoulder—as though to comfort him.

It did the exact opposite, of course, and he silently cursed every god in creation for putting him in this untenable position. If he acted on his impulses, he'd be sorry as hell the second after he climaxed. If he didn't act on his impulses, he'd be even more afflicted.

In some misguided attempt to act the gentleman, he eased away, putting a small distance between them. Perhaps she wouldn't notice and he could slip away and sleep in the other room.

She did, though.

Clutching his shoulder, she pulled him close once again, slid the quilt from his shoulder and nestled against his naked back. Clenching his teeth, he silently counted to ten backward in every language he knew while her breasts burned into his flesh.

All he could think of was mounting her and plunging deep inside her over and over and over again, until he couldn't move, until she couldn't move, until every urgent, ravenous desire scorching his senses was sated. His cock was so hard his spine ached up to his ears and if he knew any useful prayers he would have prayed like hell for help.

Don't, he kept telling himself. *Just don't.*

You'll live if you don't fuck her.

Maybe.

He wasn't sure of anything right now.

Then he felt her move again, felt the quilt slip down farther, felt her soft silky mound against his buttocks and any further gentlemanly motive fell victim to lust. Rolling over, he took her face in his hands and kissed her gently. He intended to woo her softly, but sharp-set lust wasn't so easily tamed when they lay flesh to flesh. His kiss deepened with feverish haste, ravenous need and opportunity fierce stimulus.

She came awake—but not in fear . . . lazily, as though intrigued by the violence of his passions, and tranquil and yielding, she uttered the smallest of sighs.

"Hello," he whispered, his breath warm against her mouth.

"Konnichi-wa." She half smiled.

As they lay side by side, he felt her smile under his hands, the inhalation of her breath, the inherent acquiescence in her quiet greeting. But he wanted sanction too—or perhaps only the pretense. "Do you know what you're doing?" he whispered.

"Yes . . . no . . ." She shivered faintly as a streak of longing quivered through her senses. "It doesn't matter."

He wasn't about to ask for clarification. "You're cold. . . ." he murmured, pulling up the quilt.

"No." She stopped him. "I'm warm; you're too close." Or her dreams had been too graphic.

"Should I move?" He already knew the answer, the scent of female arousal pungent in his nostrils.

"I should say yes . . ."

"But?" His voice was assured, impudence in his gaze.

He was too confident; she should refuse. "I don't usually—I mean—this is . . . very—disconcerting," she stammered, trying to repress the ravenous desire coursing through her blood. "Do you suppose the food was drugged?" she blurted out.

"If it were, I'd have an excuse," he gruffly replied. If he were sensible, he'd leave her alone.

"We shouldn't," she said, as though reading his mind.

"You're right." Abruptly sitting up, he stared off in space as though some remedy to his frustration lay just beyond the lantern glow.

"And yet."

His gaze snapped around. "And yet, what?"

"Never mind."

He was about half a world past "never mind," his throbbing erection immune to practicalities. On the other hand, did he really want to get involved? Or more to the point, what would she expect of him afterward? "Perhaps we could work something out," he heard himself saying as though he were negotiating the price of rim-fire cartridges. "It depends," he said.

Coming up on her elbows, her gaze took on a sudden directness. "On what?"

Her tone had changed—no cowering female here discussing the liabilities of having sex. "On how you feel about continuing relationships," he replied bluntly, meeting her candor with equal frankness.

She suddenly smiled. "Are you saying my attitude concerning this relationship might be a deterrent to your lust?"

He shrugged. "It could be."

"It certainly doesn't look like it," she murmured, surveying his blatant arousal—his heartbeat visible in the pulsing veins—the magnificent size effectively obliterating any further thoughts of liabilities she might have. "I didn't think you"— she paused, the unspoken word, *barbarians,* hanging in the air—"westerners had sexual reservations. You wouldn't be monkish, by chance?" Christian missionaries were numerous in the country.

"Not at the moment," he noted drily, his glance flickering downward to his upthrust penis pressed hard against his belly.

"Do you find me unattractive?"

"On the contrary," he grumbled. "If I hadn't met your father I probably wouldn't be so polite."

His gallantry was oddly endearing, his powerful body and stark arousal irresistible, her fevered senses rashly focused on consummation. "Women have amorous liaisons in my world. Please, there's no need for politeness."

"Meaning?"

"You know what I mean, Captain. Make love to me." Her eyes held his, an unconscious note of command in her voice.

"Is that an order?" he drawled softly.

"Did I offend you?"

He hesitated briefly, weighing masculine pride against sexual satisfaction—not a long debate. "I don't take orders, Princess. Just a warning," he said, mitigating his rebuke with a faint smile.

"I understand," she replied, smiling back. "Would you do me the great honor of making love to me, Captain Drummond? I would be ever so grateful. Is that better?"

He grinned. "I'm getting the impression you'll say anything to get your way."

She'd never had to in the past, her every whim instantly accommodated. "Wouldn't you?"

"No."

"How commendable." Her brows rose. "A man of such honor selling arms."

He tipped his head in the faintest reproof. "If

you want something from me, Princess, you're going to have to be a touch more tactful."

"Sex is sex. You and I want the same thing. Why be so disobliging?"

"I don't know," he replied, wondering himself why he was so obstructive when he'd been fucking a great many ladies for a great many years without so much as a second's hesitation. "Maybe it's your tone."

"Come, Hugh-san," she said in a sweet cajoling murmur, the dulcet accents thick as honey. "Please, let's not argue anymore."

Patently willing, she half reclined on the soft quilts, her long black hair gleaming in the lamplight, her pale skin lucent ivory against the crimson silk, her slender form and plump breasts lushly curvaceous, her thighs open in invitation. And instead of giving in to temptation, he found himself wondering how often she did this—ordering men to make love to her.

"Could I say something to help you decide?" she whispered, arching her back slightly, her breasts rising in perfect delectable mounds.

Abruptly jettisoning any further equivocation, he rolled over her, pulled her arms flat so she tumbled onto her back and settled between her legs with a supple, effortless grace. Braced above her, his powerful shoulders blocking out the light, he nudged her thighs wider to accommodate his hips. "Why don't we decide instead," he murmured lazily, "how much you can take. . . ."

"What a delicious thought. . . ." she purred, the captain's bold gaze offering her whatever she wished, his enormous sex hard against her pulsing cleft, the ostentatious means to that end. "I'm so very happy we're in accord. And in the hopes of improving any future *rapprochement,* I most humbly apologize, *mon capitaine,* for anything I may have said."

Her lapse into perfectly accented French was artlessly playful, the inflection lightly teasing, reminding him that he was treating this dalliance much too seriously. "No need to apologize," he said with a flashing smile, back on familiar ground, casual sex his speciality. "It was my fault entirely."

"How sweet," she whispered, lifting her hips slightly, her sleek, turgid vulva sliding up his rigid length.

He smiled. "Not exactly. Pure selfishness, darling." The affectionate word slipped easily from his tongue. Hot cunt pressed hard against his cock had that effect on him.

"Am I your darling?" Her smile was delicious.

"You are right now," he said with cheeky impudence. "I look forward to your company aboard ship." Or, more precisely, to fucking her from here to Paris.

The tiniest of frowns marred her pale brow. "Provided we reach your ship."

"Don't worry. We'll get there." For a man who had captured a record ninety-seven Union vessels in some of the fiercest engagements of the Civil War, the short distance to Osaka wasn't insurmountable.

His calm assurance brought tears to her eyes.

"Hey, hey . . . everything's fine." He gently touched her cheek. "We're going to get there."

"How embarrassing," she whispered, sniffling.

"I don't usually cry—especially . . . I mean—at a time like this—when—"

"I'm not easily fazed," he said, smiling faintly, moving his hips so she could feel his undiminished arousal. "As you can see. And you have reason enough to cry after all you've been through, so you set the pace or say no if you wish—I'm understanding as hell."

"What I want more than anything is to forget everything that's happened—if only for a few moments. I don't want to remember right now or live in fear or worry about tomorrow." She raised her tear-filled eyes. "I want escape, Hugh-san . . . and forgetfulness—please . . ."

For a man who had restrained his desires much longer than he'd thought humanly possible, he was more than willing to comply. "We'll escape together," he whispered, understanding the need for deliverance—perhaps as subject as she to memories he'd rather forget. "To better times and sweeter dreams," he murmured, kissing her gently.

Her mouth was lush and soft, her sigh of surrender warm against his lips, her arms sliding around his neck velvet assent.

"I want the sweet dreams to start right now," she whispered, biting his lip in a feverish little nip, pulling him closer.

"Now-now?" he teased.

"Yesterday-now, if you want to please me."

"Or myself," he breathed, entering her a heartbeat later, giving her what she wanted, what they both wanted—sweet oblivion and forgetfulness.

She moaned softly, the warm glow of carnal pleasure inundating her senses, enveloping her soul, effacing fear and dread. "Thank you," she breathed, sinking into a soft blissful cloud of balmy rapture. "Thank you, thank you, thank you . . ."

"My pleasure," he whispered, forcing his way in by slow, silken degrees, each small measure of ingress riveting, whetting his appetite for more, making him harder.

Unthreatened and safe, she basked in the unequivocal joy, exhilaration, the glory of unalloyed passion. Perhaps the captain was her reward for surviving; perhaps he was her gift from the gods. "More," she breathed, greedily arching up into the captain's long hard length, "please more, more, more . . ."

Afraid he might hurt her, he curbed his impulse to respond as he would have liked. "There's plenty of time," he murmured, tamping down his lust, easing forward another infinitesimal distance, watching the rosy flush of desire creep up her throat and face, gauging when he could next exert additional pressure. Her cunt was unbelievably tight, the engorged head of his penis so compressed he could feel the contact points jar his senses with every beat of his heart. Not that he was complaining. In fact, he was seriously considering sending Sunskoku a lavish thank-you gift.

Tama was also infinitely grateful, enchanted by the captain's magnificent size, every nerve in her body focused on the delectable pleasure he offered. Whether slumbering impulse or charitable spirits had guided her to his bed, she gave thanks—for his strength and power, his gentleness, his very noteworthy virility. And with a quiver of liquid heat, she melted around him.

The princess was almost too small, half his size if that, and so fucking tight it was going to take nerves of steel to keep from plunging headlong into her sweet, honeyed cunt. Gritting his teeth against the inclination to please himself too swiftly, he counted to ten once again, then slid forward another constrained distance.

She gasped.

"Sorry," he breathed, marginally withdrawing.

"No—no." Her hands resting on his lower back forced him back. "Don't stop."

Easy to say, he thought, every muscle in his body tense with restraint. He wasn't sure she was capable of taking him all. Worse, he wasn't sure he was capable of caution.

But even as he was contemplating their rueful disparities, she suddenly dug her nails into his back and went completely still beneath him.

Whimpering faintly, the first orgasmic flutters lapping at the verges of her sensory receptors, she suddenly sucked in her breath as the floodgates began to open. Panting in unconscious rhythm to the building delirium, orgasmic splendor trembling on the brink, she clung to the captain with increasing frenzy as ecstasy rippled upward and surged through her vagina in powerful waves. And when the full, violent impact of her climax exploded in a fierce, unbridled paroxysm, she screamed and screamed and screamed—the fevered sound rising in a high-pitched crescendo that hung in the air for long, endless moments.

Christ, she was fast—an impetuous, white-hot wildcat, easily aroused, quick to orgasm, lush and wet and more than willing—her tightness having yielded nicely on climax, his cock currently buried hilt deep.

Sexual compatibility might not be a problem after all.

Correction. Wasn't a problem.

Definitely good karma.

Killers on their trail aside, meeting the princess might have been the most fortunate of encounters. Now, all he had to do was make her climax a few more times and she'd be so soft and pliant he'd slide in and out smooth as silk.

Not a difficult assignment, as it turned out; the princess was insatiable. Although, there came a time—after the princess had had several more orgasms—when he considered his gentlemanly duties discharged. Or perhaps the point of no return had come. In any event, it was an opportune occasion, for the princess was begging for release—*again,* and his cock, about to explode, was buried deep inside her. "Let's try this together," he whispered, his splayed fingers slipping on her hips, both of them sleek with sweat, their hearts racing. He watched her face, waiting for that exact, precise moment, gauging rhythm and depth, waiting for her to peak—almost . . . almost . . . he could feel her orgasmic flutters begin, her eyes were shut tight, her breathing nearly stopped. Tense with waiting, he restrained the pressure of his climax a second more. There—there—THERE! The floodgates opened, his climax rushed downward, and they met in that rare, transcendental zone of consciousness where earth, spirit and passion blended in a perfect, endless, soul-stirring orgasm.

Moments later, gasping for breath, his elbows

locked to hold him upright, Hugh struggled to draw air into his lungs. *So this is what it's like,* he thought, understanding for the first time why poets wrote poems. And if he were a praying man, he'd pray for strength because the Princess of Otari was going to be the hottest little piece he'd ever had on board the *Southern Belle,* bar none. Which meant Paddy would have to run things because he intended to lock himself in his cabin with the greedy little minx and not come up for air until the coast of France hove into view.

Tama had never subscribed to the Zen tenet of living in the moment. But right now, she was inclined to embrace the maxim because feeling this good was sheer unadulterated heaven. "I might need you again," she murmured, the captain's undiminished arousal inside her the most luxurious sensation, every throbbing vaginal cell acutely aware of his sizeable presence. "Do you mind?"

"Not in the least. Now or a minute from now?" Lust was infinitely accommodating.

She smiled, her hips moving in a slow, gliding undulation. "It feels as though you've already started, Hugh-san. . . ."

"How about that," he whispered, the poet in him trying to find the appropriate word for what he was feeling. "I need you closer, though," he breathed, gliding deeper, the phrase "unbridled debauch" front and center in his brain.

"Like this?" she whispered, blissfully impaled, pressing her palms into the dip of his spine to heighten the pleasure. She was unutterably bewitched, all the rumors of the barbarians' lack of finesse dispelled by the captain's uncanny ability to anticipate her every wish. *Like that.* "Ummm . . . stay there . . . exactly there—forever and ever and ever . . ."

Perhaps it was a mistake to offer such license to a man just coming off a fortnight of drinking, his nerves strumming and raw.

Or then again, maybe they were the perfect match.

Cramming her full, he kept her filled to surfeit as they made love fiercely, softly, swiftly, slowly—continuously . . . She was unquenchable, frenzied, heedless to all but desire and he was more than willing to oblige her until such a time as even a man of his virility needed pause. Rolling away, he sprawled on his back and said in a rush of breath, "Intermission."

"Whatever you want," she panted, flinging her arms over her head and shutting her eyes, letting her last orgasm blissfully dissolve.

Now there was a tantalizing phrase, Hugh thought, and gazing at the dainty princess with the huge appetite for sex, he smiled faintly. Hours till morning—hours more of exploring the princess's delectably hot cunt. It almost made one believe in nirvana.

Slowly lifting her lashes, Tama turned her head, smiled back and in a voice still warm with post-coital languor, whispered, "I think my luck has turned. . . ."

"Mine as well, Princess."

His slow wink was barefaced provocation, a promise of pleasure she found herself unable to resist. She blamed the captain, of course, for her unusual sexual craving. On the other hand, she decided, blame wasn't the precise word to describe the enormous pleasure he incited. The insistent pulsing between her legs a case in point. For which she needed surcease. "We truly are safe here, aren't we?"

"Absolutely."

"No one will come in to disturb us?"

Did she mean servants? The abbot? The Mikado's army? He wasn't sure, but basking as he was in a state of unbelievable contentment, it didn't matter. "We're safe here, no question."

"Perfect. Then I may have my way with you undisturbed."

In contrast to what, he thought, repressing a grin. Had not the past hour been unconstrained enough? But infinitely polite, he lifted his hand in a gesture of compliance. "Be my guest."

"You're wonderfully accommodating," she murmured, her voice sultry and low.

"I never argue about having sex."

"My good fortune."

"Ours," he pleasantly offered, the term *mutual pleasure* never more apt than when in close proximity to the randy Princess of Otari.

Rolling on her side, she reached over and ran her finger lightly down the length of his penis. "And perhaps his as well . . ."

He sucked in a breath at her touch no matter how gentle, his nerve endings skittish, overstimulated, keenly attuned after their recent fuck-a-thon.

"How polite he is," she whispered, watching his erection rise. "He's waking up to say hello to me."

His lustful energies stirring back to life under her deft massage, his penis quivered, moved, inching upward with each beat of his heart until the upthrust contour took on the slight curve of optimum extension.

"You're showing off . . ." She stroked the flaunting proportions. "How sweet."

He groaned softly, arching his spine against her exquisite touch, wondering what would give out first—his rutting brain or his cock.

"Look. He's getting bigger still," she breathed, coming up on her knees, her gaze rapt with delight. Not that he noticed, with his brain on fire. Not that she gave him the time to take a note, for she grasped his erection in both hands and exerted pressure gently downward, then up and down once more with less gentleness, forcing the bulging crest upward in a surge of dilating blood vessels. "Is this all for me?" she whispered.

He drew in a sharp breath. "If you want any of it"—he said on a suffocated exhalation—"I'd suggest you stop before it's too late."

"Stop this?" she teased, dipping down and licking the massive, crimson head.

"You're pushing your luck." His voice was strained, every muscle tense with restraint.

"Very well, I'll stop. There. Is that better?" she murmured, releasing her hold.

Before he could decide if it was better or not, whether he wanted what she wanted or some other variation on the theme, she slipped downward between his legs, braced her forearms on his thighs and offered him a beguiling smile.

"Keep it up and you're going to get a mouthful," he said gruffly, her cheeky smile only inches away from his cock.

"I have this urge," she purred, touching his testicles with a light brushing stroke.

"It's your call." Consummation was a hard, pounding rhythm in his brain.

"Is that a warning?" she replied playfully, lightly grasping his erection, gazing up at him over its turgid height.

His fingertip brushed her mouth. "Why don't we save time. It's not going to fit in there."

"Indulge me, Hugh-san." Sliding upward slightly, she drew the glistening crest closer, slowly encircled the flared flange with her tongue, and licked a slow path down the underside where the nerves were most sensitive.

He groaned, a low inarticulate pleasure sound from deep in his throat, the animal sound echoing through her heated senses, triggering an intensified pulsing in her vagina. Her hands tightened on his rigid length and, looking up, she met his fevered gaze. "I'll make him fit."

"I know where he'll fit better." His voice was taut, his carnal urges curbed with effort. He couldn't remember when last he'd considered fucking himself to death a reasonable goal.

"Let me lick him clean first," she whispered, her lips hovering over the swollen crest, her gaze holding his. "Do you mind?"

They both knew what his answer would be.

"Do whatever you want." His mouth quirked in a flashing smile. "Within reason." And he waited, breath held, for her mouth to move that infinitesimal distance more.

Her lips touched him, molten pleasure emanated throughout his body from that finite point of contact, and lucid thought gave way to delirium. Cupping her head in his hands, he held her captive, forcing himself deeper into her mouth, size restrictions no longer a concern.

And where she should have taken offense at such brute coercion, a jolt of hot, urgent desire flared through her brain and sensual receptors, and most powerfully through her throbbing vagina—as though she were helplessly in thrall to the barbarian captain—to lust—to unbridled prodigality. There was no explanation for her insatiable need, not fear or the lack of it, not fatigue or loneliness, her craving an uncontrollable madness.

His grip tightened, ramming the head of his penis against the back of her throat and she moaned softly, the feverish ache in her swollen sex heightening wildy, as though she were a willing handmaiden to his carnal pleasure. His prodigious size was flagrantly arousing; she was half choking as she moved on him and all she could think of was feeling that monstrous cock deep inside her. Personal gratification suddenly became a priority. She began pulling away, familiar with having her every desire met.

"Uh-uh." He held her firmly in place. "Please me first, before you get this."

Flame-hot desire coursed through her senses at his softly uttered threat, a drenching rush of moisture bathing her heated core as though readying her for her reward. She quickly obliged him, sucking, licking, nibbling with renewed fervor.

His eyes were shut, his hands lightly cupping her head as she moved up and down, the oscillating rhythm of her mouth and tongue, the light friction of her teeth the focus of every frenzied nerve in his body. Until she bit a fraction too hard.

"Bitch." Jerking back, he glared at her.

"I'm sorry," she whispered. "It was an accident."

"It better be."

She was trembling, her lips cherry bright and glistening. "Please," she whispered.

He could still feel the stinging nip. "Please, what?" he growled.

"Please make love to me."

"This isn't love."

"Please have sex with me."

"Get over there," he grunted, suddenly wanting to leave his mark on her in the most primordial expression of male power and fill her with come. A ridiculous, irrational need. He barely knew her. It shouldn't matter who did what to whom.

The princess wouldn't have agreed, selfishly intent on her own pleasure. Aflame with longing, she quickly lay on her back and spread her legs wide. "Hurry!"

"Wait," he muttered, still in the grip of his autocratic impulses.

"Right now!" she hissed, her royal prerogatives difficult to suppress for any length of time.

And suddenly it *did* matter who did what to whom, his response to fiat predictable. They were going to do things *his* way. Pushing her thighs wider, he bent his head.

Realizing his intent, she squealed in outrage, shoving hard at his shoulders.

Ignoring her efforts to dislodge him, he pushed her back down, held her firmly in place with one hand on her hip while he opened her drenched pubis with his other hand, her squirming resistance only offering him better access to her succulent flesh. Understanding how best to subdue her defiance, he instinctively centered his attention on her clitoris. His talents for cunnilingus had been honed to perfection years ago in Peachtree county and further refined in the brothels of the East. The consummate combination of technique and performance had never failed to please. Tama's struggles quickly ceased, her hands fell from his shoulders, her squeals altered to soft little cries, then heated purrs as the captain's deft caresses glided over her pouty flesh and pulsing tissue, and her clitoris swelled under the delicate friction of his tongue.

He took care not to move too fast nor exert excessive pressure, his gift for proper rhythm masterful, and very soon, the princess was meekly submissive, paying homage to his expertise with little, yielding whimpers.

Raising his head, he came to his knees and waited. Her eyes flared wide in shock and dismay. "Don't stop," she pleaded. "Please, please, don't stop."

"Make up your mind," he said brusquely, inexplicably needing abject capitulation.

"I want you any way at all," she whispered, shuddering with need.

"You're sure?" he drawled.

"Yes, yes, *yes!*"

Assuaged or perhaps beyond waiting himself, he moved swiftly, guiding his penis to the dewy folds of her sex and plunging foward so quickly she gasped. Sobbing in gratitude, she clung to him, immune to all but sensation, her panting cries warming his throat, an undercurrent of breathy hysteria in the sound.

While less vocal, the captain was no less fevered, his orgasm too long constrained, his fierce thrust and withdrawal likely to be of short duration.

They were both on the veritable brink after such protracted foreplay—mere milliseconds from climax, the silence punctuated only by the sound of labored breathing.

She screamed.

Hugh's first swelling surge responded on cue.

And the confluence of his ejaculation and her ecstasy flowed together in a shimmering, seething, glowing rapture.

When Hugh finally lifted his head, a smile curved his mouth. "Did you like that?" he teased.

"I'm not sure." A playfulness imbued her tone. "Should we try again?"

"Until we get it right?" He moved faintly inside her so she could feel his undiminished interest.

"If you don't mind . . ." she uttered on a soft breathy sigh. "My apologies if you do."

"It's not a problem."

Her cloudless gaze met his. "We should celebrate this rare and felicitous accord."

"I think we already are," he whispered, and bent to kiss her.

It was a light, buoyant kiss, a summertime kiss fragrant with sweet delight. But brief moments later their inexhaustible passions occasioned more heated caresses.

"I'm sorry," he murmured, courteous and gallant, conscious of their brief acquaintance. "Would you rather rest?"

"I'll let you know when I want to rest," she whispered, arching up to lightly brush his lips with hers.

Fortunately he was familiar with sleepless nights. He grinned. "Welcome to the party."

And for the remainder of the night, hidden away in their own private Elysium, they surrendered to their wild, unblushing passions. Driven by inexplicable desire, they mated in a bacchanalia of bold, reckless indiscretion—caught in the grip of an obsession so extreme they felt as though they were captive to some spell.

A startling revelation for two people not given to flights of fancy.

But glorious and fine and much too enchanting to question.

Near morning, sated and content at last, they fell asleep. She lay atop him, her head resting in the curve of his throat, his arms around her, and like babes in the wood, they slept.

She'd never allowed herself such unconditional release—never in memory.

Exhausted, the captain slept like the dead.

At midday—the eleventh chime of the old Dutch case clock in the corner having just died away—they came awake with a start. The tramp of feet and muffled voices resonated overhead, the scraping sound of heavy objects being moved shattered the silence of the grotto.

Tama went tense in Hugh's arms.

"They can't get in," he whispered, stroking her back. "You're safe."

"I know." But she found herself trembling as though she were the most faint-hearted woman. As though she wasn't capable of holding her own in combat against any man. Struggling to quell her apprehensions, she forced away her inchoate fears, reminding herself she'd wakened from a deep sleep. She wasn't thinking clearly. *Breathe slowly, concentrate—listen, they're already moving away.* But she'd feel safer armed, and slipping from Hugh's chest, she plucked her swords from above her futon. "How many do you think are up there?" she asked, resting on her knees beside him, her gaze lifted upward.

"It doesn't matter. They can't find the entrance." Levering up on one elbow, he tossed a quilt around her shoulders and then lay back down. "Are you hungry?"

She stared at him, her eyes huge in the dim light coming through an ingeniously disguised transom on the Amida statue's base. "How can you think about food at a time like this?"

"They're leaving—hear that? And I haven't eaten much lately." His diet had been essentially bourbon for weeks. "The abbot will see them on their way," he murmured, touching her arm in reassurance. "He's an accomplished courtier. If not for his *tozama* heritage he might have been shogun himself. And a damned sight better one than the last one."

"Anyone would have been," she muttered testily,

the effete young man more interested in poetry a disaster for the country.

"Your father shared your opinion, yet was loyal. Why?"

"My father distrusted the opposition more. They're blatant opportunists as you no doubt know in your line of work. Satsuma and Choshu were buying weapons and ships years before anyone else, currying favor at court with money and lies. And now they control the Mikado."

"While your father preferred a more representative government—advanced thinking for a man in his position. Most great lords would resent giving up their feudal privileges."

"He understood what was best for the future of our country."

"A benevolent man."

Her expression softened. "As are you, Hughsan. In so many delightful ways."

"Thank you. Your benevolence pleases me as well. But remember, you're paying me. I'm not entirely charitable."

"Why shouldn't I pay for your services?" She set her swords aside, the noise upstairs having died away. "Although if you think yourself well paid, may I be more demanding?"

He grinned. "Is that possible?"

"I don't know." Her voice was sultry and low. "You tell me."

He stretched in a glorious display of hard, rippling muscle and blatant virility. "I'm more than willing to serve as stud, Princess, but my minimum requirements are some food and sleep on occasion."

"Of course. You'll find me amenable on both points."

He held up his hand, taking issue with her noblesse oblige. "It's not about you being amenable to me. Is that clear?"

She assumed a demure pose. "Yes, sir. I understand."

"And don't be coy," he said, scowling faintly. "You're not the type."

"What type am I?" A sportive light gleamed in her eyes.

"Selfish as hell, intractable, headstrong, prone to give orders and"—he winked—"sweeter than sweet."

Winking back, arms akimbo, she fluttered her eyelashes in teasing flirtation. "How sweet exactly, Captain Drummond?"

His gaze narrowed. "How the hell old are you?" Rosy-cheeked and tousled, she suddenly looked very young. He hoped like hell he hadn't fucked some fifteen-year-old last night.

"I'm twenty-two, twenty-one in your years."

"Married?" He probably should have asked before.

"Does it matter?"

"I suppose it's a little late. Are you?"

"No."

While not precisely shocked, he *was* surprised. The Japanese married young—particularly those from prominent families where influential alliances were traditional. "That's unusual, isn't it? Unmarried at your age?"

"My father allowed me freedom to make my own choices and no one appealed."

"But you've obviously had lovers." She'd been neither a virgin nor shy.

"Every aristocratic lady has lovers, Hugh-san. How else would we experience the delights of love?"

"Some women wait until marriage."

She looked at him, his tone having taken on a cool brusqueness. "Are you suggesting I should have waited?"

"No, of course not. I spoke out of turn."

"Are *you* married?"

"No." A curt, brusque reply.

"Ah."

He scowled. "What the hell does that mean?"

"Nothing." She schooled her features to a bland mask. "I look forward to your company on our voyage, Hugh-san. I could not have found a more gracious captain."

Would she have slept with any captain who gave her passage? The sudden thought was disturbing.

"I wouldn't have, Hugh-san," she said with a knowing smile. "I only sleep with men who intrigue me."

"I didn't say anything."

"In Bushido, one learns to study an adversary's expression in order to survive. What he thinks, he does a second later."

Less steeped in the warrior culture, Hugh had learned the technical skills, but perhaps not the art of Bushido. "I apologize. I didn't mean to offend."

"I'm not offended. I do as I like, Hugh-san. As do you."

It unnerved him momentarily to have met a

woman not geisha trained in the art of seduction but a beautiful, refined, intelligent woman who viewed sex with the same nonemotional criteria as he. "I appreciate your candor," he said, when he wasn't so sure he did. Although, sensibly, he should. No undue sentimentality, no lasting ties had been his byword since the war. "Do you know whether your brother is still in Paris?" he abruptly inquired, preferring to change the topic to something less problematical.

"We received regular letters from him until recently," she answered, recognizing his withdrawal—and understanding. "I expect he's heard the news of the northern alliances' defeat by now. He has friends at the French embassy."

"You don't think he might be on his way back here already?"

She shook her head. "He left for love of a woman he couldn't have married if he'd stayed. She was an eta, a caste unsuitable for a noble. They have a son now. He won't leave them." She smiled faintly. "And he knows I can take care of myself. I could defeat him in swordplay by the time I was ten."

"If he won't leave his family, what makes you think he'll return with you?"

"He is rightful Lord of Otari. He has to," Tama firmly said. "In any event, the caste system will be eradicated soon and his wife can take her place by his side. Like other disgraced lords, we will be forgiven in time. But come, Hugh-san, we must be on our way," she said, rising to her feet.

Reaching out, he caught her ankle and tumbled her back down, rolling over her with a comfortable familiarity. "There's no rush," he murmured, kissing her cheek lightly, adjusting himself between her thighs. "We have to wait for dark, anyway."

"No, we don't," she protested, pushing against his chest. "They won't be expecting us to move in daylight. We'll have the advantage."

Ignoring her efforts to dislodge him, he shook his head. "We'll have the cover of darkness at night. A better advantage."

"Then you travel at night and I'll meet you in Osaka."

"How are you going to accomplish that if I won't let you up?"

"Like this." Jamming her forearm into his Adam's apple, taking him by surprise, she slipped away in a supple twist of her body.

His hand closed around her wrist before she'd come to her knees. "Perhaps we could compromise?" he murmured, his grip inflexible against her squirming attempt at escape.

She glared at him. "I don't want to."

"Wrong answer."

"Yes, then."

"If you want me to take you to France, you have to actually mean it." While he admired her reckless courage, he'd survived in a dangerous profession for many years because he didn't take unnecessary risks.

"If you insist, I mean it," she muttered.

"Smart girl." Although not taken in by her response, he preferred a truce, however fraudulent, to useless contention. "Why don't we discuss this with the abbot," he suggested, releasing her and dropping back onto the mattress. "He knows the area."

"If we didn't travel together, we'd be less conspicuous. You realize that."

"You forget you have an army on your trail."

"I can hide better than you. I'll manage."

"And I have a Spencer rifle. We stay together." He didn't care if she was the best swordsman in Japan and smaller than he, she couldn't take on the sheer number of men in pursuit. Two were better than one if they were attacked, and his Spencer was better than both of them.

"It sounds as though you've decided for us," she retorted huffily.

"Unless you think you can swim to France."

"You can be most unaccommodating," she snapped.

"I don't recall you saying that last night."

"Last night you didn't argue with me."

"Or maybe you didn't mind what I said as long as you had what you wanted."

"Exactly. Unlike now," she replied crisply.

At the sound of footsteps next door, Hugh reached for his robe, relieved to have an excuse to leave. "Stay here," he ordered, sliding his arms into the sleeves.

"Of course, whatever you say," Tama muttered.

He shot her a glance, opened his mouth to speak, thought better of it and, tying his robe as he turned away, strode from the bedchamber.

Left behind, Tama sullenly considered the captain's uncompromising, vastly irritating behavior. Orders, orders, orders—he didn't seem to understand she'd spent a lifetime *giving* orders, not taking them. And while she realized a certain courtesy was required toward the man helping her flee the country, it was nonetheless grating to have to be *so* complaisant.

Now, where were her clothes?

She found her peasant garb washed and carefully folded in the small adjacent bathhouse. Quickly washing, she donned the tunic and trousers that had helped make her invisible these weeks past. Then taking her short sword, she cut off her hair to shoulder length, tied a scarf around her forehead and packed her swords.

Unlike the samurai and nobility who had their hair dressed daily, peasants wore their tresses conveniently short. And with the gauntlet of her enemies between here and Osaka forewarned and on the lookout, she needed every advantage to melt into the crowd.

Chapter

9

Entering the adjoining room, Hugh found the abbot waiting, his serenity intact despite his recent visitors.

"I hope the chief inspector's men didn't disturb you," Lord Yabe said.

"No—although the princess was nervous briefly."

"They were insistent on a full search—so I obliged them. They found nothing, of course."

"Do you think they're gone?"

"So they led me to believe. I expect they left spies behind."

"The princess is advocating we leave this morning. I told her it's unwise."

The abbot nodded. "It certainly is. Give Hiroaki's men sufficient time to tire of their surveillance first. Tomorrow, we have a group of pilgrims setting out for the shrine at Lake Biwa. You could join them."

"Unfortunately, my size and face will give me away. I'd prefer leaving as we came—in the dark of night. If your men could help clear our way of Hiroaki's spies."

"A simple enough task, Hugh-san. My men have been without excitement since the end of the war. Although rumor has it Satsuma is dissatisfied with their position in the government. We might be at war again before long."

"Sooner rather than later would serve our purposes, but I doubt Satsuma will be so obliging as to begin their rebellion tomorrow. I *would* like to be nearer Osaka though, so when my ship is ready to sail we won't have so far to travel. Somewhere out of the way and rustic would suit—a dwelling that a princess would be unlikely to visit."

"Our hermitage near Ibo might be suitable."

"How far is it from here?"

"Ten hours, traveling fast."

"We'll need supplies for a week."

"Certainly. Whatever you need."

"And you're welcome to whatever you need from my next shipment of arms. I'm in your debt," Hugh said, his broad smile indicative of his good spirits. "I haven't slept so well in years."

The abbot had received a full report on his guests' nocturnal activities. "I'm happy we could be of assistance. I trust the princess had pleasant dreams as well."

"Yes, I believe she did."

An underlying current of male understanding permeated the brief exchange, the abbot a man of cosmopolitan tastes despite his forced exile.

"Perhaps you and the princess would like to join me later for tea or dinner or a view of the gardens at—"

A commotion erupted outside the small parlor, curtailing the men's conversation, and a moment later the door slid open to disclose the princess caught in the grip of two brawny, armed monks.

"I wasn't going anywhere. I just wanted some fresh air," Tama muttered, giving the two silent guards a glowering look.

The princess was dressed and armed, her motives plain.

"Perhaps we could take a stroll in the gardens later," the abbot offered. "Once we know that your enemies have, er, vacated the premises."

"You need a keeper, Princess," Hugh growled. "Or shackles."

"You forget, Captain, I made my way to Edo without your help!"

"If you'll excuse us, Abbot," Hugh said, taking Tama's hand and holding it despite her efforts to shake him off. "We have some matters to discuss."

"Why don't I send a message when it's safe to walk our grounds once again. Forgive me, Princess, for our excess of caution. But Chief Inspector Hiroaki is a devious man."

"I understand, Lord Yabe. Thank you for your concern."

"Until this evening, then. I'll inform you, Hughsan, as to our success with the, er, extraneous issues outside our walls."

"Thank you. We'll wait here until we hear from you." Hugh's grip tightened as Tama tried to wrench away.

Avoiding the princess's gaze, the abbot bowed and left.

The moment they were alone, Tama turned on Hugh, her eyes snapping with anger. "Kindly release my hand," she said, each syllable coldly implacable.

"Not until you promise to obey me," Hugh brusquely muttered, disinclined to chase after her into Hiroaki's web of assassins.

"I don't need your permission to leave," she spat.

"If the abbot's men hadn't stopped you, you'd be in a cage now, on your way back to Edo. This place is ringed with spies."

"I'm capable of avoiding them."

"Only if you can fly."

"I beg to differ with you," she retorted testily.

"Don't you always. Although, you're wrong in this case. So you're staying inside until nightfall— willingly or not. I'm going to let go now," he said, slowly loosening his grip. "But don't run again. You won't get far. And I'll really be pissed if you make any more trouble for the abbot. Understand?"

Her expression was mutinous, but she knew better than to disagree with every temple monk on the lookout for her.

"Once it's dark, Hiroaki's spies will be killed and we'll be free to go. So cool your hot little temper and take advantage of a day of rest because we'll be moving fast tonight. I'm about to have breakfast. Would you care to join me?"

"Do I have a choice?"

"Certainly. You may eat alone or not at all. Suit yourself. But I'm not playing nursemaid to a stu-

pid young lady who could get us killed. So behave
yourself and don't embarrass me."

"Embarrass you! I am Princess of Otari, you
graceless man!"

"Listen, you spoiled bitch," he growled. "You're
not only embarrassing me, but the abbot as well.
Mind your damned manners."

"How dare you speak to me like that! How dare
you—"

Palms up, he stopped her tirade, his gaze flinty.
"Before you say another word, consider who's taking you to Paris. I have no tolerance for bitches."

"Only for women who always say yes," she retorted testily.

"As long as we understand each other," he said
grimly, and then he walked away before he lost his
temper completely.

They stayed in separate rooms for the rest of the
day, neither willing to cry pax, both stubborn and
moody. When the abbot came to fetch them as twilight fell, he smiled at the obvious signs of tension
between his guests. But recalling lovers quarrels
with the benevolent hindsight of middle age, he
remembered how sweet it was to make up and en-
vied the young couple their reconciliation.

As they walked with him through the temple
gardens, their conversation was well mannered,
but desultory, the coolness between them palpable. They admired the tranquil ponds and graceful
bridges, the dark pines, the austere sand gardens
used for meditation, the small pavilions scattered

throughout the landscape where tea ceremonies or prayers took place in the midst of nature.

But they were both careful to direct their comments to the abbot rather than to each other, their politesse taut with undercurrents of reserve.

On their return to the grotto, the abbot took it upon himself to lecture them on the merits of forgiveness. Surveying them with the sufferance of a parent for recalcitrant offspring, he said, "If an old man might make a suggestion, my children, it would be wise for you to put your differences aside. Your journey ahead is perilous, your enemies formidable. You can't confront them alone, Princess, while you can use Lady Otari's help, Hugh-san. Come now," he asserted, his hand resting on the hilt of his short sword as though reminding them of what lay ahead, "make amends."

"I apologize," Hugh offered urbanely, obliging his friend.

"I'm sorry," Tama murmured, understanding that courtesy was essential to one's host.

"Good; it's settled." Regardless that their responses might be token, Lord Yabe hoped it was indication of a chastened anger. "Even if my men eliminate the spies outside our temple, there will be others waiting in the wings. You need each other."

"Perhaps I need the captain more," Tama acquiesced graciously.

Damn right you do. But Hugh was too polite to speak aloud. "I appreciate your good sword arm, Princess."

"Excellent." The abbot's gaze swung from one to the other. "Your survival odds have risen considerably. Now, let me see that my men are set loose," he said with a smile. "Once their mission is complete, I'll come for you."

And with a bow, he turned and left.

With the abbot's departure, the painted screens lining the walls of the parlor seemed to close in on them, the pine forests and mountain landscapes depicted on the gold ground taking on an impenetrable, charged presence in the lantern light. Or perhaps alone once again all their unresolved conflicts came to the fore.

An awkward silence fell.

The mechanism on the ancient case clock whirled loudly in the hush.

"Did you eat today?" Hugh inquired, speaking first, their imminent departure bringing the question to mind.

"Yes."

Another small silence.

Tama slanted a look at him from under her lashes. "Did you?"

"Yes."

"Good."

He smiled faintly, their stilted exchange ironic after the singular intimacies they'd shared last night. "I heard you sharpen your swords."

Her mouth curved into a fleeting smile. "I heard you humming."

"Sorry."

"You have a very nice voice."

"I didn't realize I was humming. I must have been packing my ammunition."

Her brows rose. "Singing while gathering your ammunition? Is that normal for you, Hugh-san?"

"There's nothing normal about my life." He lifted his hand. "This place a case in point. Things happen; I deal with them."

"Or I come along and you deal with me."

He tipped his head in sardonic assent. "Which is why we need more ammunition."

"I've put you in a great deal of danger, haven't I?" A twinge of guilt assailed her.

"Nothing I can't handle."

"You're very gracious."

"Just realistic. The abbot's men are good at what they do. They'll clear our way."

"I promise to be less troublesome if that will help."

He blew out a small breath. "I'll try to be less dictatorial."

"Do you mean it?" The words came out before she could censure them.

He smiled. "Don't ask. I haven't had much call for good manners lately, I'm afraid."

"While I've been ill-behaved."

"So we're not exactly perfect." He held out his hand. "We'll begin again."

She hesitated briefly and then slid her fingers through his.

His hand closed, the warmth between them palpable. "Friends?"

She nodded. "Friends."

"We'll get to Osaka. My word on it."

"Thank you, although we must be without emotion once we leave here. For survival, Hugh-san. You understand, don't you?" Not wishing to damage their newfound accord, her gaze was tentative.

He understood. In the heat of battle, only

adrenaline and instinct saw you through, all else was distracting. "You will be my comrade in arms once we leave here, Princess. Nothing more— until we reach safe haven."

"Safe haven," she murmured. "How nice that sounds. . . ."

Chapter
10

Hiroaki received a preliminary report from his trackers while entertaining a party of government officials at the Green House. Two of the men, assistants to the Mikado's councillors, gave him up-to-date information on the shifting intrigues at court. They were well paid, but as apt to relay information back to the Mikado's council as not, so he schooled his face to give away nothing as he perused the message. The trail of the princess had gone cold at the Shin-Shiu monastery. Some men had stayed at the temple complex in surveillance roles. The remainder of the troop had dispersed to continue the search.

The chief inspector felt like screaming or hitting something or ordering the stupid men sitting across from him to leave. But he couldn't, of course. No one knew of the search for the princess and until she was safely in his hands, no one would. A man didn't rise to a position as powerful as his without a pristine record of success. What-

ever mistakes he might have made were buried—
literally.

The atmosphere in Sunskoku's richly appointed
quarters in the Green House was festive, the numerous geishas she oversaw that evening the most
beautiful in Edo. Waving her hand, she summoned a maidservant to pour more sake for the
inspector. And when he looked up she smiled as
though she didn't know he'd received bad news.

Hiroaki often made use of Sunskoku's apart-
ments to entertain his more important associates,
her reputation as the leading *tayu* in Edo adding
luster to his name. The little mistress he spent
most of his nights with was seventeen, fresh as dew
and adoring, but incapable of playing hostess to
senior members of the court. Nor would she have
noticed the minute change in Hiroaki's expression as he read the note. Sunskoku, on the other
hand, had more reason to be vigilant. Both her
own and her family's future depended on Hiroaki's success or failure.

Sliding closer to him on her knees, she leaned
in enough to murmur in his ear. "Have your guests
begun to bore you? Would you like the girls to take
them to private rooms?"

The inspector gave no indication he'd heard
her, responding to one of the official's drunken
jests with a smile—adding a coarse comment of his
own that generated another round of ribald laughter. But a moment later, he waved away the maidservant offering him a tray of sweets and stopped
the musician playing the samisen with a nod. "I
fear an early morning meeting requires me to bid
you good night," he said, keeping his voice casual

and mild. "Could I interest you men in some further amusements in private rooms?"

Sunskoku signaled the geishas with the merest dip of her head and they all began pulling their male companions to their feet with whispered words of seduction. The Green House employed only the most charming, accomplished geishas and the inebriated bureaucrats were guided from the room before most fully understood what had transpired.

As the door slid shut on his guests, Hiroaki reached for his sake cup. "It's a wonder anything gets accomplished," he muttered, "with the ignorant louts in positions of authority." Lifting his cup to his mouth he drained it.

"Your Excellency deserves better than to be burdened with men of such mediocrity," Sunskoku said soothingly, picking up the sake bottle from the brazier.

"Perhaps soon I can have them all banished from court."

"If your search goes well," she noted quietly, watching his eyes as she leaned forward to add a small portion of wine to his cup.

"It's just a matter of time," he replied, careful to give nothing away.

"The senior council will reward you handsomely, Your Excellency, once the prisoner is in your hands."

With that possibility less certain at the moment, a faint tic flitted over his jaw. "Did the captain mention his sailing plans?" he asked in a studiously offhand tone.

So that was his bad news. The princess was still

at large. If she'd been captured, the captain's sailing plans would be irrelevant. "We did very little talking, Your Excellency. Captain Drummond wasn't a conversationalist." Whether she knew or not, a man like Hiroaki didn't inspire loyalty. "If you had told me you needed his departure schedule, Your Excellency . . ." she murmured mendaciously.

"Yes, well . . . who was to know at the time." Hiroaki set down his cup. "Advise me immediately if any of your informants hear rumors concerning the captain. In the meantime, don't go far," he added, rising to his feet. "I may need you."

"Yes, Your Excellency." She bowed low. "I await your summons."

For a brief moment, he'd considered staying the night. He'd paid the brothel a fortune for Sunskoku's contract and the most beautiful geisha in Edo, renowned for her sexual talents, was at his disposal. But sweet little Aiko was refreshingly naive, so young she'd not yet been tainted by corruption—stark contrast to the perfidious liars and sycophants prevalent in his world. And after the galling news recently conveyed to him, he needed a refuge from artifice and treachery.

The geisha before him too much a paragon of deceit.

"If you ever dare lie to me," he said peevishly, letting his guard slip for a moment before recovering himself. "Which I'm sure you won't," he added, his voice once again silky smooth. "We both understand the game, don't we, my dear."

"Distinctly, Your Excellency." Her tone was softly agreeable, her gaze open.

He looked at her for a potent moment, his expression unreadable, and then turning, he walked from the room.

With not so much as a *ryo,* a gold coin, of payment for the cost of the evening's entertainment, she thought resentfully, her smile vanishing. And he'd given her warning not to fail him—his comment about lying a patent threat. If his pursuit of the princess proved a failure *and* if word of it were to surface, the chief inspector would have a great deal of explaining to do. His position would be at serious risk, every prominent office subject to court intrigue, double dealing and betrayal, every councillor on the alert to advance a relative at someone else's expense. The moment it looked as if Hiroaki had failed at his job—at the very least—he would be replaced by someone's cousin or uncle or brother. At the worst, he would be exiled or ordered to commit *seppuku.*

Her heart began beating faster, no calming thoughts or attempts at reason sufficient to still her racing pulse. This might be the beginning of the end for Hiroaki, his countless enemies just waiting to pounce, the possibility of failure very real against an adversary like Hugh-san. The captain dealt with men of Hiroaki's ilk every day in his business—unscrupulous, ruthless men. And the fact that he'd survived so long wasn't due to luck.

Since she'd been paid to spy on him, she'd overheard many conversations between Hugh and his first mate and she knew the captain had a dozen vessels plying their trade between America and the Orient. He'd spent the last several years battling the pirates of the China Sea, Macao, and the Straits of Malucca, all vicious predators who gave no quarter. And he'd not only survived, but prospered.

Hiroaki, cowardly schemer that he was, may have finally met a man who couldn't be cowed or bought off or threatened with physical harm.

Sitting amidst the resplendent decor of her chambers, the gold-leafed panels and painted screens, her lacquer chests filled with extravagant silk robes, her luxurious bedding piled high in the wardrobes next door, Sunskoku seriously considered leaving it all behind for the first time. She could take nothing with her if she fled. If she packed even the smallest parcel of belongings, it would give her away. There were eyes everywhere watching her in her gilded cage.

If she ran—the prospect still too terrifying to actually commit to—she would have to warn her family somehow. Not an easy task when they lived in a distant fief. More difficult still when they would have to leave the country with her or die.

Professional trackers would be hired to bring her back if she fled, her contract representing a huge loss for the brothel. Simultaneously, assassins would be sent out to murder her family—their fate tied to hers. Fear of such reprisals was an effective means of controlling the geishas. Not that Sunskoku hadn't thought of flight anyway. In fact, it had been a constant in her mind from the first day she'd entered the Yoshiwara.

What she'd never quite managed to contrive was how to save herself *and* her family.

Although if Hiroaki's star began to fall, she might no longer be at liberty to make a choice. He would need someone to blame and she would be convenient.

Which meant she'd need an accomplice. Someone like Yukio perhaps—one of the handsome young enforcers the brothel employed who professed undying love for her. As did any number of men, she reflected cynically . . . when what she really needed was loyalty and trust.

However . . . if the princess wasn't captured in the next few days, she would have to risk asking him to warn her family.

She shut her eyes against the headache beginning to form at her temples, cursing men like Hiroaki who were never satisfied. Who never had enough power, or money or fame. Who always wanted more. In this case, his reach may have exceeded his grasp, and most irksome was the fact that he might take her down with him.

On the other hand, a small voice inside her head noted, flight might not be necessary if Hiroaki was to meet an untimely death.

Her eyes opened and she quickly looked around as though the small voice might have been overheard in this house where nothing was secret, where the walls had ears—and peepholes.

Composing her features, she rose from her knees.

She was sleeping alone tonight—at her small cottage outside the Yoshiwara.

Where a modicum of peace was possible.

She'd wait until morning to make any decisions.

And time enough to consider murder, she reflected, when all other avenues were closed.

Chapter

11

Even with the abbot's assurance that all of Hiroaki's assassins had been garrotted, Hugh waited until the moon slid behind a cloud bank before taking Tama's hand and slipping through a small gate near the stable block.

Standing motionless outside the walls, he listened to the night sounds for a lengthy interval before dropping her hand, signaling she stay behind him, and moving forward. They traveled at a slow trot, a pace both could keep up indefinitely, moving through the forest on the paths described to them by the abbot. There was enough of a moon to light their way and before long, their eyes were so accustomed to the dark, even if the moon were covered by clouds, as it was from time to time, it didn't affect their speed.

They'd been on the trail for nearly an hour when Hugh put out his hand and came to a stop. Pointing to his ear, he nodded in the direction from which they'd come. Straining her ears, Tama listened, her brow furrowed. Nothing.

She shook her head.

He held up his finger, telling her to wait.

A second passed, two, three, four, five, six, and then she smiled.

She'd heard it.

He put up his hand again—two fingers raised, then three, his brows arched in query.

Once she'd heard the sounds of running, however faint, they thundered in her ears. She held up three fingers and nodded decisively.

He grinned.

And she realized he'd been testing her.

Silently, with hand motions alone, he made her understand his plan. And moments later after he'd left conspicuous indication of their passage in disturbed pine needles and a broken branch, they were waiting fifty yards beyond a curve in the trail, crouched in the underbrush.

The sights of his Spencer repeating rifle were trained midway between their concealed position and the curve in the trail. He wanted all three trackers to be visible before he fired. With the capability of firing seven rounds in ten seconds, he could get them all if he could kill the last man first and block their retreat.

Barely breathing, he calmly waited. Three were manageable.

Tama had her swords ready should she need them, but she understood avoiding hand-to-hand combat was to their advantage. *Immature strategy is the cause of grief.* That was a true saying, the great Mushashi warned. She was willing to wait.

The first ninja came loping down the path, certain of his prey, no longer concerned with concealment, the second and third mere strides behind. They were moving fast, as though they could already scent victory.

Hugh squeezed off the first shot, the last ninja dropping with a fifty caliber round between what was left of his eyes. The second man had half turned to run when the top of his head disappeared in an explosion of blood and bone and flesh. The ninja in the lead dropped into a crouch, hoping to make a smaller target. But Hugh could hit the bull's-eye at a thousand yards. The lead assassin died before he could draw his sword.

"Go!" Hugh hissed. "I'll catch up." If there were reinforcements ahead, the ninja wouldn't have been traveling so fast. She was safe.

Tama didn't hesitate. He was proud of her. And as she raced away, he approached the three trackers, his Colt revolvers drawn; he knew of too many foreigners who had been killed by samurai they'd presumed dead.

But at close range, there was no mistaking death.

Quickly searching them, he didn't expect to find anything and he didn't. Ninja carried only weapons, not identification. Yet, he was curious why the chief inspector was mounting such a massive chase. Surely the princess wasn't the only noble from the defeated clans remaining free.

Although, she was one of the wealthier ones.

And the smell of money always brought out the vultures, didn't it.

Catching up with Tama a few minutes later, he pulled her to a stop. "There're three less on our trail. No identification, of course."

"If any more are in the vicinity, they would have

heard the rifle report. Should we change direction?"

"When it's closer to daylight, we will. Right now, we have to stay ahead of them. Are you able to pick up the pace?"

"Yes."

"You lead," he said. Because there were bound to be more coming and this time the assassins wouldn't be as likely to walk into an ambush.

Their path was clear, the rolling landscape no longer densely wooded, and they were able to travel a considerable distance before Hugh came to a stop.

"I heard," she said.

"Can you fire a revolver?"

"If I have to."

"What does that mean?"

"It means I prefer my swords, but my father's armory was complete." She smiled. "We had Spencer rifles too."

"Care to tell me how many are behind us this time?"

"Five. Bigger men than last time. That's why they're slower."

"But they haven't stopped coming."

"Nor will they. Failure means death for them."

He swore softly, although he was as aware as she of the samurai code.

"I'm sorry for bringing this plague down on you."

"If we get out of here, you can show your appreciation."

His voice was so gruff she didn't know how to interpret his statement. "I'm at your service, Hugh-san," she said as amends.

He grinned. *"Now* you're suddenly obliging."

"It's all about timing," she said, grinning back.

"If we had a few more seconds, I'd call you on that."

"Once we're on board your ship, you may call me anytime."

"I'm holding you to that promise," he murmured, handing her one of his revolvers. "It's cocked, so take care."

"Six rounds, forty-four caliber, firing speed eight seconds. I think I can manage."

"You target the one in the lead, I'll take care of the rest."

"They won't be strung out like last time."

"No kidding. Now, I hope you don't mind getting wet."

He'd waited for suitable terrain before stopping, the marshland before them offering optimal concealment. Moments later, they were squatting up to their necks in cold water, their feet sunk into the swampy muck, their weapons resting on hillocks of marsh hay that lay around them in great sweeping drifts.

After what seemed a very long time—the trackers must have reconnoitered carefully this time—Tama saw a single figure approach the path over the marsh. As she questioned Hugh with a glance, he warned her off. *Don't shoot.*

The first man was bait. If they fired, their positions would be compromised and breaking out of this muck quickly was impossible.

As the lone man made his way down the pathway, they waited.

The ninja stopped after several yards, turned and waved.

He was a damned tempting target silhouetted against the moon.

But their caution was rewarded a second later when a flash of movement on the eastern perimeter of the marsh responded to the wave. And then another on the western perimeter, followed by a fourth shockingly close to them.

Dammit, Hugh muttered to himself. Where was the fifth man?

A nightingale cooed overhead and to the left . . . there. Right above the entrance to the marsh.

His gaze met Tama's and he nodded.

As her shot rang out, Hugh took out the man closest to them first, swinging his rifle barrel around to target man two and three in rapid sequence. He was counting on the assassin in the tree to take a second or two to decide whether he should stay where he was or drop to the ground. Just. Like. That. Hugh's fourth shot caught the ninja in the head, mid-drop. In terms of making sure your enemies didn't get up again, he preferred the head shot.

"I may have gotten the one closest to us too," Tama murmured, confident enough of their shooting skills to come to her feet. "I'm freezing."

"You'll warm up soon enough. We're going to have to really move if we want to get far enough ahead to change direction. We should head east soon and we need to do it without trackers."

Tama was hauling herself out of the water before he'd finished speaking and this time he didn't pause to verify their kills.

They ran full out.

Just before dawn, they reached their destination, coming up the trail to a small rustic pavilion overlooking a waterfall. The thatched-roof dwelling and gnarled pines clung to the rocky precipice seemingly in defiance of gravity.

In terms of defense it was perfect, Hugh contemplated gratefully. One way in, the long uphill trail clearly visible from above.

"Do we dare go inside?" Tama murmured, viewing the precariously placed structure. "That rookery looks as though it might tumble down the ravine any minute."

Hugh grinned. "You go in first. You're lighter."

"Thank you very much. For that, I may go in and lock the door behind me."

"Lot of good that will do you," he said softly.

"Are you telling me I can't keep you out?"

"I don't think you want to."

That particular low, husky intonation triggered highly susceptible receptors in her body, receptors apparently immune to danger. "Is it safe?" she asked, reason not quite as ready to avail itself of mindless pleasure.

"Is what safe?"

"Us. Here. This place."

"Yes to two and three. I'm not so sure about us."

"Because?" Her voice was teasing now.

"Because I have this overwhelming need to ravish you with or without your consent."

"What makes you think I'd refuse?"

He laughed. "Indeed. So do we eat first or second? I'm starved on both accounts."

"Is some order required?"

"Nothing's required, darling." He held out his hand and when she placed hers in his without hesitation, they both smiled.

"We're alive," she murmured.

"Oh, yes. I'm feeling very much alive. By the way, thanks for your help. If I'm ever in a firefight, feel free to join me."

"You're awesome, Hugh-san. A true warrior."

"You're only saying that so you'll have your way with me," he mocked, uncomfortable with praise.

"Hardly. I can have my way with you anytime I want."

He grimaced. "Unfortunately, that's true."

"What's unfortunate about it?"

"Nothing, darling, absolutely nothing." And he meant it, which was perhaps the reason he decided to change the subject. Wanting sex was one thing. Wanting a woman without reason was something else entirely. "Come, sweetheart, we'll see how rustic these monks like their hermitages."

The rough outside turned out to be a faux peasant hut disguising a magnificent interior. The single room was composed of the most rare, beautiful materials, the uprights and cross beams of plain unpolished *keaki* wood fastened with polished brass bolts and capped with gold leaf, hangings of rare brocades embroidered with peacocks and cranes, azaleas and bamboos graced the walls, the finest rush mats covered the floor. The tokonoma alcove was adorned with a large vase of forsythia, the flowers obviously forced this time of year and so fresh, the arrangement must have been placed there recently.

"You do know the most unusual monks," Tama murmured, slowly turning around, taking in the glory of the room.

"They're not monks by choice, which accounts for their style of living."

"Does Lord Yabe hope to be pardoned someday?"

"He's certain of it." Hugh smiled. "And I suspect, if he isn't, he'll see that his enemies suffer for their obstinacy. He intends to be free one way or another. Like you."

She sighed softly. "In due time, Hugh-san. Right now, it's enough to have survived another day."

"All you have to do is plan what you're going to say to convince your brother to return. I have no intention of dying. Nor will you."

"I adore your certainty," she said, opening her arms wide and twirling in lighthearted cheer. "Thank you ever so much."

"You did your share tonight. You don't have to thank me. Now, are you going to feed me or not?"

"You mean there are no servants here? What are we going to do?" she wailed playfully, coming to a stop.

"It's as good a time as any to learn the fundamentals, Princess. Look in those cupboards and take out anything you think is edible. We'll figure it out."

Chapter

12

As the search moved into the second day, Hiroaki was tortured with doubt. Could he call off the search or was it too late to have his actions go unnoticed? Perhaps it would be safer to shift the focus of his pursuit from the princess to Captain Drummond. He could concoct some treasonous charges that would give him reason to have sent out such a massive hunt. Or could Lord Yabe at the monastery become the object of his investigation?—a thought he rejected almost immediately. Lord Yabe had powerful allies, his pardon already making its way through the necessary channels.

The chief inspector grimaced.

None of the answers were palatable, not with so many of his men aware of the object of his search. Damn the American gunrunner. If Drummond hadn't suddenly taken center stage in this drama, the princess would have been long since captured.

Instead, as of Hiroaki's last report an hour ago,

he had upward of thirty men dead or wounded and the princess and captain had disappeared.

Disappeared! He couldn't believe it! In a country this size? In the limited area between Edo and Osaka? Although, apparently even the American's crew didn't know where he was, he'd been told by an informant. The captain's ship was at anchor near Osaka and the *Southern Belle*'s new cook was going to earn a small fortune when and if he discovered the whereabouts of the elusive captain.

Hiroaki stared out the window. Edo Bay was choppy this afternoon, the sky overcast, a chill in the air. Although it wasn't the cool weather making his blood run cold; it was the thought of his enemies lining up to witness his very public fall from grace. He'd actually stayed home last night in the event he'd meet some of his colleagues who might ask him questions he'd rather not answer. He hadn't spent an evening under the same roof as his wife . . . for years—although he'd not so lost his consequence as to speak to the lowly merchant's daughter whose dowry had financed his initial climb to power. But he couldn't be home two nights running. He would have to go out and be seen.

A second evening in the bosom of his family would cause undue speculation, and so drastic a change in the patterns of a lifetime would have the spies chattering. He couldn't afford the gossip.

Not with messengers arriving on the hour.

His enemies were sure to know something was afoot.

Sunskoku would have to serve as decoy for him tonight.

Let everyone observe him in fine spirits, being entertained and amused by the reigning beauty of the day.

Whom he owned body and soul.

Hiroaki's summons came very late, much later than etiquette allowed, and if it had been anyone but the chief inspector requesting her company, Sunskoku would have refused. She had her reputation to uphold. A geisha of her consequence expected rigid protocol be observed.

Her intended entertainment had to be canceled, the patron who had been expecting to spend the evening with her consoled with an appointment the following night. And while her servants scurried about, making sure Hiroaki's favorite dishes were prepared, his prized wines heated, the musicians he preferred engaged, Sunskoku readied herself to be gracious to the man who held her life in his hands.

Her years of training in specious flattery held her in good stead when she greeted him, her welcome one of warm delight. "How kind of you to grace us with your presence, O-metsuke," she murmured, kneeling before him, bowing low, her forehead touching the mat.

"I feel the need for some entertainment," he replied gruffly, bidding her rise with a wave of his hand. "My duties become too onerous at times."

"A man of your consequence, my lord, requires leisure from the burden of his many cares. May I offer you some relaxing music and wine?"

He stared at her for a moment as though he'd not heard her words, his gaze dour, and just as she was about to speak again, he said, "Why not," in a tone so abrupt and curt, she felt a small chill run up her spine.

Had she done something to offend him?

Was he here to chastise her?

She felt for the small dagger in her sleeve pocket as though for reassurance.

"Send your servants away," he ordered.

Fear gripped her heart, but she obeyed, no sign of her agitation visible.

"Sit," he commanded next.

And she sat.

Sinking down on one of her luxurious cushions, he allowed himself a quiet sigh. "I am assailed by stupidity and incompetence," he muttered.

His sigh gave her courage. Was he here tonight like so many of her clients—to find solace from the cares of the world? "If I may help in any way, Your Excellency, you need but ask," she murmured.

His gaze was shuttered once again, his small concession to humanity quickly shrouded. "Some wine, perhaps," he said, wishing he was looking at the unassuming little Aiko instead of this stunning creature coveted by every red-blooded man in Edo.

And yet appearances must be maintained.

There was something in his tone, an infinitesimal undercurrent of hesitancy never before heard that made Sunskoku conjecture that she might have been given the smallest of chances to escape. With the raw courage that had allowed her to thrive in a culture of brutality and violence, she said bluntly, "If you haven't found the captain yet, would it help if I were to try to find his first mate? The man knows me. I could approach him with ease."

Hiroaki understood what she meant by approach. What man alive would turn her away? And the quick spat of anger that had erupted when she'd dared to broach covert matters immediately dissipated before the possibility of success she offered.

"Do you know where he is?"

She knew better than to answer yes, although she had her spies too. "I don't. I thought you might."

"As a matter of fact, I do," he replied, watching her closely.

Sunskoku had been sold into the world of the Yoshiwara when she was eight and trained for four years, at which point her virginity had been sold to the highest bidder. She could have concealed her feelings from God himself. "Then, perhaps, I could be of assistance to you," she said calmly.

"What if his first mate doesn't know where the captain is?"

"He will eventually. And I doubt he'll mind if I stay for a time."

"No, I don't suppose he will," Hiroaki noted drily. "I'll send two men along should you need assistance."

"How kind of you," she observed, when she knew they would be a major obstruction. "When would you like me to leave?" She gave him an artless smile, her expression innocent of guile. "Or I should ask instead, where would you like me to go?"

If he was being deceived, she was a superb actress. "Osaka," he said, because it didn't matter if she knew or not so long as she delivered the information he needed. Particularly since no one else seemed capable of the task. "And I want you to leave immediately." For the first time today, he felt a renewed confidence, the celebrated courtesan unlikely to be refused admittance to the captain's vessel. Perhaps he would have good news soon. He came to his feet in a surge of energy, the possibility of spending the rest of the night with Aiko more agreeable than exchanging half-truths with Sunskoku. "Send any information you discover immediately," he ordered, walking past her without a nod of recognition or a farewell, confident she understood what was expected of her. More confident she knew the consequences of failure.

As his footsteps echoed down the hall, Sunskoku swore if she ever attained her freedom, she would never again deal with rude, arrogant men who looked through her with disdain. Buoyed by hope, however tenuous, she sent for Yukio and began packing. She could take very little, although a journey to Osaka under the O-metsuke's orders would at least require a modest wardrobe—allowing her to remove more than she thought possible a short time ago. She could hide a portion of her gold in her robes. Enough hopefully to buy her way to freedom.

When Yukio arrived she told him nothing more than that she would require his escort to Osaka. "I'm traveling on a mission for the chief inspector. His men will accompany us. But I want you for my personal bodyguard."

As would the brothel, Yukio understood, their most celebrated geisha would not likely be allowed such a journey unaccompanied. "My pleasure," he said, bowing gracefully. "When do we leave?"

"I need someone I can trust," she said, double entendre in her words.

"I am trustworthy," he replied, knowing as she did, that the walls had ears. "You needn't fear the chief inspector's men."

She smiled at his tactful reply. "Perfect. We may be gone for a week or so. Pack what you need. I have orders to leave immediately." Then Sunskoku sent for her maid to deliver a message to the manager of the brothel.

Within minutes, the madam arrived, full of questions, although Hiroaki's men had spoken to her already.

"If you wish to know more, question the chief inspector," Sunskoku offered, knowing how unlikely that would be. "He's sending me to Osaka on some private matter. The circumstances are not for your ears. Yukio and two of the inspector's men will accompany me. Your property will be well guarded."

The woman who managed the prestigious brothel had once been a celebrated beauty like

Sunskoku. Past her prime, relegated to a servant's post and salary, she was officious and resentful. "We'll expect you back soon."

"You'll expect me when the chief inspector tells you to expect me," Sunskoku retorted, having borne the brunt of the woman's wrath too many times in her youth to accede her position of power. "If you have any confusion about your role in this endeavor, take it up with the O-metsuke."

"We'll be watching you," snapped the thin-lipped crone. "Don't forget who trained you and made you the most celebrated *tayu* in Edo."

"Don't worry. I'll never forget who trained me," Sunskoku replied bitterly. "I remember every whipping and beating, every insult and degradation."

"Ungrateful slut. You'd be in the rice fields burdened with a drunken husband and ten children if we hadn't bought you."

"Let's just say I'm as grateful as you are for your life. Now if you'll excuse me, Lord Hiroaki instructed me to dress well for this assignment. I have some packing to do."

She knew they'd be watching her, but she'd already secreted what she could of her gold; the rest would have to be left.

"You're fast," Yukio said with a smile when he returned a short time later to find her seated on one of her wicker baskets, waiting.

"Lord Hiroaki's in a hurry," she said blandly. "I am but an instrument of his decrees."

The smallest flicker of disbelief flashed in Yukio's eyes, but his voice when he spoke was as mild as hers. "His men are waiting downstairs. We're to ride, so the inspector must consider this mission urgent. Wear a warm cloak."

Chapter

13

"I have some pleasant news, my lord," murmured pretty little Aiko, looking down modestly before meeting Hiroaki's gaze once again and smiling.

The chief inspector was seated across from his young mistress, the small table between them strewn with food and drink, his brain fuzzy from too much sake. But he was relaxed for the first time in days, Sunskoku already on the road south per his most recent messenger, a favorable outcome to their mission highly likely. The *tayu* was a woman of many accomplishments.

He could almost taste success. Which added an element of gentleness to his tone. "Tell me your good news, little one."

"I'm pregnant, my lord. And the abbess at the temple assures me it's a boy."

"Ah." His first thought was she would be ungainly soon and less appealing, but she looked so sweetly joyous, he found himself almost wanting to please her. "How delightful, my dear," he said. "You'll make a very pretty mother."

Hiroaki had twelve sons and eight daughters by his wife and various concubines. He needed an obedient mistress more than another son, but it never paid to speak with candor. So he smiled instead and beckoned to her. "Come here, my pet, and show me your belly. . . ."

He would have the housekeeper put a drug in Aiko's morning tea to terminate her pregnancy. Time enough for her to have a child when he tired of her. Which was not the present case. Her sweet innocence amused him or perhaps distracted him from the violence of his world. "Have you thought of any names?" he inquired gently.

Chapter

14

At their first post stop, Sunskoku suggested Hiroaki's men have a cup of sake to stave off the cold and she and Yukio would see to acquiring fresh horses.

Despite the chief inspector's orders to make the journey with all haste, the night was cold and wet and miserable. His men hesitated only briefly. "And see that you don't rifle through our packs," one of the troopers warned. "I'll have your heads if you do."

Glaring at the two samurai sauntering off to the warmth of the inn, Yukio hissed, "Arrogant bastards. I'd like to see them try to take my head."

"Their arrogance will be their downfall. But we need them for the moment so don't let your temper get out of hand. Give the stable boys this—" Sunskoku handed him a large coin. "I want good horses, not the kind Hiroaki is willing to pay for. I'll wait for you over there."

The small shed beside the stable door offered shelter from the storm and privacy.

A few moments later Yukio joined her. "Now tell me what's really going on." Shaking the sleet and rain from his cloak, he leaned against the rough wall and half smiled. "Because this is a helluva night for you to be on the road, Hiroaki's orders or not."

"I don't know what you mean." She tipped her face upward, artless innocence in her gaze.

"This is more than a mission for Hiroaki," he said bluntly, innocence unlikely in his world. "So tell me or I'll make some excuse and return to Edo."

"You wouldn't," she challenged. "The Green House will sack you—or worse."

"I'll think of something. The old hag who runs the place likes me," he said with a wink.

"You haven't!"

"Spare me your shock. We both do what we have to, to survive." Yukio's mother had been murdered when he was young, and alone and destitute, he'd turned to petty crime. He'd been strong for his age and quick of mind. Before long, the local yakuza had seen his potential and brought him into the fold.

"Forgive me. I don't like her, that's all."

"No one likes the *obasan*. What's that got to do with anything? Now, where are we going and what do you want me for?"

"Can I trust you?"

"Can I trust *you?*"

There was a small pause while both gauged the extent of their danger. For two people who had been cast into a brutal world as children, trust was an equivocal word.

"What I need from you could cost you your life."

"My life is at risk every day."

His expression gave away nothing of the man. "Why did you come? You didn't have to."

He shrugged. "You know why."

"I hear words of love from every man I meet."

"No doubt. The difference is, I mean it."

"More fool you, perhaps. Look," she said with a small sigh, perplexed by talk of love. "I'll be honest with you because everything is at stake." She shut her eyes briefly, wondering whether she was jeopardizing her life by confiding in him. The yakuza dealt cruelly with traitors. Would he risk so much for her?

"Your luggage is too heavy for clothing alone," he pointed out, his tone blunt and factual. "You're not coming back, are you?"

Fear glittered in her eyes for a fleeting moment as she tried to recall who had handled her baskets.

"No one touched them but me," he offered gently.

"Can you read minds?" she breathed, her pulse beginning to race, the punishment for geishas who took flight often that of being placed in the meanest cribs on the waterfront.

"I can read yours because we both live with the same fear. And we both overcome it a hundred times a day." He quickly surveyed the stable yard, conscious of the peril in what he was about to say. "I'll go with you anywhere. Do anything for you. You have but to ask."

She'd heard such protestations too many times; perhaps she was inured. "What I want and need right now," she said simply, "is for you to warn my family and take them away from Owari."

There was no need to explain the reason why. "I'll find someone to go."

"I was hoping you would."

He shook his head. "I'm not leaving you. Where you go, I go. But Noguchi will do anything I want, no questions asked. If I send for him, he'll overtake us by morning. Especially if Hiroaki's men prefer the warmth of the tavern to a cold night on the road."

"I doubt they'll dare stay in there long."

"We could have their sake drugged."

"Could we?" Noguchi would have time to reach them.

Yukio smiled. "Money buys everything, you know that."

"How much?"

"They'd kill for ten *ryo*. Three should be enough to slip a sleeping potion in some sake."

Her gaze narrowed. "You know these people."

"Why do you think we stopped here for fresh horses?" he said with a grin.

"You're absolutely wonderful," she murmured, experiencing gratitude for the first time in years, finding herself almost believing in hope.

He gently touched her chin and lifted her face. "I will expect something from you in return."

"Of course. Anything."

"I want you to think about love."

She'd expected something more conventional and achievable. "I'm not sure I can," she said. "It's been too long."

"I just want you to try." He ran his finger down

her cheek, the tattoos on his hand dark against her pale skin. "You might like it."

Her bewilderment was plain. "How can you feel something so alien and remote?" she inquired, each word tinged with doubt. "How is it possible after all we've been through?"

Cupping her face in his hands, he bent low, so their eyes were level. "There's no explanation." He smiled. "You've bewitched me."

She laughed softly. "You're crazy; I knew it."

He shook his head. "It's a glorious enchantment. Wait and see."

"So sure," she whispered, a winsomeness to her voice.

"You'll like it," he murmured. "Believe me."

Even if she did, it wouldn't last, she thought, a dearth of love and kindness in her world. "If you say so," she replied ambiguously, not wishing to offend him when she was in need of his talents.

"Afraid to gamble?" he teased.

"Deathly afraid. Terrified."

"Then stay here and don't move." Dropping a light kiss on her mouth, he stepped away. "I'll take care of everything."

Well schooled in self-control, she quickly regained her composure and smiled. "I'm so very glad you came along."

"Not as glad as I. But be warned," he declared brusquely, "I'm here for good."

Her emotions in tumult, she watched him walk away, his tall, broad-shouldered form exuding a kind of confidence she could only wish for, his wind-tossed hair and long-legged stride a pithy display of his boldness and spirit.

Taking chances had been beaten out of her long ago. And yet here she was, with a rash and reckless man telling her to treat her life like a throw of the dice.

She shivered faintly, from the cold or fear, she wasn't sure.

But she was glad he was with her, pleased he could laugh in the face of danger, and in a portion of her brain where she'd locked away feeling long ago, she allowed the smallest glimmer of joy to break through.

Chapter
15

Shortly after breakfast the following morning, the fair Aiko was doubled over in pain, her face white with fear, the child she'd so wanted being cast from her body. She sent Hiroaki a note pleading for his presence, but he only responded with a message of condolence brought by his personal physician who had orders to stay in attendance as long as he was needed. With regret, the chief inspector informed his mistress, his schedule was filled with meetings for the remainder of the week.

That same morning, Sunskoku and Yukio waited for Hiroaki's men to wake from their drugged sleep. They'd made a rough bed for themselves in the stable in the event the samurái had overcome the potion and appeared during the night. But it was late morning when Hiroaki's retainers arrived, surly, unapologetic, and intent on exerting their authority. Having long ago learned to offer bland visages to the world, neither Sunskoku nor Yukio responded to the troopers incivilities.

The samurai class had been raised to its exalted position by the first shogun in 1192, but since the Battle of Sekigahara in 1600 and the consolidation of power under the Tokugawas, the prestige of the samurai had steadily eroded. Although, until recently, if a samurai felt insulted by someone of a lesser class, he could kill that person with impunity. Hiroaki's men were still operating under the old traditions.

Not that loyalty to their overlord didn't take precedence—and in this case Hiroaki's orders kept their churlishness within bounds. But amidst great grumbling and small tyrannies to their inferiors, the troopers were finally mounted and under leaden skies the party took to the road.

Anticipating the events at his mistress's and wishing to be well away from them, Hiroaki had reached his office early that morning. Although not a praying man, he'd stopped briefly en route at a shrine, and offered up a prayer for the success of his mission. So much was at stake this time, the prize so valuable, he was willing to use whatever means necessary to ensure a favorable outcome to his quest.

His normal means of operation was already functioning, his vast spy network committed almost in its entirety to finding the princess. To that purpose, he had his principal secretary summoned the moment he reached his office.

Pacing while he waited for his man to arrive, Hiroaki chose to dwell on the positives rather than the negatives of his pursuit, collating the various rewards that could come his way should events transpire as he planned. He also ran down a list of enemies he would see banished from court—an amusing conceit that offered pleasant respite from more daunting concerns. He was deep in a mental review of which new estates he might purchase with his prize money when his secretary was announced, his mood lightened enough by his musing to greet the man with a rare smile.

Hiroaki's odd smirk was so shocking the poor man racked his brain for what possible cunning lay behind the unusual sight. Was the chief inspector drunk? Or trying to throw him off the scent of something ominous? Was he setting some trap? Quickly running through the recent events in his life, the secretary tried to recall if he might have botched some assignment.

"I need an update on the search for the princess," Hiroaki said briskly. "As well as any new reports since last evening. I assume no one outside this office knows of our activities," he added casually.

The spy felt his fear evaporate, his master's curious behavior explained. The chief inspector was worried about the repercussions of possible failure. "Everything is quiet, my lord. Nothing is known of the search outside our private network."

"You're certain."

He couldn't say abject terror kept Hiroaki's spies mute. "I'm certain, my lord."

"Good. Good." The chief inspector's relief was visible.

A troubling sight to his subordinate who understood how damning visible emotion could be. It meant the man's nerve was gone. An unpleasant revelation that could be an antecedent to disaster—the ripple effect of any failure sure to engulf all those working for the inspector.

"I can expect some further news of our quarry by the end of the day?"

"One would expect so, my lord. We're scouring the country."

It wasn't the precise answer Hiroaki wanted. "This must be kept secret at all costs," the chief inspector reiterated, a grimace creasing his cheek.

"Yes, sir, I understand."

"There's no margin for error," the inspector growled. "You realize lives depend on the success of the search," Hiroaki added ominously.

"I understand, Your Excellency." It was the usual threat against failure, but Hiroaki's chief spy also understood that this time Hiroaki's fate could be in the balance.

It made one begin to choose sides.

"Well, get on with it," Hiroaki ordered crisply, waving him off. "And send in my breakfast."

Chapter

16

While the location of the princess was causing concern in various quarters, the object of Hiroaki's search had just come awake. And while the gloomy skies and wet weather may have dampened the spirits of those pursuing her, the princess rolled over in bed, looked at the drizzle outside and said brightly, "Don't you just love the rain?"

"At times like this I do." Drawing her into the circle of his arms, Hugh gently kissed her. "Did you sleep well?"

"Very well, indeed, thanks to you." Countless orgasms had had a narcotic effect on her. "Did you?"

"Yes," he lied, more awake than not during the night in the event Hiroaki's men had followed them. "Are you hungry?"

"Always with you." She smiled. "It's the strenuous exercise."

He grinned. "Getting here?"

"And staying here. I smell hot tea."

"And miso soup. I thought you might like some

warm food before you take a cold shower under the waterfall."

"Unlike you, I do not subscribe to Tendai principles. Take your cold shower alone."

"What if I made it worth your while?"

"Are you saying I can't heat water?"

"This is faster."

She glanced outside at the drizzle and snuggled deeper under the quilt. "How much worth my while?"

"I think I can guarantee you won't be cold."

Her expression brightened. "Is that so."

"It's a fact."

"You're much too assured. I should take offense at your expertise."

"Why would you want to do that?"

She smiled. "You're right. May I wear this quilt down to the water?"

"Be my guest."

But he fed her the soup a spoonful at a time before they left, the exercise punctuated with kisses and salacious promises and before long, she was warm enough to discard the quilt. "You did that on purpose," she murmured, regarding him with a sportive glance.

"I didn't want to ruin the quilt in the mud." He held out his hand. "Ready?"

"Oh, yes, Hugh-san, I'm more than ready. Perhaps we should delay our departure for a minute or so. . . ."

"I know your minutes," he replied with a roguish smile. "You kept me up half the night."

"I assume that wasn't a problem for you."

"You assume correctly. However, you need my come washed off you."

"Are you saying I smell?"

"Of course not. I'm merely suggesting we wash off a layer or two before we start all over again."

"I like the idea of starting over again."

"Why am I not surprised?" he said drolly. And without further comment, he took her hand, pulled her to her feet, and led her outside.

He was right, although she didn't tell him so because he was much too confident already about his abilities, but the air felt warm on her heated skin, and as they stood under the chill water some moments later, she found herself appreciating the coolness. Particularly so after he began soaping her between her legs and never more so than when he followed that washing with the promised reward. He was clean and she was clean as he held her in his arms, her legs wrapped around his waist, his erection buried deep inside her and temperature was no longer an issue. She was flushed with urgent desire, each rhythmic stroke matched to the undulations of her hips, he up and she down, deep, deep, deep, the reverse oscillations following in prodigal gorging splendor, over and over again with such unbridled fury that when she climaxed she was left almost inert.

"Are you all right?"

He was breathing hard and looking worried. "Fine." She mouthed the word, the air in her lungs insufficient to enunciate it properly. "Perfect . . ."

But he carried her back up the trail to the hut, not sure the ice-cold water and fierce pumping of her heart were compatible.

And she lay unresisting in his arms, which worried him more.

"I'm sorry," he murmured as he laid her down on the bed. "That was too much for you."

She shook her head and smiled. "Never."

"Greedy little vixen," he whispered, covering her. "Sleep now and I'll give you more when you wake up."

"Promise?"

"Promise."

Her eyes were half shut, her voice the merest whisper. "I feel different with you."

He didn't need an explanation. He knew what she meant. And that worried him too.

He watched over her for a time as she slept and after assuring himself she wasn't harmed by the cold and excessive stimulation, he dozed off himself, the last few days having been almost entirely sleepless.

Waking sometime later, Tama took pleasure at the sight of him sleeping beside her. His beauty was breathtaking, his tall, rangy body hard-muscled and powerful, his ruffled curls enchanting. He had little of the strange foreignness of the blonde or red-haired men who came to her land. His swarthy looks were in a more familiar mold, although certainly no one would consider him common. His size alone set him apart, along with the stark beauty of his eyes. She'd noticed that first about him that night in Edo, although she'd not consciously recognized that assessment until now. Perhaps their peaceful surroundings allowed her the luxury of reflection. Perhaps she was already half in love with the man who had saved her life so many times. Perhaps every woman who looked on him fell in love. Or maybe only after having sex with him.

And why not? He was exceptionally skilled.

But he stirred in his sleep just then, and not wishing to be caught staring at him like some besotted young maid, she rose from the bed.

"Come back," he murmured, his eyes still shut.

"I'm going outside to practice," she said, desiring to extricate herself from her unwanted feelings of neediness. She couldn't afford to be emotionally bound to him, no matter his allure and benevolence. "I won't be gone long."

"I'll practice with you." He was instantly wide awake.

"That's not necessary. I usually practice alone."

"You wouldn't be afraid of some friendly competition, would you?"

"I'm not afraid of any kind of competition."

"Perfect. I could use some practice. One sword or both? Which drill do you prefer?"

"You choose. It doesn't matter."

He was on his feet instantly with the kind of fluid grace only superb conditioning allowed. And digging in his pack, he extricated two swords that had clearly been made by a master.

Slipping on his trousers, he followed her outside. The drizzle had lightened, the surrounding forest half shrouded in mist, the small clearing where she stood waiting brilliant green against the vaporous haze. Barefoot, he approached her and bowed as was customary before a match.

"Be my guest," she said quietly, bowing in turn, her hair tied back with a cord, her small feet in a perfect middle stance, her heels strong, her toes floating. "I'll defend."

She was indulging him as though he weren't completely competent. "I may be better than your brother."

She half smiled and tipped her head. "Why don't we see?"

He moved into the attack.

She parried, her blade sliding up his long sword with precision, holding him motionless blade to blade as the flint and spark hit with surprising strength for a hovering second before slipping away.

"Very good," she said. "Now let's do them in order. First technique."

They closed ranks, striking with their long swords, deflecting to the right, striking again, their swords up then bouncing down before they stepped apart.

"Second technique," he murmured, his guard in the upper position. "Your turn." Their swords met in a perfect synchronized rhythm, his from below, hers sweeping downward to block him.

And so it went through the third technique, each varying and adjusting their speed and stance, the position of their sword arms, striking, parrying, slapping, holding back, trying to anticipate their opponent's intent and tactic. So evenly matched in skill and expertise, they checked each other's blows with an unwavering tranquillity and calm, their sword work like a perfectly choreographed dance.

But despite the balanced rhythm, the proper execution required strenuous maneuvering and soon they were both sweating, their hair damp from the mist and their exertions, their sword grips wet from their palms.

"Two more techniques, Princess," Hugh panted.

"Come and get me. . . ." Breathing heavily, she tossed her head to dislodge a heavy fall of hair from her forehead. "Maybe you'll only get the chance for one more."

She was phenomenal, but he was one of Master Kodama's best pupils and he planned on finishing the fifth technique as well. His smile was impudent. "Maybe you're wrong."

She shifted her stance and lifted her chin in challenge.

He shifted left instead of right and it took her a split second to veer and meet his attack. She deflected his blade with a smooth parry, jumped back and grinned.

"Almost," he said, quickly closing.

Once again she met his attack and slipped away, but he kept coming, forcing her to parry over and over to meet his headlong offensive. He drove her back, forcing her toward the tree line, relentless in his assault, surprising her with a flurry of swift, fierce *katsu-totsu* strikes and stabs.

Until he held her hard against the rough bark of the tree, his two swords pinning her to the tree. "Now, then," he gasped, his chest heaving, "I think I deserve an apology."

"For what?" Her temper showed in eyes; she wasn't familiar with defeat.

"For thinking I was like your brother." His smile was cheeky.

"Very well; you're not like my brother. Now let me go."

"I might require a little reward as well."

She knew what he meant. "I'm not in the mood."

"That shouldn't be a problem."

"It is a problem. Release me."

"What if I said no. What if I said I'd like to have sex with you now."

"I dislike tyranny with my sex." But she'd felt him move against her ever so lightly and her traitorous body was responding as though it had no scruples.

"I wouldn't think of being a tyrant," he murmured, dropping his swords to the ground. "See— I'm harmless."

The hard length of his erection pulsed lightly against her belly, the wool of his trousers and her thin cotton pants insignificant barrier to her rapidly accelerating arousal. "I have my swords. What if I were to tell you to back away?"

"If you really meant it, I would."

"You needn't be so insolent. Don't women ever say no?"

He just smiled and lifted her swords from her hands. "I'm not sure it's a good idea to say no to sex."

"A philosophy that has held you in good stead, no doubt."

"So far," he murmured, reaching for the buttons on his trousers. "And admit, you're not really serious about not wanting sex."

"I might be."

"Or you might not be," he corrected softly, letting his trousers slide down his hips and legs, "if you can have this inside you." She couldn't help but look, he knew. "You like to come," he whispered, kicking his trousers aside. "And he likes to make you come. . . ."

He was lightly stroking his upthrust penis, the engorged erection reaching to his navel. It was impossible not to want that inside her; it was impossible to say no when her vagina was pulsing to the beat of her heart. When the fierce ache of desire surged upward in welcoming ripples. When he could make her climax like no one else. "Maybe just this once," she said.

His gaze swung upward and for an infinitesimal moment he debated taking offense at her tone. That useless option swiftly discarded, he said, "Fine," in lieu of voicing his more predacious resolve. "Take off your trousers." Perhaps he was taking offense after all.

"Pardon me?"

"You heard me." His voice was ultrasoft.

Unlike his alluring erection, she thought fretfully.

"I could masturbate, I suppose. It's up to you." Circling his erection with his fingers, he slid his hand downward, the swollen head flared higher, and she gasped. "Changed your mind?" he inquired silkily.

She didn't reply; she wouldn't give him the satisfaction. But she untied the cord at her waist, stripped her pants away and waited.

"Ask me."

"You're impossible," she said, heated and low.

"Ask."

"Give me that." A crisp command.

"Ask nicely."

She silently met his gaze, the only sound that of the mist dripping from the trees.

It was a Mexican standoff. He understood the concept even if she didn't. He also understood that look of longing in her eyes. "Never mind," he said and began turning away.

"Wait."

He swung back.

The part she wanted swung back a fraction of a second later. "I would very much like that"—she pointed—"inside me. Sir," she added with a smile.

Whether the deference in her smile was feigned or not was incidental. "My pleasure, Princess," he said gently, and reaching out, he grasped her around the waist. "I really mean it," he whispered, lifting her upward slightly, bending his knees enough to introduce the head of his penis between her legs, targeting her pulsing cleft with the expertise of considerable practice. There . . . exactly there and he pressed upward, burying himself in a swift ascent as the princess clung to him and whimpered with pleasure.

He was going to have to get a grip on his lust, he thought, his mindless need for her dangerous. He couldn't afford to be constantly in rut—for reasons other than the immediate peril it put them in with regard to their enemies. He didn't wish to be constantly aroused. It was a juvenile distraction for a man of his responsibilities. But she pulled his mouth to hers and whispered against it, "Could I please come more than once . . ."

And suddenly, all bets were off.

"You let me know when you've had enough," he murmured, feeling himself swell larger and longer, a volatile need to fuck himself to death an unpromising, irresponsible reaction.

Maybe tomorrow he'd become more circumspect, he thought, settling into a hard, steady rhythm.

Or maybe the day after that, he reflected, ramming in deeper as the princess began to scream in climax.

Or, what the hell—there was no need for an immediate decision, he decided, as his orgasm began peaking.

And as the glorious splendor jolted his body, he gave up any pretext of rational thought and absorbed the soul-stirring pleasure.

Chapter
17

Sunskoku and her party arrived in Osaka after two days of hard riding in poor weather. Having been soaked through for most of the journey, Hiroaki's men were more than ready to find lodgings and get into dry clothes.

Their orders were to guard the *tayu* to Osaka and see that she returned to Edo when her mission was complete. Hiroaki had not, however, given explicit instructions on their duties while she was aboard ship.

With Sunskoku settled in her lodgings for the night, Yukio offered to take the men to a teahouse he knew and give them gratis an evening of entertainment. It wasn't an invitation any red-blooded man could refuse. Particularly when it was offered by a *wakaimono,* a Yoshiwara enforcer, who better than most, knew the best brothels in town.

The evening began with several drinks . . . and then several more . . . until Hiroaki's men didn't know where they were or who they were with.

Leaving money for their night's pleasures and giving orders to keep them there until morning, Yukio set forth for Sunskoku's lodgings. He was looking forward to her company free of the chaperons they'd had with them since Edo.

Just short of the inn, a young man fell into step beside him.

Yukio glanced at him. "You made good time."

"Owari is practically on the way."

"And you saw the family to the port of Nagoya?"

"They're on their way to Hong Kong as we speak. Frightened, but aboard."

"All of them?"

"Down to the last grandmother. A remarkably handsome family, by the way."

"I assumed as much. And living in relatively good conditions."

"Paid for by their daughter."

"Of course."

"So when are we leaving?" Noguchi inquired.

"We?"

"You didn't think I'd stay behind, did you?"

"I wasn't sure you had a yen to see the world."

"Good friends are hard to find."

"That's true." Yukio looked at him and smiled. "We're going to the States, I believe. Or at least eventually. Captain Drummond's business is based there."

"What if he doesn't want us on board?"

"We'll have to change his mind."

"In his business, he's well armed."

"But a reasonable man, I hear."

"Unlike our employers."

"Exactly. I was thinking he might need body-guards."

Noguchi grinned. "Certainly, he does right now."

Yukio shot him a questioning look. "You wouldn't happen to know where he is?"

"I might be able to find out."

"If it takes money, just tell me how much."

"Let me ask around. I cut my eyeteeth in this town."

Noguchi had grown up on the streets of the sea-port, only arriving in Edo two years ago as body-guard to a yakuza captain who was opening a new operation in the capital. On his employer's sud-den demise in a power struggle over territory, Noguchi had found work with Yukio.

"Are you staying with us?" Yukio asked as they approached the inn.

"I've a friend in town. I'll see you tomorrow."

"A woman friend, from the look of your grin. If we're not here, we'll be on board the *Southern Belle*."

"Don't worry. I'll find you."

"If the captain and the princess arrive, we'll be swiftly weighing anchor, I suspect. Don't go far."

"You're always in sight, my friend," Noguchi said softly.

"Good. At some point, I might need some help with Hiroaki's men."

Noguchi grinned. "They won't be coming with us, you mean?"

"Something like that. I'll see you tomorrow." Bowing faintly, Yukio turned into the gate of the inn.

*   *   *

"I thought something happened to you," Sun-skoku said nervously as Yukio entered her bed-chamber a few moments later.

He'd stopped inside the doorway, charmed by the sight before his eyes. She wore only a simple robe, her hair unbound, her face devoid of cos-metics, and he thought her more beautiful than ever. "Not likely when you're waiting for me in bed," he said softly.

Her brows rose in mockery. "How original."

"I didn't know that was a requirement."

Taking note of the sarcasm in his voice, she said, "Forgive me, I'm on edge. So much depends on everything falling into place, on so many people obliging us. On Hiroaki's men staying out of the way."

"They're in a drunken stupor at the moment. They won't wake till morning."

"When we'll be gone."

"As early as you like."

"I wish we could go now."

"The crew of the *Southern Belle* would probably shoot first and ask questions later if we were to try and board tonight."

"I know, I know, but"—Sunskoku blew out a breath—"I wish it was all over. Safely. And we were at sea."

He'd never seen her like this, tense and fearful, almost shaking. He'd only known her as the re-fined and restrained courtesan, the center of all eyes, the glory of the Yoshiwara. "We'll get on board safely. All it takes is money. Don't worry."

"I wish it were that easy. I wish words alone

would calm my fears. I wish I weren't so frightened. I never am, you know—or was . . . before . . ." Her voice trailed off.

He understood what the Yoshiwara could do to a person. And perhaps it pleased him more than he thought possible to see the flesh and blood woman with fears and insecurities beneath the elegant facade of Edo's most renowned geisha. "We'll sit up till morning if you like and leave at dawn."

"Could we—I mean . . . how childish I sound, but I'm afraid to go to sleep in case I don't wake up in time—or Hiroaki's men come back before we leave . . . in case any number of things might go wrong. . . ."

"It's not a problem. You have tea, I have sake, the brazier is stoked. You can tell me your life story till morning comes," he said with a grin.

"For your information," she replied, trying to smile in return, "my life will begin the moment Drummond's ship weigh's anchor."

"Fair enough." He swept off his cloak and tossed it aside. "Then it's my story tonight," he said, a teasing light in his eyes.

"Perhaps we should make up some stories. They might be more pleasant."

He looked up from pouring himself a cup of sake. "I intended to. You didn't think I'd tell you the truth, did you?"

"Having lived with deceit so long, I'm not sure I like to hear you say that."

"Then we'll talk of more pleasant things—our life stories better suppressed. Have you eaten?"

"I tried." She waved her hand at the untouched tray of food.

"Actually, I have some very good news for you," he said, sitting beside her on the bed. "Your family is safely away."

"Why didn't you say so before?" she exclaimed, wide-eyed.

"I forgot." The sight of her always blinded him to mundane affairs.

"Tell me, tell me everything!" Sitting beside him, her hands clasped tightly in her lap, a note of urgency rang through her voice. "I want every little detail."

"I don't know much. Noguchi reached your family, brought them to Nagoya and saw them aboard a ship bound for Hong Kong—surreptitiously, of course."

"Everyone?"

"Down to the last grandmother, he said. They'll wait for you in Hong Kong."

Tears came to her eyes, trembled on her eyelids for a moment and then poured down her cheeks as she tried to choke back her sobs.

Taking her in his arms, he held her close. "You can cry, sweetheart, no one can hear."

He knew, she thought. And she allowed herself to cry as she'd not allowed herself for years. She cried for her family and for the loss of her childhood, for the joy of knowing those she cared for were safe. "You're a very fine man, Yukio-san," she whispered, sniffling away her tears, her chin resting on his chest. "You're the most compassionate, beautiful man in the world and if love truly exists, I will love you for all you've done for me."

He didn't want her gratitude; he wanted more. But had he not survived the Yoshiwara for a decade? He was a patient man. "I was happy to help," he murmured, wiping away her tears with his sleeve.

"You may have anything you want for what you've given me," she whispered, kissing his cheek.

He knew what she was offering, but he wanted her passion, not her benevolence. "There's time enough for that once we're free." His smile was indulgent. "Right now, we should think of a way to get our gold to the ship without having it stolen by bureaucrats."

She pushed away and looked at him earnestly. "Are you serious?" Her savings were too hard won to lose without a fight.

"The gauntlet of officials can be expensive, unless . . ."

"What, what? . . . Tell me!"

Her excitement was that of an impatient child and he wondered whether her early training as a geisha had arrested adult emotion or whether she was finally allowing herself to respond with true spontaneity. "We could pay a fisherman to take us out past the official barriers. I understand it can be done for less than the harbor master's bribes."

"Well, we'll do that, of course." She glanced at her luggage. "How much can I take? May I take it all?"

"Yes, take it all."

"How do you know all this?"

"Noguchi was raised in Osaka. I've listened to all his stories."

"Fortunately, you don't have much luggage."

"I sent my valuables ahead."

"Ahead? How did you know where—" She smiled. "The walls have ears, don't they."

"And eyes," he added, looking amused. "I probably know more about you than you do yourself. For instance, you snore when you have too much sake."

"I certainly do not!"

"I could be wrong," he quickly acceded. "But you're very beautiful when you're sleeping."

"That's better," she said, her embarrassment mollified. "So you knew we were bound for Osaka?"

"The moment I heard Hiroaki give you orders. I made it a point to be close by whenever he visited. He's a dangerous man."

"You were my guardian?"

"In a manner of speaking."

She smiled. "And a voyeur?"

He grinned. "That too. Although, just for the record, I'm much better."

"So I've heard."

"Just a thought for later. You have too much on your mind right now."

"And you don't?"

He grinned. "I'm pretty focused."

"Then don't drink anymore."

"I don't get drunk. You're safe with me—and from me." The last thing he wished to do was frighten her more.

"How can you be so kind?" she whispered, almost undone by his gentleness, the men she'd known invariably selfish and demanding.

"I want to." A man of discipline, he'd learned long ago to wait. "I don't need sex."

She surveyed his handsome face and strong

young body, taking in the pattern of tattoos visible on his forearms and hands, scrolling up the back of his neck to the base of his ears. How much did one have to endure to be so adorned? How nerveless was he? "I don't need sex, either, although I'm not sure I really know what it is."

"I'll show you later."

"What if I said now," she murmured, testing her power.

He smiled faintly. "You don't mean it. Wait until you do. You'll like it more."

"On how many occasions have you *liked* it?"

"Now why would I tell you that? Let's just say, I have a feeling we'll get along just fine."

"Arrogant man."

He grinned. "Just realistic. Would you like some tea? It's going to be a long night." A *real* long night, he reflected, not used to restraining his lustful desires. "Should we play a game of go?"

"For money?"

"Of course. I'll lighten your luggage for you."

"Not likely. I'm very good at go."

His lashes lowered over the amusement in his eyes. "Is that so?"

"I won a thousand ryo last month."

"Then I'll have to be on guard," he said pleasantly, this man who gambled and won on everything from go to the date the cherry blossoms would bloom.

"I brought a small board along." It was inlaid ivory from the Heian period. "It was a gift I couldn't part with."

His gaze turned resentful. "A gift from someone special?"

"From my old teacher before he died." The most celebrated courtesans were expected to write poetry with a fine hand and a creative flair.

"Ah. Tadayasu." The old courtier fallen on hard times had taught Yukio to read and write, as well. In fact, he'd become a mentor of sorts, living in a house Yukio had bought for him. "He taught me too." His slow lazy smile held a hint of challenge. "Why don't we see who learned the most. . . ."

Chapter

18

Early the next morning, at the same time Noguchi was softly knocking at Sunskoku's door, Hugh came awake. Lying motionless, he listened for the sound again, not sure whether he'd been dreaming or not. Shit. As the black-clad figure crashed through the door, he lunged for his Colt, rolled over Tama with his finger on the trigger and emptied his revolver into the assassin's head.

Then he breathed again. One down.

But there was never only one ninja, and grabbing his second revolver, he whispered, "Don't move," to Tama as he eased away.

Ignoring him, she pulled her long sword from under the futon and came up on her feet in a combat stance.

He wanted to say, *They'll see you naked. Get dressed,* but understood how irrelevant nudity was when they could be dead seconds from now.

Raising her sword to shoulder height, she swung

the tip to her left and nodded her head. Hugh heard it too—the light breathing barely audible. Carefully calculating size and height in the direction of the sound, he marched four quick rounds up the wall.

A scream echoed in the pre-dawn grayness.

Then a thud . . . and silence.

They looked at each other but neither smiled in triumph. This was only the beginning. There were more out there somewhere, waiting like them.

An ominous hush enveloped the hut, only the crash of water striking the rocks below breaking the silence. And even that had a distant sound, as though separate from the catastrophe in the making.

Hugh began dressing, his movements swift and economical, and Tama followed suit. If they survived this attack, they would have to take flight. A messenger would have been sent back for reinforcements.

Dressed moments later, their weapons in hand, they waited to meet the next onslaught. But nothing moved outside the hut—not a rustle or utterance, no sight or sound indicated the position of their enemies. Packing their few belongings in the interval—ammunition most critical for their escape, Hugh rechecked their weapons and they waited. . . .

None of their pursuers had been armed with modern weapons, the ninjas' reliance on the traditional methods of warfare still the governing standard in Japan. That disdain for foreign prowess and weapons might very well be Tama's and his salvation, Hugh understood.

If they weren't attacked in large numbers.

If their ammunition held out.

If neither one of them was seriously wounded.

Far too many unknowns this far from the coast.

But the initial setbacks had given rise to caution in their attackers and when the ninja finally mounted their assault, they came en masse, smashing through the walls of the lightly built structure from different directions.

The small interior space hindered defense, the possibility of being overrun perilously real. But the option of misgivings didn't exist and relying on instinct and skill, Tama and Hugh sighted in and fired automatically.

One ninja went down, then another, but a third and fourth were almost on top of them by now, their swords raised high, their attack screams rending the air.

Shoving Tama behind him, Hugh shouted, "Run!" as the last round left the chamber of his revolver. Deft as he might be at reloading, half seconds weren't enough and hurling his weapon at the ninja nearest him, he jerked his short sword from his belt. "Get the hell out of here!" he yelled, feeling Tama's presence. Prepared to make a stand to give her time to escape, he needed her to fucking GO RIGHT NOW. "Go, go, go!" he cried, parrying both ninjas' sword thrusts as he retreated, wishing he had his long sword. Swinging to the right to avoid decapitation, he stumbled and began to fall. . . .

Both ninja rushed him, howling in triumph, their swords sweeping downward for the fatal blow.

Leaping over Hugh, Tama arrested their onslaught, wielding her swords in wide horizontal sweeps to force them back. *He who enters to attack is a hawk,* Musashi said. *You must appreciate this.* Without fear, she charged them with her swords and body, her inner spirit calm, cutting straight upward, aiming for their hands, shouting, "Ei!" as she initiated and delivered the strike, her razor-sharp blades slashing through flesh and bone like butter. As the ninjas' swords fell from the stumps of their wrists, she swiftly thrust at their hearts, her offensive unwavering, the ridges of her blades square on, plunging the cold steel through their chests with unflinching resolve. As the light died in the eyes of her enemies, she jerked out her blades and yelled, her victory cry strong and clear. This is called *"sengo no koe."* The voice is a thing of life.

"Christ Almighty, that was beautiful to behold," Hugh murmured, coming to his feet. "I owe you," he added with a smile.

"It was but a small repayment for your many acts of defense on my behalf, Hugh-san," she said solemnly.

Quickly surveying the bodies strewn on the floor, he nodded toward what was left of the door. "We can discuss our debts to each other later. Right now, we'd better get the hell out of here."

"Is it safe to leave?"

"Those four would have come in with reinforcements if there were any," he noted, picking up his revolvers. "Not that more ninjas won't be on our trail soon enough." Dextrously reloading his revolvers, he slipped one in his holster, handed Tama the other and picked up their pack. "Ready?"

She nodded and began moving toward the door, skirting the puddles of blood on the tatami mats when a hand shot out from the sprawl of bodies and caught her around the ankle.

She froze. The wounded ninja had his dagger poised.

Hugh didn't move. With the ninja's life draining away he had nothing to lose; Hiroaki's man had one chance yet to succeed in his mission. Could he draw and fire in time or would the ninja's deadly blade strike Tama first?

For a breath-held moment, time seemed suspended.

Then Hugh moved in a blur, drawing, firing, diving for Tama—willing the man's blade to falter.

The stiletto flew through the air and Tama fell hard as he pushed her down.

For a fearful moment he thought she'd been hit.

"You're crushing me," she muttered.

He felt like laughing, and if Hiroaki's pursuit weren't still fully operational, he would have indulged his sense of humor. Easing away instead, he carefully surveyed her for knife blades. "You look unscathed."

"Other than some broken ribs," she grumbled, coming to her feet.

"You're welcome," he said drily.

"Thank you—of course," she said quickly. "Very much."

He tipped his head in acknowledgment. "Now, should we try our exit once more?"

"I'm ready. And more alert."

But just to make sure, he put another round into each ninja's head. "A few less on our trail," he murmured, picking up their pack.

"But we've survived another day, Hugh-san," she said with a small smile. "I, for one, am grateful."

"I'll wait to be grateful until I'm aboard ship," he muttered, gesturing at the broken door with his rifle. "After you."

Hoping to stay ahead of their pursuers, they didn't stop to rest that day, traveling a circuitous route, backtracking from time to time, shifting direction often, moving at a hard, steady pace. Neither spoke, nor were so inclined, their thoughts occupied with matters of survival.

Although occasionally, Tama's musing would shift to scenarios of revenge. Reared in a culture that exacted vengeance for a wrong, she not only had her father's death to vindicate, but Hiroaki's unrelenting malice to avenge. And at the moment, the chief inspector was at the top of her vendetta list—greedy coward; he didn't even have the courage to lead his troops.

Hugh had more prosaic concerns, the arcane concept of blood feuds beyond the canons of a man who had operated of late with the profit motive as his guiding light. Right now, he was hoping their ammunition lasted until Osaka because he had a cargo of silk that should be on board. And if it was, he'd be a helluva lot richer when he unloaded it in London.

Chapter

19

While Tama and Hugh were literally fighting for their lives, Sunskoku, Yukio and Noguchi were at a waterfront tavern negotiating the price of transport to the *Southern Belle*.

"We're willing to pay you fairly for passage," Yukio declared, "but we're not interested in buying you a new boat. Understand?"

The two fishermen understood perfectly. One didn't argue with yakuza enforcers. "We'll have to meet you down on the quay, though," the younger of the two men murmured, looking across the dingy room at the owner who was eyeing them with considerable interest. Although enveloped in her cloak, Sunskoku's beauty drew attention. "You're not the usual customers on this part of the waterfront. You're attracting notice."

Yukio nodded. "Our business is finished. The terms are half now, half when we're on board your boat." He slipped a small leather pouch to the fisherman.

"The American steamship has sent small boats

ashore every day. Are you the ones they're waiting for?"

"Thank you for your cooperation," Yukio said, ignoring their question. He stood up. "We'll be on the quay in ten minutes. You may go."

As the two men scurried out, Yukio strolled over to the tavern owner who tried not to look frightened as he approached. Yukio shoved a gold coin across a rough table. "You never saw us. And Kenkaichi is a friend of mine, so don't be tempted to talk to anyone about this." Kenkaichi was the head of the crime syndicate in Osaka and well known on the waterfront where a certain percentage of each cargo went into yakuza coffers.

White-faced, unable to find his voice, the owner nodded.

Returning to his companions, Yukio escorted Sunskoku outside and they stood at the entrance to the ramshackle building, surveying the fishermen readying their boats.

"Everyone's looking," Sunskoku whispered, tremulous with nerves, their party the cynosure of all eyes, such well-dressed strangers uncommon. "It's becoming light. What if Hiroaki's men find us?"

"Relax, sweetheart. We're safe." Yukio glanced at Noguchi. "Tell her Hiroaki's men won't find us."

"They won't."

"How can you be sure?" Sunskoku clutched her cloak around her as though shielding herself from danger. "If they discover us trying to leave, we'll die a slow, agonizing death. You know how vicious Hiroaki is, how everyone lives in fear of—"

"Hiroaki's men are dead," Yukio said quietly. "No one will be coming after us this morning."

She went ashen. "Are you mad! You can't mean Hiroaki's men! His revenge will be terrible!"

Yukio gently guided her toward the quay. "They just disappeared, sweetheart. Hiroaki won't know of it for days."

"Disappeared?" she whispered, at once fearful and relieved.

"They decided to go for a swim last night and drowned."

"They should have known they were too drunk to swim," Noguchi added with a *tsk, tsking* sound.

"I suppose if we were to run, people will notice." Sunskoku felt the urge to throw off her pattens and sprint for the fishermen's boat.

"I wouldn't recommend it." Yukio squeezed her arm lightly. "Look, there they are—with their boat. Another few minutes, don't look around, just walk slowly. That's the way." He rebalanced his grip on the heavy basket he was carrying and glanced at Noguchi, who was trying to look as though the two baskets he held were lighter than they were. "Look, they're hoisting the sail. And the breeze is blowing out to sea. We'll be out of the harbor in no time."

She knew why he was talking in that calm, soothing voice and she was grateful, the possibility of freedom so close now she could almost taste it. "Tell me no one is after us," she whispered.

He glanced around, caught sight of the tavern owner standing in his doorway and hoped the man wasn't stupid. If he chose to turn them in to the harbor police, they'd be in trouble; on the other hand, he'd be dead.

Yukio hoped the man understood.

Noguchi had made all the necessary arrangements last night, his local compatriots also of help in disposing of Hiroaki's men.

The yakuza brotherhood took care of their own.

Moments later, Yukio was helping Sunskoku into the small vessel, and after finding her a sheltered seat aft, he ordered the fishermen to cast off. As the shore slowly receded, he and Noguchi scanned the waterfront for any signs of pursuit. But their departure was uneventful as it should be with well-laid plans, the breeze was cooperative, and very soon, they were coming up on the large steamship at anchor in the harbor.

As the fishing boat approached, several crew members targeted them with rifles. A man shouted at them, warning them off.

"Ask for the first mate," Yukio ordered, leading Sunskoku to the bow. "Tell them Captain Drummond sent you."

As Sunskoku's words rang out in both English and Japanese, Paddy abruptly appeared at the rail and recognizing her, he immediately gave orders to bring up the visitors.

"Once we're on board, get under way," Yukio commanded the fishermen. "And speak of this to no one."

They nodded mutely, knowing better than to involve themselves in yakuza business.

The moment their passengers began to ascend the gangway on the side of the ship, the fishing boat pulled away.

Paddy McDougal waited at the top of the stairway, his expression dour. "You're a long way from home," he murmured as they stepped on deck, his gaze on Sunskoku. "And don't tell me the captain sent you. He don't trust you none."

"We're here because we might be able to help him."

"And how might that be?" Paddy inquired skeptically, surveying the two men with her—roughneck thugs, from the looks of their tattoos.

"We know Hiroaki hasn't found the captain yet. In fact, the chief inspector sent me to Osaka to see if I could discover his whereabouts from you."

"We can be of help with your search," Yukio offered. "The yakuza has informers everywhere."

"Hiroaki has trackers following the captain. We know that," Sunskoku asserted.

"Thanks to you," Paddy noted coolly.

"I had no choice. He threatened me and my family."

"She did what anyone would do to survive," Yukio interposed. "But we come in peace. We can help; we have access to information you don't. Consider being reasonable for your captain's sake, if for no other."

With foreigners fair game to every hot-blooded samurai with a hatred of the invaders, Paddy knew the help they offered was invaluable. And yet.

"How do I know I can trust you?" he said, scowling. "The Yoshiwara ain't exactly a breeding ground for church folk."

"We came to you at great risk." Yukio stood almost eye to eye with Paddy, his height unusual. "Noguchi and I will go ashore alone or with you in your search for the captain and the princess. But, there's very little time," he bluntly added. "Hiroaki's ninja are hot on their trail."

"Any suggestions where we might find them?" Paddy growled. He'd been to Oen's teahouse almost every day and she'd not seen or heard from Hugh.

"The captain was making for Osaka, was he not?"

"He were making for a teahouse he knows but he never got there."

"When we left Edo, Hiroaki hadn't yet found them. Take me to the teahouse and let me speak with the women. I may be able to discover something."

"That I couldn't, you mean," Paddy grumbled.

"Doing business with foreigners can be dangerous for anyone who deals with them. I'd suggest you let us ask the questions, but the sooner we leave the better. The guards Hiroaki sent along with us have been eliminated, but their disappearance won't go unnoticed for long. A day or two at the most."

Paddy's gaze was calculating. "You killed them and I should trust you?"

"Hiroaki's men would have caused trouble. It was necessary. If you could see to Sunskoku's quarters," he murmured politely. "She'll be safer on board while we're gone."

"I ain't made up my mind yet," Paddy said gruffly.

"Sunskoku's very fearful," Yukio pointed out. "She's risked her life to help save the captain and the princess. It's no little thing." His voice was without inflection, but the fact that he cared for Sunskoku was clear.

If anyone knew the lay of the land, it was the yakuza, Paddy knew, the crime syndicate's reach extensive. "Very well. She can have my quarters for now. I'll bunk with the bos'n."

"We thank you." Yukio bowed formally, his expression grave. "Once the lady is in her room, we're at your disposal." Bending low, he spoke to Sunskoku rapidly in Japanese and she nodded twice before murmuring something in return.

Yukio shook his head and then looked up at Paddy. "She'll be happy to wait here until we return," he said.

Before long, a launch drew away from the *Southern Belle*, the crew rowing hard against the waves. And soon after landing, a small party rode away from the waterfront, mounted on the best horses Osaka had to offer.

Chapter

20

"How much—farther?" Tama panted, drench-ed with sweat, concentrating on putting one foot in front of the other, sheer will keeping her moving.

"Two ri if we don't run into trouble. Do you want to rest?"

"Yes, of course—but we can't."

"I could carry you."

"Not with—the pack—and your rifle."

"We'll stop for five minutes, then," he said, com-ing to rest under a towering pine. "We can both catch our breaths."

"I find—it—very—annoying," she gasped, "that you're—not—even breathing hard."

"My legs are longer than yours. You have to work harder."

"Thank you—for the explanation," she snapped, out of breath and out of temper, and in general annoyed that the captain looked as though he could keep up this pace for the next month or so without so much as breaking a sweat.

"We're staying ahead of them," he said gently, squatting down so his face was near hers as she rested head down, panting, her hands on her knees. "If we reach Oen's in good time, they won't know where we went to ground. There's thirty thousand souls in the town."

He was being gracious, stopping for her, being politely encouraging. She needn't be so peevish. "I'll be ready to go again in a minute."

"It's not much farther. Then we'll have food and a hot bath." He grinned. "How's that for incentive?"

"A bed's all the incentive I need right now."

"Done."

She stood upright and drew in a deep breath. "Lead on. I can stand anything for another hour."

But when they came within sight of the teahouse, Hugh put out his hand and brought them to a stop in a nearby alley. The lantern above the entrance gate was missing.

"Someone's been here or is here," he murmured. "The lantern is taken down." Oen had contrived the signal in the early days when the trade treaties had only recently opened Japan to foreigners and it was risky for westerners to be seen in Ko.

Tama slumped against the shop wall bordering the alley. "Now what?"

There was a plaintive note in her voice he'd not heard before and Hugh glanced at her. "We have to take a short detour." Oen would have left a message at a nearby shrine as she had in the past.

"I'll wait here."

"You can't." Lifting her into his arms, he added, "It's not safe." And silently giving thanks for the early darkness of winter, he began retracing their steps to the Shinto shrine they'd passed.

Too exhausted to protest, Tama gave in to her fatigue and allowed herself to appreciate the captain's strength. "There will be an additional stipend in your retainer, Hugh-san," she murmured, smiling up at him.

"It's only two streets away," he said, smiling back. "This is free."

Coming to a halt a short time later near the back wall of a temple property, he set Tama down near an ancient yew with sprawling branches that spread over the stonework and out into the narrow lane.

Crawling under the low branches, he searched for a small crevice in the trunk. Pulling out a twist of paper, he scrutinized the brush stroke over the knot, the smooth flow of ink evidence it hadn't been opened. Untying the knot and spreading out the twist of paper, he read: *Government ninja are in wait. Paddy is at Cecil's.* Oen had signed it with her cipher.

Allowing his pulse rate a few moments to subside, he tore up the note and buried it. Returning to Tama, he squatted down beside her so she could see him in the diminishing light. "I was left a note. We have unwelcome visitors at Oen's. But the good news," he added, at her sudden alarm, "is that Paddy is waiting for us at Cecil's. And I expect he's armed to the teeth."

Exhilaration and fear simultaneously flooded her brain, separating one from the other impossible in her weariness. But Cecil's would be their goal; that she knew. "How far?" she whispered, trying to gather her energy.

"Eight or ten blocks." She was pale with exhaustion, the distance perhaps too much for her. "If you can't walk, I could carry you."

"But we'd be more conspicuous."

He didn't reply immediately. "Yes," he said finally.

Her nostrils flared as she drew in a deep breath. "I'll walk," she declared firmly.

But spies were everywhere, informers from Edo to Osaka on alert for the captain or his crew. Paddy and his party had been followed from the moment they'd come ashore.

Cecil's pub was owned by an Australian who had come to Japan with the first traders allowed in after the ink was dry on the treaty of fifty-four. Already fluent in Japanese when he'd arrived, he'd been well connected enough in the China trade to have been tolerated inland when no white man was safe outside the foreign legations. He knew and was known to everyone in the expatriate community, from the roughest navvies to the titled diplomats. His liquor was top rate, his games of chance honest, and the rooms upstairs offered the most beautiful tea hostesses on the coast.

And everyone at Cecil's that night knew the captain and the Princess of Otari might make a run for the pub. Rumors of their expected presence in the area had been bruited about all day.

Yukio and Noguchi had associates posted in all the nearby streets, as did Hiroaki's network of spies—the cook on board the *Southern Belle* having jumped ship. Yukio was to give a signal if the captain and princess were sighted. With westerners in Japan by necessity well-armed, those at Cecil's that evening were more than willing to add their fire power to assist in the captain's rescue.

Everyone—both friend and foe—was waiting.

Leaving Tama hidden under a nearby bridge, Hugh approached the perimeter of the district where Cecil's was located, reconnoitering. Nothing but shuttered houses and silent streets met his gaze and he swore under his breath.

Something was wrong . . . seriously wrong. Not even a dog was out.

Searching for a superior vantage point, he climbed a tall pine to better survey the empty streets. If any living being inhabited the area, they were well hidden or locked away inside their homes. The sound of piano music lent an eerie note to the deserted scene, the familiar passages from a popular mazurka being played at Cecil's faintly heard. The lanterns strung along Cecil's veranda roof twinkled in the distance, but the vacant thoroughfares separating him from the famed pub were starkly ominous.

Close and yet so far. Scrutinizing the urban landscape, he tried to devise some strategy that would allow them to reach Cecil's alive. But, no matter from which direction they approached, they would be solitary figures on the streets.

They might as well put a target in the middle of their foreheads.

Or—a sudden thought appeared like a scene from a magic lantern show.

Why not have Cecil's the target?

Descending the tree, he went to fetch Tama, explained their dilemma and led her back to the pine where he helped her climb up onto one of the lofty branches. "Hold on and wish me luck," he said, giving her a quick smile. "Let's see if I can bring my crew to us."

The distance to Cecil's porch was pressing the maximum range for his Spencer. If ever he needed a steady hand and a good eye, this was the time. Bracing the barrel of his rifle on a branch, Hugh sighted in on one of the porch lanterns, held his breath and gently squeezed the trigger.

The rifle blast shattered the abnormal silence and in the darkness one of the lanterns on Cecil's porch disintegrated in an explosion of light. Quickly sighting in once again, he fired and another lantern blew apart and this time the porch began filling with men.

He took great care with his next shot, the fifty caliber cartridge capable of blowing a man apart even at this range and the porch was crowded with milling patrons. Aiming at the lantern above

Cecil's sign, directly over the entrance to the building, he carefully pulled the trigger.

Any of the shots would have been incredible on a clear, sunny day with a stationary firing stand, but to thread the needle in twilight conditions from a swaying tree could only have been accomplished by a first rate marksman.

"It's the cap'n!" Paddy shouted, pointing in the direction of the shot. "Ain't no one can shoot that straight from that far!"

At the sight of Cecil's patrons surging out into the street, Hugh fired a final shot to give them his position and took note of a number of men coming out into the streets and pointing in their direction.

Unfortunately, not all of them were from Cecil's.

Aware of the interest they'd garnered, not all of it favorable, Tama put out her hand. "Give me one of your revolvers, just in case your men don't get here first."

"We still have ammunition." He didn't say it was limited.

"Good," she said drily, nodding at the black-clad men racing toward them from several of the side streets. "Because it looks as though we might need it. Which ones do you want?"

"Wait until they get closer. No sense in wasting shots," he said in what he hoped was a casual tone.

But his nerves were better than hers or perhaps he was simply aware of their depleted ammunition supply, because Tama fired before Hugh did. Two ninja went down, then two more, and suddenly they began falling from auxiliary, unseen gunfire.

The streets cleared of ninja in record time and were suddenly quiet again.

Until the customers of Cecil's came racing down the main thoroughfare leading to Hugh's makeshift firing stand.

Hugh smiled at Tama. "That bed you were looking forward to is coming into range. We'll be sleeping aboard my ship tonight."

"I am overjoyed," she replied, trying hard to suppress her tears. "My thanks to you, Hugh-san. I could not have reached Osaka without you."

It was a huge concession from the woman who had insisted she could make better time without him. "Nor could I have," he said with genuine sincerity. "We make a good team."

The foreign contingency was beginning to swarm around the base of the tree, shouting and hurrahing and carrying on like men who had had a drink or two or ten.

"Hey, there, Cap'n!" Paddy shouted. "Are you comin' down or what!"

The procession back to Cecil's was triumphant, the westerners swaggering and rejoicing in their success, the style of men arriving early in foreign lands adventurers all. It was necessary for Hugh to relate the story of their journey, or at least an edited version several times, as it was necessary to buy several rounds at Cecil's long mahogany bar in thanks and appreciation before the party bound for the *Southern Belle* could finally take their leave.

The five miles of open road between Cecil's and Osaka was posted at regular intervals with yakuza who fell in behind Hugh's party as they passed. By the time they arrived in Osaka, there were a thousand men in their wake.

A testament to the power of the yakuza, to Yukio and Noguchi's influence, and to hard-earned Yoshiwara wealth.

Chapter

21

The *Southern Belle* was under way within minutes of their return. Wanting to be well out of range of any government vessels should Hiroaki choose to exert his power, Hugh gave orders to sail out to sea rather than take the usual route through the Inland Sea to the Shimonoseki Straits. He didn't want to take any chances they might be fired on by the Choshu shore batteries.

After escorting Tama to his cabin, Hugh saw that she was made comfortable, finding her a robe and nightshirt, a brush and comb, ordering her bath water and food, pointing out his liquor cabinet and small library. "You have everything you need, now?"

"Yes, more than enough, thank you."

He was standing at the door, one hand on the latch. "You needn't wait up for me. It might take some time to arrange our sailing schedule."

"Don't expect me to wait up for you," she said with a small smile. "I'm practically asleep on my feet."

The sight of her standing in his cabin caused him a moment of unease. It wasn't normal for a woman to be there. He guarded his privacy—or at least he had in the past. And now he'd be damn near living with Tama on the weeks-long voyage to Europe. What the hell was he doing? Since the debacle of his marriage he'd avoided any suggestion of permanence in his amours.

"Did I say something?" Tama inquired, surveying Hugh's faint frown.

"No—not at all," he said quickly. "Business matters." He smiled. "They never go away. I'll see you in the morning." And he walked from the room.

As the door clicked shut, Tama curled her toes in the plush carpet and scrutinized what Hugh referred to as his home. It was a large suite of rooms—a parlor, study, dining room and bedroom, the furnishings oversize to accommodate his height, the decor non-Western, Bengali perhaps, a certain opulence in the materials used. The wardrobe in his bedroom had taken up an entire wall—he was a man of fashion apparently—and one of intellectual tastes, as well—his books lining the walls of his study. His bed had startled her in its dimensions. More familiar with futons, the grand canopied bed seemed to fill the room. Like his scent—a fragrant blend of musk and ambergris.

But the verbena-scented bath water that had been carried into the bedroom was more potent lure to her weariness and she moved to the porcelain tub set before the fire with pleasure. How nice it was to be warm again, to have the amenities at her disposal. Opening the closures on her peasant jacket, she began to undress, dropping the worn garb on the floor, gazing at it for a moment, the plain padded cotton both familiar after so many weeks and alien to the life she'd always known. How far she'd come from her palace home. But regret was useless, she told herself, climbing into the tub. She must keep her thoughts on what lay ahead. Sinking into the warm, fragrant water, she exhaled in a long, blissful sigh.

Every muscle in her body ached after their grueling race for Osaka, her weariness all-consuming. Leaning back against the curved headrest, she offered up a brief prayer of thanksgiving for being alive. Certainly some benevolent gods had helped her through the last few weeks.

And with her voyage about to begin, she'd soon see her brother and his family, she thought with a smile. In spite of all the pain and sadness that had brought her here today, there was solace in knowing she and her brother together would restore the family's honor and name. They would rebuild their home and make a new life for themselves on the Otari domains.

She was confident of Komei's help. He had a son now to carry on his name. He was duty-bound to continue the princely line.

She had but to see him and he would understand.

In due time, she promised herself, it would all come to pass. . . .

She came awake shivering in the chill bath water. Glancing at the clock, she was surprised at the lateness of the hour. Quickly rising, she dried herself before the glowing coals, pulled one of

Hugh's nightshirts over her head, wrapped herself in his robe and built up the fire. After a brief detour to eat a few morsels from a tray left nearby, she climbed up into Hugh's canopied bed and fell asleep again almost before her head touched the pillow.

Hugh had bathed and changed and after a swift survey of the sea charts to set their course, he joined Paddy for drinks in the officer's lounge. They discussed all that had transpired since Edo, beginning with Paddy's grumbling account of the silk merchants' intransigence. Apparently only threats of violence had finally produced the silk—just loaded yesterday. Hugh described their journey south without offering any information on what was obviously his relationship with the princess.

She was staying in his cabin—that was clear as could be, Paddy thought—and also a first. But he also knew better than to ask any questions.

The men agreed that the appearance of Sunskoku and her friends was extremely opportune as was the help they received from their friends at Cecil's. And then they went over the various commissions given them by Cecil's patrons. Whenever anyone left the foreign colony for the outside world, they were sent off with a list of "Necessities."

"You get to buy the red silk underwear for Cecil's ladies, though," Paddy said with a smirk. "I ain't puttin' *myself* in that embarrassing situation."

Hugh grinned. "But I don't suppose you'll mind looking at it in situ once we bring it back."

"That's somethin' else entirely, now, ain't it," Paddy drawled, leaning back in his chair and raising his whiskey glass to Hugh. "Hell, I might even put in an order for myself. That little Etsu would look right fine in purple silk."

There was a infinitesimal moment of silence, both men thinking the same thing—the princess center stage in their minds. Not that Paddy would ever dare broach the subject of Hugh's paramour with him. While Hugh had no intention of alluding to the word relationship *or* paramour.

"What say we ask the yakuza boys to join us?"

"Took the words right out of my mouth," Paddy replied instantly, grateful for an opportunity to shift to safer ground. "They look like they might like a taste of your bourbon."

When Yukio and Noguchi arrived, Hugh thanked the men for their assistance in protecting them from Hiroaki's men. "The princess and I appreciate everything you did. Hiroaki was relentless in his pursuit."

"The chief inspector will soon no longer trouble us," Yukio declared.

"We're nearly beyond his reach now." Hugh glanced out the porthole to the starry sky. "Or we will be soon."

"As you say," Yukio murmured with a faint nod. "And we thank you as well, Hugh-san, for your hospitality."

"Let's drink to that," Paddy proclaimed jovially, passing the bottle around, well ahead of everyone else in his imbibing. "To a smooth-as-silk operation," he said, lifting his glass to the two yakuza.

"To new friends," Hugh proposed, raising his glass.

"To the future," Yukio offered, his English tinged with a Dutch accent.

Pipes were passed around along with the liquor and they spoke about the current state of the government for a time, everyone agreeing that no one could be certain what was in store for the country, all the powerful families still jockeying for position.

At the third circuit of the bourbon bottle, Hugh broached a more personal issue. "Do you have any plans—not that you necessarily would have after leaving Edo so precipitously," he politely added. "But if there's anything we can do to help, you need but ask."

"Sunskoku's family is en route to Hong Kong. If it were possible to stop there, she would be grateful," Yukio noted. "Beyond that, we have no plans."

"Are you thinking of staying in Hong Kong?"

Yukio shrugged. "Who knows."

"You're welcome to stay on with us if you wish. The princess and I are both beholden to you for our lives."

"It depends on Sunskoku. What she wishes, I will do," Yukio said quietly.

"I see." The man was obviously in love; Hugh wondered if the beautiful Sunskoku was as enamored. She didn't seem the type.

"We thought you might be in need of bodyguards," Noguchi interposed.

Yukio looked embarrassed. "That's enough, Noguchi. We are not in need of charity. We have funds."

"If you want to become a merchant," Noguchi noted disparagingly, undeterred by his friend's reprimand.

Yukio gave him a sharp glance. "We are yakuza. We will survive."

"I've never had bodyguards."

Noguchi looked surprised. "In your business?"

"Forgive my friend." Yukio scowled at Noguchi "He is without pride. If you wish, we'll leave you at Hong Kong."

"What do *you* wish?" Hugh inquired, intrigued by the reserved young man whose occupation he would have thought precluded such civility. "Naturally, I'm in your debt."

Yukio smiled suddenly. "I would like to see Europe where the cities are built of stone. We have sufficient money to pay for our passage and live well once we arrive." Yukio had converted his gold to Bengal diamonds in Edo and had them conveyed to Osaka by a friend. His nest egg had been waiting at the inn when they arrived. "On the other hand, life could be dull doing nothing. Noguchi and I only know combat and defense."

"Have you studied Bushido?"

"Of course. Although firearms are a better defense," Yukio declared, refilling his glass.

"Perhaps we could train together on the voyage to Europe."

"As you wish."

"And I'm thinking, perhaps we could use some bodyguards after all, Paddy," Hugh noted with a small smile.

"It would be our pleasure, should you so choose," Yukio politely replied. "In the meantime, I will discuss the placement of Sunskoku's family with her. They may not wish to travel to Europe. It is for them to decide. But she wishes me above all to convey her gratitude to you," he added in the same polite delivery. "She has long wished to leave the Yoshiwara. As have I."

"We all have things we wish to leave behind, do we not, Paddy?" Hugh said, tipping his head toward his first mate.

"Damn right. My shrew of a wife for one," Paddy noted, tossing his drink down.

Hugh grinned. "Paddy had the misfortune to marry while under the influence one week in Dublin and woke to find himself shackled. He's been at sea ever since."

"And as long as I send money back, the bitch don't care none."

"A match made in heaven," Hugh teased.

"I don't intend to marry," Noguchi firmly declared.

Yukio smiled at his friend. "That's because you like variety."

"As you once did," Noguchi challenged.

Hugh lifted his brows. "You've changed your mind?"

"Yes, because of love."

Yukio's calm assurance begged the question, "How does the lady feel?" The query was prompted by several drinks of bourbon or perhaps by Hugh's need for an answer to his own susceptible feelings.

"She will agree." Yukio's tone was soft. "I will take care of her. As you have taken care of the Princess of Otari."

Hugh choked on his drink.

"Did you not protect the princess on your dangerous travels? Did she not rely on you?"

Hugh's moment of discomfort passed. "Yes, of course." His voice was studiously casual. "I did."

Yukio had seen what he'd seen—the way they touched and spoke, the looks that passed between them, and if the captain and the princess weren't intimate, he'd give away his fortune to the next beggar he met.

Not likely, that.

Chapter

22

The first night on board Hugh almost sat up all night, reluctant to join Tama in bed, as though the simple act of sleeping with her might compromise his independence. But eventually, weary of the discomfort of a chair when he had a perfectly good bed, he slipped under the covers. But he didn't wake her, tossing and turning instead, trying to deal with the distinction between wanting and having. There was no question he desired her. The question was, rather, how much she might expect now that they were essentially living together.

If he didn't have sex with her again, would his freedom be restored?

If he didn't have sex with her again, would he survive the journey?

His dilemma unresolved, he finally fell asleep near morning.

Yukio had no unresolved issues concerning his sexual intent. He was sleeping with Sunskoku tonight. And to that purpose, he prepared himself with an almost ritual solemnity, bathing with care, washing his hair, combing it with scent like his hairdresser always did, wearing his best for the woman he loved—had loved for years.

She was waiting for him, seated on a chair, dressed in her most splendid gown like a well-trained courtesan.

He smiled. "I didn't surprise you."

"I'm beyond surprise," she replied gently.

"I understand. I brought you a present." Walking to her, he offered the small lacquerware box on his open palm.

As she opened it he stood motionless, watching her.

"How lovely." She touched the jeweled hair ornaments. "Thank you," she said, looking up at him. "Would you like some sake?"

He shook his head. "I've drunk enough. The captain invited us for some of his whiskey. Would you like some sake? I'll get it for you."

Her lashes lifted. "Would you wait on a woman?"

"Why not?" He smiled. "Or one woman, at least. Are you nervous?"

She shrugged faintly. "I'm not sure. Possibly."

"Don't be. I have no expectations."

She laughed softly. "Are you being rude?"

"Hardly. I just meant we have our whole lives before us. One night can't matter."

"I *would* like some sake, if you don't mind."

He moved to the small table where a tray had been arranged with sake and cups, poured her some and, returning, bowed and handed it to her.

"Please, sit down. We only have chairs, I'm afraid—the floor is cold."

He sat, his hands in his lap, his feet evenly spaced, his back straight, and watched her sip on her sake. "Does the liquor help?" he politely inquired.

She nodded.

"Would you like more?"

"Yes, please."

He poured her another cup, presented it to her with the same quiet dignity, and sat down again.

"How old were you when you first had sex?" she asked in a swift breathy query.

"I forget. Old enough."

"I was twelve."

"I'm sorry."

She took a deep breath to suppress the tears suddenly welling in her eyes.

Instantly, he was at her side, taking the cup from her hand, setting it down, lifting her in his arms. "I won't hurt you." Moving back to his chair, he sat again holding her in his lap. "We've escaped from the misery imposed on us. We can do anything or nothing. We can dream again. Don't be afraid."

"It's been so long. I don't know how to dream."

"I'll help you. You need but ask."

"What would you do if I kissed you?" she asked instead.

He smiled. "Enjoy it."

"And then what?"

"I would wait for you to kiss me again if you wished."

"Would you really?"

"Of course. I have no predatory intent."

"I thought all men were predatory."

"Not all of them." Although he'd known more than his share.

"What if I invited you into my bed?"

"I would grow faint with desire like Lady Kasa and go."

She smiled at his allusion to the ancient love poem. "While I am so confused in yearning for you like Tzumi Shikibu," she answered in kind.

He gently touched her hand. "Love and longing is never simple. But those historic lovers felt the beauty too."

"What do you feel?"

"Unconditional love," he said without hesitation.

"For me?"

The uncertainty in her voice pained him; she'd been abandoned by her family so young. "For you," he said quietly.

Her bottom lip began to quiver and, drawing her close, he held her in a gentle embrace.

"Kiss me."

The words were so faint, he wondered for a moment whether he might have imagined them. But she lifted her face to him and he understood.

He kissed her the first time with hesitancy, fearful of frightening her. But her lips were softly yielding, her small sigh a breathy flutter on his mouth, and he dared to kiss her again. And then again in a long, slow sweetness that curiously heated her senses more effectively than the most skilled manipulation.

She felt a warmth seep downward from his

mouth and hands, from the scented heat of his body, a delicious, drifting sensation of comfort and bliss, of something more, as well. She felt a quick, faint ripple of desire and longing—brief at first, as though she were wakening to spring or her heart was coming free from the dark night of her past. And then he pulled her closer still so his powerful, strong young body touched her everywhere—became a source of delight to her, and she was dazzled. She'd not realized she was capable of passion; she'd never before felt desire. It was astonishing. "Guide me on my way," she whispered, taking his hand, leading him to her bed. "You've set fire to my heart." And eager now to lie with the man who could make her world rich with feeling, she reached for his erection.

While she might not know love, she knew a thousand ways to please a man.

"Wait," he said, brushing away her hand. "I've not come so far to be wild and driven. I want to remember this night. With your hair down for me," he whispered, lifting a pin from her hair, and then another, raising a shiny tress to smell its fragrance before letting it fall to her shoulder. "And your pure beauty unclothed." He slowly undressed her as she stood shivering—from longing and need—removing the many layers of kimonos one by one, slipping her sandals from her feet, combing the tangles from her hair with his fingers, kissing her mouth and eyes, her rosy cheeks and pale smooth throat. And before long she was panting with desire and laughing with delight at the notion that she was panting for sex. "You've unlocked my soul. . . ." Her voice was filled with joy.

He smiled, pleased he could give her joy. "Soon, you can end my longing and torment," he said lightly, lifting her on the bed. "And I will glimpse your soul."

"And I yours?"

"Perhaps," he said mildly, beginning to undress. He didn't say he'd locked the door on his years ago.

She watched his disrobing, fascinated. The men who could afford her weren't young men, nor beautiful. She was enthralled with Yukio's stark beauty and hard, young body, with the flaunting spectacle of his tattoos that covered much of his body, the showy adornment of his penis particularly intriguing. A phoenix, wings spread, was emblazoned on the enormous, turgid length.

"Let me see," she whispered, wiggling her fingers at his resplendent erection, thinking with a stabbing tenderness that it must have hurt. "Did it hurt?"

He smiled. "I was young and swaggering—intent on showing my valor."

She lifted her hand in a sweep up his body, feeling an ache of affection. "And the rest? How strong you are."

He shrugged. "All done years ago."

"I've never seen a man like you. Come closer."

He obliged, but stood just out of reach, skilled as a lover, less certain of how to deal with love.

"I want to touch you."

"Are you sure?"

She slid her finger up her vulva and lifted it to him, the pearly essence of arousal glistening on her fingertip. "Does this look sincere?"

"Yes." But he didn't move.

"Are you going to keep me waiting?"

"No," he said, moving to the bed and sitting beside her, the hallowed hour near, his heart drumming.

When she touched the cascading wings on his phoenix, he sucked in his breath. But when she dipped her head to take his penis in her mouth, he cupped her chin in his palm, lifted her face to him and said, "I don't want that. We're doing this together. I'm not a client."

"You're too sweet. You're going to spoil me."

"I'm going to spoil you all night," he murmured, easing her back on the bed, gracefully sliding between her legs, his weight resting on his forearms, his dark eyes luminous. "And all day and for the rest of the next week unless I die of exhaustion in the meantime."

Unfamiliar with youthful resilience, she trembled faintly at such profligate largesse. "Is that possible?"

"Let me show you," he murmured, easing the head of his erection into the liquid rapture of her melting cunt.

Smiling, compliant, dissolving with virgin desire, she arched up to meet him, wanting something she'd never wanted before, wanting it with naked desperation and longing, her hands fluttering along his muscled arms to draw him nearer. "Don't make me wait," she pleaded.

And he began living the dream he'd always dreamed.

* * *

Hugh came awake the next morning from what he thought was a dream, only to find blissful reality in the form of Tama seated astride his hips, his penis buried deep inside her succulent warmth.

"Good morning, Hugh-san," she said, with sunshine-bright cheer. "I hope you don't mind me waking you."

How could he mind when flame-hot desire coursed through his blood, when her lush, young body was drawing him in and her dewy cunt was just a bit tight so his cock was throbbing in bliss? Dismissing his uncertainties of the previous night as highly irrelevant when his cock was buried deep inside the charming princess who could never get enough of it, he answered, "I don't mind at all," gripped her hips and held her firmly in place as he thrust upward.

She uttered a blissful sigh.

He groaned softly.

And they greeted the new day with a tumultuous round of fierce, turbulent, wild and wondrous sex.

As he was trying to catch his breath sometime later, she turned to him and said, "I hope you don't mind me sleeping in your bed."

"Not in the least," he said with complete honesty. "It's my pleasure."

And so the voyage to Hong Kong continued in a love-tossed sea of great love and affection, the two young couples enamored with each other and with the larger delight of bewitching rapture and passion.

Sunskoku was inclined to worry occasionally about her family's reaction to being plucked from their lifelong home, but Yukio soothed her concerns, telling her there was time enough to deal with any problems once they reached Hong Kong.

Hugh and Tama by mutual agreement decided to enjoy the gift of their cloudless sexual relationship without reserve. As to other more mystifying feelings beginning to infiltrate their defenses—they chose to ignore them.

All in all, it was a gem-bright journey of shining days and starry nights.

Chapter

23

On the same night, nine days later, that those on the *Southern Belle* viewed the twilight mist settling over the hills of Hong Kong, Aiko was breathless with anticipation. Hiroaki was coming to visit—the first time she'd seen him since her tragedy. The physician had finally pronounced her hale and healthy and her great sadness at the loss of her child had been tempered by her belief in the gods and fate. She was young, her old nurse had said. She would have many children yet.

"Did you have the special fish prepared?" she excitedly inquired of her housekeeper. "And the sweets Hiroaki likes? Are the flowers arranged and the incense ready?"

"Yes, yes . . . everything is in readiness," the housekeeper replied, pleased to see her young mistress in good spirits once again. She was a sweet child, much too good for a man like Hiroaki, but such was the way of the world. No one in her position dared question his or her betters.

"Go and see that the cook is preparing the duck

properly. Last time she didn't make the sauce with
enough spice for the O-metsuke. Go . . . go, he'll
be here any moment!"

The old woman ran down the corridor toward
the kitchen, willing to follow her mistress's orders,
but certain the cook would do as she pleased like
she always did. But the chief inspector had person-
ally selected the cook, as he had the entire staff, so
who was she to question the woman's credentials?

As she returned from the kitchen some moments later, the O-metsuke was just entering the
house with his retinue and on seeing her, he dismissed his bodyguards and beckoned her over.

"You've spoken of the potion to no one," Hiroaki murmured, watching the housekeeper with
a hawklike gaze.

"No, my lord. I have been silent."

"Is your mistress well? Physicians often tell you
what they think you want to hear. I want the truth."

"Lady Aiko is completely recovered and very
pleased to see you again, my lord."

"She had no ill effects from the drug?"

"None." His gaze was terrifying, as though he
could see right through her brain. "She's young,
my lord, and quick to regain her health. She will
have other children someday."

"No, she won't. I have no interest in brats.
Understand? And should she become pregnant
again, I want word of it immediately. If necessary,
you will see that her pregnancy is terminated
again."

"As you wish, my lord. You need but give me my
orders."

"Yes, yes, I know. Now, where is she?"

"In her parlor, my lord."

"See that my men are fed." And with a wave he dismissed her.

As Hiroaki tossed his cloak on a wall hook and set his long sword in the rack by the door, Aiko crept back down the hall, her hand clamped over her mouth to stifle the anguished cry that had risen in her throat, the loathsome words she'd overheard almost too much to bear.

But even as she retreated down the corridor and slipped back inside her parlor, an awful, pitiless need for retribution gripped her senses. How could he—the man she'd given up her life for . . . how could he treat her so cruelly? Had he no charity or tenderness that he could take from her something so precious when she'd given him *everything*?

Breathing deeply, she forced herself to a fictitious calm, dropping to her knees, bowing her head as he would expect, adopting the pose of a faithful woman greeting her lover.

The door slid open and she looked up shyly, forcing herself to smile when the effort was excruciating.

"Ah, my little one. How lovely you look this evening. Have you recovered from your misfortune?" The chief inspector went to her, lifted her to her feet and drew her close.

Sliding her arms around his waist even as she felt the hate inside her grow, she lifted her face to his and offered him a gracious mask. "I am quite recovered, my lord. As you would wish."

"As the spirits would wish, little one. Is the world not a little brighter now that you are well again," he said gently.

"My world is brighter, my lord, now that you have returned to it."

"My duties have been onerous, my sweet," he said with a dramatic sigh. In fact, the past weeks had been fraught with near disaster as he'd frantically covered his tracks in the calamitous and luckless pursuit of the princess. The Yoshiwara had to be assuaged, his ninja reassigned to remote domains where loose tongues would go unheard, those closest to the search executed to ensure their silence. But all had ended well; the senior councillors were ignorant of his failure to find the Princess of Otari.

"Then, you must enjoy your leisure tonight, my lord. Let me see that your favorite wines are in readiness. Sit near the brazier and warm yourself. I shall return shortly." Her smile was honeyed as she guided him to a soft cushion by the brazier, a plan of vengeance beginning to form in her mind. As she glided from the room, she offered him a deceptively sweet smile redolent of future pleasures.

Hiroaki leaned back against the pillows and reached for his pipe. Now this was how a man should be treated, with deference and respect—and perhaps just a little awe. He'd found the perfect little wren in Aiko . . . faithful, decorous, and her dewy little cinnabar cleft was delightfully tight.

Lighting his pipe, he inhaled deeply. Life was as it should be.

* * *

In the early days of their liaison, Aiko had once thought the chief inspector had deserted her and in the deep throes of passion and despair, she'd bought poison from the apothecary, intending to end her life. But Hiroaki had returned, bearing lovely presents, explaining that her fears were unfounded and promising to send her love poems if ever he was gone so long again.

Her thoughts of suicide had instantly vanished.

But the vial of poison remained tucked away in a small drawer.

Forgotten.

Until now.

Moving swiftly down the corridor, she entered her dressing room, dismissed her maid and went to the small chest where her fans were kept. Kneeling before it, she pulled out a drawer, felt beneath the tissue-wrapped bundles and pulled out the vial.

Without a moment's hesitation, she slipped it into a fold of her obi, and rose to her feet. She hadn't realized she could hate with such fury. Nor plan murder without conscience or guilt. But then, she'd never lost a child before. A child she'd wanted desperately, a child she would have loved and cared for, who would have loved her in return. A child who had been taken away from her for the most venal, selfish of reasons by a man without compassion or humanity. By a man without a heart.

She was shaking faintly—from rage, not fear—

and standing utterly still for a moment, she consciously drew a shroud of calm about her. It would require composure to see this spectacle through to the end; she had no illusions as to her fate once the chief inspector was found dead in her bedroom.

But she would face death with equanimity, knowing she'd destroyed the monster who'd killed her child.

How dare he, she thought calmly, opening the door to the hall.

How dare he presume to strip her life of meaning.

Her blood was like ice in her veins as she returned to her bedchamber, her nerves steady. A kind of peacefulness and tranquillity had settled over her. "All is in order," she declared serenely on entering the room. "The wines will be here soon," she added as though she'd actually spoken to someone on the staff. "Would you like a fresh pipe while we wait?" She smiled. "Or perhaps a small cup of tea? I have the cakes you like."

"As you wish, child," Hiroaki murmured, charmed by her docile homage. "Perhaps a cup of tea would be pleasant on a winter night."

Aiko busied herself readying the tea and arranging a tray of cakes, smiling over at Hiroaki from time to time, talking to him of the mundane activities of her day, lulling him into restful doze with the sound of her voice. She glanced over her shoulder before she took out the vial, but his eyes were half closed, pipe smoke wreathing his head. And she picked up the thread of her monologue, describing her afternoon walk in the imperial gardens—one drop—whom she'd met and talked to—two drops—the snow-dusted pines and swept paths—a third drop for good measure—the condition of the pond, half frozen over so the swans had to be taken in to their winter pens.

Putting in a smattering of jasmine petals to scent the tea and disguise her additions, she turned around with the tray in her hands and placed it on the small table near Hiroaki. "Try a cake, first, my lord. The cook made them specially for you." She offered him one on a fine lacquerware plate.

As he took it, she set the cup of tea at his elbow and picked up a pink sugared cake herself. Nibbling it daintily, she spoke of missing him in his absence as he ate. "I hope your duties won't require such long hours in the future," she concluded sweetly.

"A man of my consequence is much in demand, my pet. So few are capable of making weighty decisions." He set down the remains of his cake and picked up his teacup. "Aren't you joining me?" he asked.

His pleasantry was so unusual, Aiko momentarily took alarm. Until the dispassion that had brought her to this point with levelheaded calm reasserted itself. "When I finish my cake, my lord. Pink sugar cakes are my favorite." And so saying, she smiled and took a fashionably small bite.

Hiroaki carried the cup to his mouth and paused. "How pleasant—jasmine," he murmured, and took a sip.

And her heartbeat resumed, her apprehension not for herself, but for possible failure. She wanted him dead.

The teacup was small. Three sips later it was empty.

She took care not to alter her tone of voice or her smile as she continued regaling him with the prosaic dealings of her life. She complimented him on the flowers he'd had sent to her, telling him how much she appreciated his thoughtfulness. "I particularly enjoyed the lilies, so delicate and fragile. Are you feeling unwell, my lord? You look pale. Would you like a cover against the cold?" Rising, she carried a quilt over to him and draped it over his shoulders.

"I'll be fine," he murmured, blowing out a breath, trying to sit up a little straighter to ease the constriction in his chest.

"You've been under so much pressure, my lord. A rest will do you good. Lie down on this pillow," she said softly, slipping a pillow under his head.

"You're a sweet child," he whispered, his breathing becoming difficult.

"Thank you. Shut your eyes and sleep."

Whether a nuance in her tone gave him warning or whether he recognized the effects of poison after having ordered it administered so many times, his eyes flared wide in terror and he tried to rise.

"No," she said, her dulcet tones accompanied by a hard shove. "You won't be going anywhere."

He opened his mouth to shout for help and she clamped her hand over it with fixed purpose. "You shouldn't have killed my child," she said, adding the weight of her body to the pressure of her hand. "You shouldn't have done that to me."

He was gasping for air. But she didn't relinquish her hold, slowly pushing him into the pillows, watching him die, his face turning red, then blue, then purple before his lungs gave out. She could have been watching a river flow for all the emotion she felt.

She was numb.

He had taken away her life.

And now that he was gone, she simply waited for his men to carry her away.

When the knock finally came, she said, "Enter," in a lifeless tone and neither turned around nor spoke again.

The man on the threshold came to his own conclusions after a brief searching glance and quickly slid the door shut. Standing inside the room, the silence scented with death, he debated how best to address their mutual problem. The lady appeared paralyzed or in shock. "Can you hear me, my lady?"

It was a strange man's voice without harshness, and in her surprise, Aiko swung around.

"We will help you. Do you understand what I'm saying?"

"Who are you?" She heard the sound of her voice with sudden clarity and was reassured as though she'd come back from the dead. She felt the will to live leap inside her.

"A friend."

She was about to say, *No, you're not,* but understood friendship took many forms. "How can you help? His men will find him like this and take me away and kill me."

"We will kill his men instead and move the bodies elsewhere."

She felt her body begin to warm, her heartbeat come alive. "You could? You would do that for me?"

"And for my master. He has a price on Hiroaki's head."

"As do many."

"Too many to count, my lady. His death will not be mourned. Not even by his family."

"I am in your debt."

"No, my lady, you've saved us the trouble of killing him. Stay here until I return. You're quite safe. My men have the house surrounded."

Aiko sat very still as the muffled sounds of combat resonated outside her chambers, curiously confident in the stranger's ability, confident as well that her debt to her unborn child had been discharged.

The brute was dead.

And she was alive.

The gods had taken pity on her.

When Yukio's man returned, he said only, "We will leave you in peace, my lady." And he stood aside so two men could come in and take Hiroaki's body away. "The chief inspector will be found on the road to Kyoto, along with his men, murdered by brigands. The servants have been spoken to. They will be silent. If anyone comes to question you, don't be alarmed. Nothing will trace him to your house tonight. My word on it."

She believed him as though Amida had spoken in his guise. She was that sure. "Thank you. It seems so inadequate for all you've done, but my heart is in my words."

"My master will hear of your gratitude." His bow was refined and graceful. And a moment later, he was gone.

As the oxcart slowly plodded through the streets of Edo that night, Takeo behind the reins, its contents were guarded by a ragtag group of peasants. No one would stop them or even come near, outcaste eta beyond the pale. Eta carried away the dead and cleaned the latrines—always at night so no one would be defiled by the sight of them.

On their slow passage to the Tokaido—the main road to Kyoto—Takeo had time to reflect on how best to dispose of his lucrative blood money payment. Perhaps he'd buy a property in his home prefecture or a business of his own. He could even afford to marry a rich merchant's daughter with the price Yukio had given him for Hiroaki's head.

Although it had been a long wait before the chief inspector finally visited his mistress again. After finding a job in Aiko's stables, Takeo had had to muck out stalls and do other sordid, menial work for much too long. He'd almost given up and changed to another plan when word of Hiroaki's visit had finally arrived.

He'd immediately ordered his men into place.

Although who would have thought his mission would have been discharged by the demure young lady of the house. He shrugged. It just went to show how outward appearances could be deceiving.

Lady Aiko probably deserved a share of the prize

money, he reflected. He'd have to send her some with a note—explaining the windfall in such a way that no suspicion would fall on her.

On the other hand, she was a pretty little thing. Maybe he'd deliver the money in person. . . .

Chapter

24

Their first morning in Hong Kong was sunny and bright. Hugh planned to take Tama sightseeing while his passengers tried to locate Sunskoku's family. Yukio had already contacted some of his colleagues on the waterfront and was waiting for word.

Knowing it was possible to have a wardrobe assembled in record time in the merchant capital of the East, Hugh had suggested as much to Tama that morning over breakfast.

"Are you saying I'm shabby?" she replied, a teasing light in her eyes.

"Not in the least. My robe is very fine silk. But you might like something other than your peasant clothes for sight-seeing today."

"And you no doubt know a shop for ladies' wear."

"I've heard of some," he said.

"Ah."

"There's no need for that tone of voice. I don't as a rule buy ladies' garments." That would imply a relationship of some kind—however tenuous.

"And you needn't buy mine. I have some gold."

And a fortune in pearls that she planned on selling in Europe, he knew. "I'd like to buy you *something* if you'd allow me. If not clothing, something else. As a token"—he smiled—"of my appreciation."

"If we're considering tokens of appreciation, Hugh-san, you deserve a much larger present. You are enormously"—she grinned—"enormous for one thing, but also," she added more gently, "gallant. I must have climaxed a dozen times this morning. What would you like me to buy *you?*"

"Save your money, darling. You're going to need it to fund your army."

"But not this morning, Hugh-san. I may think of pleasure, may I not?"

Her voice had taken on a sudden poignancy and he chastised himself for his boorishness. "You may think of pleasure for weeks yet, darling. And longer than that, if you wish." At base, he disliked the notion of her returning to face her enemies, anyway. "Let's make a pact. Pleasure alone for the duration."

"Yes," she said with a smile. "I agree. So tell me, Hugh-san, where is this establishment that will make me look like a westerner?"

But Tama wore a Japanese kimono borrowed from Sunskoku that first day in Hong Kong, Hugh refusing to let her wear her cotton tunic and trousers.

And they set out in a carriage for their first stop at the dressmakers.

The Frenchwoman's shop, as it was referred to by everyone but the proprietor who had clung to her memories of Paris by naming her shop Le Rue Royale, sat on a very fine property on the Peak. Rumor had it the head of Jardine Matheson had set her up in her youth and her son who now managed the shop looked more like a Scotsman than a Frenchman. But his French was without accent as were the dozen other languages he spoke, and when Hugh entered the shop with Tama on his arm, James Delaroche greeted Hugh with a perfect American accent.

Tama looked up at Hugh. "I thought you didn't come here."

"Perhaps, once, a long time ago," he murmured, meeting James's glance with a significant lift of his brows.

"And how is Mr. McDougal?" James inquired, quick to adjust his conversation to suit the occasion. "Did his wife like the gowns he purchased?"

"I'm sure she did," Hugh replied, thanking him with a smile, when the wife in question was the German minister's wife. And it wasn't as though he'd lied outright to Tama that morning. He rarely did buy gowns for ladies. But Elsa had dragged him in once and asked so prettily, he would have been a brute to refuse. "The lady needs a small wardrobe for our voyage," Hugh said in a brisk, businesslike tone. "And quickly, I'm afraid."

Hugh's lack of introductions wasn't uncommon. Many of the men who came here with a lady on their arm referred to them obliquely, for obvious reasons. James smiled. "I'm sure we can accommodate you." While the captain had exotic tastes in women, this one was particularly exquisite, pale and delicate as a rare orchid, her kimono of priceless brocade.

Tama expected no familiarity from a tradesman, so she didn't question the lack of introductions. "Please show me what women are wearing in the West," she said. "I have little knowledge of fashion. Something in silk, I think."

James indicated a table with pattern books and offered them chairs. "The publications are sent out from Paris each month," he pointed out. "You'll be in the height of fashion, no matter what you select."

After perusing several books, Tama looked to Hugh for advice. "What about this?" she asked, indicating a peony pink day gown, and he nodded. "And this?" A pale yellow evening gown to which he also agreed. "And this?" She pointed to a forest-green velvet riding habit.

"It's for riding," he said.

"Will I be riding?"

It gave him pause when he would ordinarily have given her some neutral answer that separated his life from hers. But he found himself wanting her to ride with him instead of someone else. "I'm sure you will," he said blandly, catching himself just in time. But he visualized Tama in that magnificent velvet in the Bois de Boulogne, and made some quick adjustments in his plans. "I'll take you riding," he offered.

"How nice of you."

She said it with such naivete, he felt a twinge of guilt. Although a second later he reminded himself that neither of them was naive. "It would be my pleasure, darling," he murmured, with an easy, facile charm.

She looked up at him from under her lashes and laughed, a little silvery sound. "Both our pleasures, I believe, Hugh-san. Do men wear velvet while riding?"

"I don't."

"Ah. But I may?"

"It's perfect for a woman."

"Any woman?"

He laughed. "No, only one." Glancing up at James, his smile still lighting his eyes, he said, "We'll need some riding boots as well. Green leather."

"Very good. Would the lady like a hat with or without a feather?"

"A hat. No, no hat," Tama protested. "How will it stay on?"

"A hat, James." Hugh turned to Tama. "I'll show you. If you wish to be fashionable, you'll need a hat. Your brother Komei's wife will be wearing hats."

James Delaroche's eyes widened for a split second before his gaze went shuttered. So this was the Princess of Otari. Her brother, the prince, had spent half a year in the colony before sailing for Paris. "A lady's hat is de rigeur in Europe," James observed politely.

"What a strange custom. What if I don't wish to wear a hat?"

If the princess was anything like her brother, James thought, their wealth would allow them to dress as they pleased. Although Prince Komei had been a very good customer. And in love with his wife—not the norm in the Orient. Or anywhere in the moneyed world, for that matter.

Tama was flipping through the pattern book pages with increasing disinterest. "You select some for me, Hugh-san. They all look so confining." She smiled at him and began to rise.

"If the lady would be so kind as to allow one of our women to measure her," James said, beckoning one of his shop girls over.

As Tama was led away, Hugh pushed the pattern book aside. "You decide on the gowns, James. I'll defer to your good taste. A dozen gowns if you have enough seamstresses to get them to us in two days. Otherwise, we'll take as many as you can deliver. Send the bill to my banker, as usual."

"Yes, of course. Do you know who she is?" James murmured quickly, not sure the captain was aware of his passenger's identity. He had a tendency to conduct his affairs with extreme casualness.

With their escape from Hiroaki so recent, knowing anything and anyone was for sale in the east, Hugh gazed at James Delaroche with suspicion. "How do you know who she is?" he inquired coolly.

"Her brother was a good customer while he lived here. I recognized the name. It's an uncommon one"—his brows rose—"and princely. They both have a price on their head, I hear."

"I'd suggest you forget you saw her."

"Certainly. I simply wanted you to know what rumors are about. In my business, I never remember anyone's name. You know that. But it would be wise to keep her out of sight until you sail. The Otari fortune brings out the avarice in men."

"Which is why her family is still outlawed when many clans have already been pardoned."

"The lure of filthy lucre, Captain. A merciless human failing."

"Thanks for the warning. I would have thought us beyond the grasp of her enemies."

"Don't stop looking over your shoulder. Just some friendly advice."

"Is there anyone in particular I should warn off?"

James smiled. The captain had never been a man to trifle with. "I understand the German minister is negotiating with the new government of Japan for railway lines. And port construction."

"Elsa's husband?"

"None other. He has an expensive wife, as you know. And the minister requires additional funds to maintain his, er, auxiliary household."

"His mistress, you mean."

"But of course. The minister will be given a specified portion of the contracts let—that percentage currently under negotiation between himself and the Japanese foreign minister. If he were to gain the reward for the Princess of Otari as well"—James shrugged in a particularly Gallic way—"you see what I mean about not becoming too visible."

"Among other things, I don't need Elsa coming around to visit."

"For more reasons than one, perhaps," James noted slyly.

"The princess has simply booked passage on my ship." Hugh's voice was silken and mild.

"I understand." James's expression was equally bland. "I didn't mean to imply anything more.

You're a businessman. I'm a businessman. We both do business."

Hugh glanced up to see that no one was near and when his gaze returned to James, a new gravity shone in his eyes. "I'd be more than willing to pay for any information pertaining to the princess that you might uncover in the course of your, er, business dealings." James had been born and reared in Hong Kong. Those he didn't know, weren't worth knowing. "Name your price. Anything at all," Hugh affirmed.

That magnanimity of the captain's offer must be a measure of his affection for the woman. His reputation as a tough negotiator was legendary. "I'll see what I can find out."

"I want names."

And James knew why. "Some may be highly placed."

"So? It's kill or be killed in this world." Hugh smiled tightly. "Here, more than anywhere. I just need the names and an account where you want your funds deposited. You won't be implicated in any way. But if anyone's after the princess, I want to know."

"It was a bloody war, I hear," James said.

"Which one? Hers or mine or someone else's?"

James arched his brows. "Touché. But I meant hers. Wakamatsu was a massacre, I'm told."

"She's doing well," Hugh said softly. "She's bent on revenge." He shrugged. "Not that I agree. But it gives one reason to live, perhaps . . ."

"We all do what we have to do, Captain, do we not?" Hong Kong was a merciless town to those with a heart.

"Amen to that," Hugh said, as he came to his feet. "I'll expect to hear from you, then?"

"I should know something by evening."

"Perfect."

Another one of those words with potent meaning. The dark streets of Hong Kong could often be a brutal killing field. "I'll have the gowns delivered by tomorrow afternoon."

"Thank you, on all counts. Good day, Mr. Delaroche," Hugh said in a conversational tone, seeing Tama emerge from one of the dressing rooms. "I appreciate all your help."

"My pleasure, Captain Drummond."

"Are we all finished, then?" Hugh inquired as he approached Tama. "Is there anything you'd like?" She was looking at a display of fans and gloves.

"No. Everything is very strange here."

"You'll get used to it."

She looked up at him, his voice having taken on a cynical edge. "Is there something wrong?"

"No, but I'm tired . . . I didn't sleep much last night. Would you mind if we return to the ship?"

"To sleep?" A small smile had formed on her lips.

"Am I that transparent?" he teased, grateful for her suggestive smile.

"I find that transparency very appealing."

"You don't mind not sight-seeing?"

"What do you think?"

He laughed. "I think you're going to give me a run for my money. . . ."

She looked perplexed.

"It means you can more than keep up."

"Ah . . . but then, keeping up with you is my good fortune."

"Ours," Hugh said gently, bending to kiss her in sight of everyone.

As they walked out the door, James gave his shop girls a lowering glance and they stifled their giggles.

But Hugh Drummond was in real deep, he thought.

Whether he knew it or not.

Chapter

25

Sunskoku's family had been located living in a small house in the western hills. When she arrived at the gate, all the children came running out to greet her, hugging her and chattering like magpies.

Having little memory of family, Yukio took no notice of the fact that the adults had remained inside.

But Sunskoku did. And apprehension gripped her senses.

Her mother was at the entry, but her welcome was so timorous, Sunskoku knew something was amiss. And when Sunskoku's father shouted from the parlor, her mother looked up in fear and turned and ran.

"Are we in the wrong house?" Yukio muttered, the father's rudeness raising his hackles.

"He hasn't changed."

"Perhaps he should, since you've supported them for years."

She half smiled. "What world do you live in? He is the head of the household."

"Not in my eyes."

"Please, don't argue with him. I couldn't bear it."

"I won't let him hurt you."

"He won't. He'll hurt my mother."

Yukio's jaw clenched and he inhaled deeply. He'd lost his mother to a man like that. "You're not staying here," he said, hushed and low. "I won't allow it."

"What I don't need is another man telling me what to do," she muttered fiercely.

"I ask your pardon. But, please, consider yourself. That's all I'm saying."

It was difficult to resist the quaking fear that always overcame her when her father bellowed. The fear was deep inside her. "We will talk to them," she said, taking a deep breath. "And discover what their wishes are."

"Am I allowed to speak?"

His voice was taut. She shot him a glance. "I'd prefer you didn't."

"As you wish."

The room they entered was spacious, a garden visible through a round Chinese window paned with glass, a makeshift tokonoma erected before which her father sat, surrounded by Sunskoku's family— siblings, spouses, her mother and grandmothers. "Why have we been transported to this foreign country?" her father growled.

"In order to save your lives," Sunskoku answered, her voice soft with courtesy.

He glared at her. "If you hadn't left the Yoshi-wara, our lives wouldn't have been at risk. You are an ungrateful daughter who has made our lives a misery."

"If I had died you would have been cast into poverty once again, or more likely, murdered. I thought you would have preferred this."

"There was no need for you to die. Your selfish-ness was the cause of all this turmoil and unhappi-ness."

"What of my unhappiness?" she asked quietly, a small spark of anger igniting deep in her soul. "Does not my unhappiness matter?"

"It is your duty to serve your parents."

"But only I of all your children was forced to follow the path of duty to the Yoshiwara. Why did that obligation fall on me?"

Her father's face was wrathful, his mouth twisted in anger. "Do you dare to question the head of this family?"

She didn't answer for a time, her gaze taking in the terror on the face of her mother, a small flut-ter of dread tightening her stomach. "I think I've earned the right after providing for this family all these years. I have borne the burden alone with-out complaint." Her hands were clasped tightly, her spine rigid. "Until now. Do any of you under-stand what it takes to do what I do? What repellent things are asked of me?"

"I will not hear this!" her father shouted. "You will not defile my house with such lewd talk!"

"*Your* house?" Her voice was scarcely more than a whisper. "Who do you think pays for this house and your food and clothing and everything that touches your life?" She turned to Yukio. "We're leaving."

He nodded, controlling his urge to do violence to her father only with effort.

Sunskoku met her father's malignant gaze with hauteur. "You will receive your monthly stipend and if you wish to return to Japan, passage will be given you. The decision is yours." She went to give her mother a hug. "If you ever need me," she whispered, "give a message to the cook." Yukio had his people on their staff, a precaution he'd taken of his own accord. For which she was grateful. She released her mother and stepped back. "If any of you wish to contact me, the man who brings your expense money will get in touch with me. I wish you well." She knew her mother would relay her message to the other women, some of whom might have the courage to leave. But she couldn't be responsible for so many lives anymore. She was giving herself permission to discard the onerous burden she'd carried since childhood.

She was giving herself permission to be free.

Her head held high, she turned away from the only family she'd ever known, and walked away.

As they reached the entrance gate, Yukio murmured, "I left my cloak inside. I'll be right back. Wait for me in the carriage." Hong Kong offered all the western amenities and they were enjoying them. Carriages had been forbidden in Japan.

Sprinting back up the path to the door, Yukio knocked once, pushed the door open without waiting for a reply and strode directly to the parlor. Without ceremony, he entered and, standing in the doorway like a wrathful god, looked daggers at Sunskoku's father. "Listen and listen well, old man," he growled, the low thunder of his voice resonating throughout the room. "You will lift your hand or voice to no one in this family, and if I hear that you have, my vengeance will be swift. I have my informants. So do as I say or suffer for your stupidity." Turning, he grabbed the cloak he'd deliberately left behind and exited the house at a run.

"I didn't keep you waiting long, did I," he remarked a moment later, jumping into the carriage and lounging next to Sunskoku. "You have an interesting family," he said, flashing her a grin. "It makes me feel less sad I have none."

She smiled faintly. "Was it terrible? Was I?"

He shook his head and pulled her into his arms. "You were finally sensible, sweetheart," he murmured, dropping a light kiss on her nose. "They want too much from you. You don't have to give them your soul."

She made a small moue. "I know that now."

"And I don't want it either," he said lightly. "I have enough trouble with my own."

"So we shall be independent."

"I didn't say that," he murmured with a roguish grin.

"Semi-independent, then. I no longer take orders."

"Fair enough. Semi-independent. And when we reach Paris, I'll see that my semi-independent sweetheart has a house fit for an empress."

She laughed. "In that case, I might be willing to relinquish a portion of my independence on occasion."

"When I ask real nicely."

"Yes," she purred, "because I know how nicely you can ask. . . ."

Chapter

26

After a short detour to buy some kimonos and sandals, Hugh and Tama returned to the *Southern Belle*. While his motive had been safety for the princess, he wasn't averse to her suggestion they spend the time in bed. After ushering her into his suite, he tossed the packages on the sofa, stripped off his coat, and pulled a small enameled box from his trouser pocket. "A thank-you gift," he said, offering it to her.

Taking the box from him with a puzzled look, she asked, "How did you do that?"

"There was a jeweler next door to the shop where you bought your kimonos."

"You couldn't have been gone more than a minute."

"You were trying to decide which fabrics you wanted. It didn't take long. Open it. See if you like it."

Taking the lid from the celadon-tinted box, she gasped softly. Ensconced on a bed of white silk lay an intricately carved purple jade pendant in the shape of a peony—each miniature petal exquisitely true to life, a drop of dew glistening for all eternity on one petal. "It's beautiful." She looked up at Hugh with tears in her eyes. "You couldn't have known, but my mother wore a pendant very similar to this. Thank you." Her smile quivered for a moment before she composed herself and offered him the radiant smile he knew. "I'm in your debt, Hugh-san, for any number of things. I adore this."

"Try it on." And reaching out, he took the box from her hand, lifted the pendant out and, setting the enameled box down, slipped the delicate gold chain over her head. "Very nice," he murmured, his gaze on the pale silken flesh on which the pendant lay. "Think of me when you wear it."

She was finding herself thinking of him much too much already, but not only wouldn't she tell him, she would break herself of the habit just as soon as they landed in France. But she'd selfishly decided to put off that necessity until the very last moment. She smiled up at him. "It feels warm on my skin—like you. . . ."

"I could warm you a bit more if you'd like," he said in a velvety whisper.

"I would like that very much." She began untying her obi.

If he didn't know better, if he didn't know he was in one of the more dangerous ports in the East on a ship built for war, he might be tempted to think he'd stepped into his own sweet paradise of the senses. The princess was his perfect sexual match, as eager for sex as he, as ravenous and insatiable. And unlike so many women who felt pretense was a requirement in amour, she was completely honest and artless in her need. "Let me help you," he said, almost gloating at the extent of his luck.

In all the chaos and turmoil currently prevalent in Japan, this beautiful young woman had walked into his house.

Like a gift from the gods.

He might have to think about donating some funds to a temple in Edo the next time he was in Japan.

"Have you fallen asleep already, Hugh-san?"

He looked down at the sound of her voice and met her dark enchanting gaze. "I was saying a prayer," he noted sportively.

"For me?"

Why wasn't he surprised at her percipience when the gods were clearly on his shoulder. "For having you," he said gently. "I feel lucky."

They'd agreed to be rational about their relationship, but his words gave her pleasure and she could no more ignore her feelings than he. "Good fortune is ours, is it not," she said with a smile. "Come, Hugh-san." She took his hand. "Let me show you my pleasure in knowing you."

They made love that day with a special sense of possibility, as though fate or destiny had brought them together for some purpose, as though they were allowed to revel in the simple beauty of their good fortune. And for a time, they forgot that a greater world lay outside their enchanted paradise.

But the world intruded late that afternoon in

the form of a hard rapping knock, followed by Yukio's deep voice. "A message has come, Hugh-san. It requires an answer."

While Hugh was expecting a message from Delaroche, he hadn't expected it this early, nor had he thought Yukio would be involved. But apparently he was wrong on both points. "If you'll excuse me, darling. Business. Sorry." He was already rolling out of bed and reaching for his trousers. "I'll be right there," he shouted, so Yukio knew he'd been heard.

"When will you be back?" Tama inquired drowsily, her lack of sleep over the last several weeks having finally caught up with her.

"Soon. Well—maybe not so soon," he corrected, not sure what might be required in terms of a response to James's message. "If I have to go out, I'll leave you a note. Go back to sleep."

"Ummmm," she murmured, drifting off already, numerous orgasms adding to her lethargy.

Hugh smiled. The insatiable little minx had good reason for postcoital languor. But his adrenaline was spiking in anticipation of Delaroche's discoveries and he was wide awake. Dressing quickly, he grabbed his holster and quietly left the bedroom. Buckling his Colts on his hips as he walked through the sitting room, he opened the door and stepped out into the passageway.

"One of my associates delivered Delaroche's message so naturally he came to me. Here," Yukio said, handing Hugh the note. "I assumed it was important." An understatement when Uda's men were involved. Yukio politely moved away.

"Stay," Hugh murmured, ripping open the envelope and quickly scanning the contents. "I might need your help." He crumpled the missive a moment later and shoved it in his trouser pocket. "Have you heard of Nitta Tadashi?"

"A government official. A minister. He likes young girls—very young," Yukio added grimly.

"Apparently he's here in Hong Kong negotiating a construction contract with the German minister," Hugh said. "In addition, he's offering a reward for Princess Otari's recovery. He may be working for Hiroaki or alone."

"Or for any number of people who are interested in claiming the Otari properties. But he's not working for Hiroaki. Hiroaki's dead."

Hugh gave him a sharp glance. "Since when?"

"Since I put a price on his head and left my best assassin on the assignment."

"Are you sure?"

"Takeo is to be trusted with an assignment. Hiroaki is dead, I assure you."

Hugh blew out a long breath. "That's a relief." He smiled. "One less to kill. Thank you."

"You won't be able to kill them all, Hugh-san. There are too many greedy men after the princess and her fortune."

"Would you be willing to help me with one of them? Maybe two, although the German minister is relatively harmless."

"Many ruthless men look harmless. They have assassins do their killing."

"I doubt Freddy would have the guts to give the order. What about this Nitta fellow—does he have to be eliminated or only frightened?"

Yukio shrugged. "Dead is always safer."

* * *

A man like Nitta, high profile and well known in the floating world, had made contact with those who procured young girls shortly after his arrival in Hong Kong. It didn't take more than a few hours to track him down, a word here, another there, money passing hands, a few false leads. But by early evening Hugh and Yukio had trailed the minister to a fashionable brothel on Chater Road.

"Good evening, Captain." The owner greeted Hugh with warmth as he entered her drawing room; he was a lavish spender. "What's your pleasure tonight?"

Goody Brighton was a well-preserved blonde of indeterminate age. She'd come to Hong Kong as a servant for one of the traders and decided the life offered her in Chater Road was an improvement over scullery duty. Pretty, vivacious and genuinely warm, she'd made a good living for herself until she'd married the local banker who owned the establishment. When he died soon after, he'd been gracious enough to leave it to her in his will. That largesse made up for the fact that he'd failed to mention he was already married and his family in England would inherit the bulk of his fortune.

But Goody considered her windfall more than any scullery maid could possibly expect and had not only continued the operation of the brothel, but had prospered. But then, she'd always liked men and men like Hugh Drummond had a lot to like. Not to mention the handsome Japanese with him.

"We've your favorite bourbon, Captain, and

some sake for your friend? You haven't been in town for a while. Are you looking for Lucy again? She'd be right happy to see you."

"Actually, I have some business to discuss," Hugh said, his voice mild. "We thought you might be able to help us."

"My kind of business or your kind of business?"

"Yours."

"Well, that's a relief," she said with a smile. "Come on along," she added, motioning them to follow her. "My office is private."

They followed her down a hallway to a well-appointed room that overlooked the harbor. Beckoning them into chairs, she sat opposite them at her desk looking very much the grande dame in black silk and pearls. "You look serious. What can I do for you?"

"We're looking for a man called Nitta. He's supposed to be here now."

Her brows rose over bright blue eyes. "That's pretty up-to-date information. He didn't arrive more than a half hour ago. He's offended you in some way?" That look in the captain's eye. There wasn't any doubt.

"Let's just say I want to make sure that he doesn't offend me."

"What do you want me to do?"

"We just want to talk to him."

"No killing in my place. I don't allow it."

"We'll take him outside," Yukio said.

She glanced at Yukio, a yakuza if she ever saw one, and then at Hugh. "Couldn't this wait until he leaves?"

"I just want to talk to him. Our time is a little short." Hugh regarded Yukio, his brows raised. "Maybe Nitta will be reasonable."

Yukio shrugged. He was a pragmatist. Men like Nitta weren't reasonable unless they had to be—and never for long.

"I'll rely on your discretion, Captain," Goody said with a shrug of her own. "He's not my style, if truth be told. He wanted a very young girl and I told him we don't do that here." She made an impatient dismissive gesture, her rings sparkling in the lamplight. "Men like him should have their comeuppance. So be my guest, but keep it quiet. I don't want any customers leaving." She stood, her crisp black taffeta gown rustling with her movement. "Second floor, room five. Don't frighten Molly."

When they opened the door and walked in, the girl Molly was backed into a corner, her eyes wide with terror.

"Night's over, Molly. Here." Hugh tossed her dress at her. "Goody's downstairs. Go see her. And you, Nitta, put your dick back into your pants," he said in Japanese. "We've got something to say to you."

Yukio spoke to the minister in a harsh, staccato vernacular that apparently added something in the translation, because the Japanese minister visibly blanched.

"Sit," Hugh ordered, pointing to a chair.

The man sat.

"Lock the door," Hugh murmured, and when Yukio turned the key in the lock, the minister's eyes widened in fear.

"This won't take long, and if you're sensible, you'll take my words to heart. I understand you put out a reward for information on the where-abouts of the Princess of Otari. I'd reconsider it if I were you." Hugh's Japanese was excellent and he spoke slowly so the minister wouldn't miss any-thing. "I'm taking the Princess of Otari abroad with me. And I don't want her hurt. So forget her. But if you choose to be stupid and persist in your search, I'll kill you and everyone in your family. Is that clear?"

"You should kill him now," Yukio said.

"No, no, don't, I beg of you! I will take back my offer immediately!" the minister said, his voice breaking, sweat running down his face, his gaze flicking from man to man. "I swear!"

"You can't believe a man who fucks little girls," Yukio growled. "Kill him now."

"I'll pay you anything, please!" Nitta's voice had risen to a high-pitched squeal. "I promise my search will be called off . . . you have to believe me, please, please! Be merciful! Don't kill me! I have money— tell me how much you—"

"Oh, Christ," Hugh muttered, turning away from the trembling man in disgust.

The minister had lost control of his bowels.

"Now I'm going to have to buy Goody a new chair."

Following Hugh as he moved to the door, Yukio murmured, "You're making a mistake."

"It won't be the first." Walking out into the hall, Hugh scanned the quiet corridor. "We'll leave a tail on him. If he makes a wrong move, screw him."

"You're the boss."

Hugh shot him a look as they moved down the corridor. "I'm just being cautious. Goody doesn't like scandal attached to her house." Stopping at the top of the stairs, Hugh paused, the opulent drawing room below awash with beautiful women and wealthy men. He grimaced faintly, people like Nitta reminding him what lay beneath the scented luxury and ingratiating smiles. "We'd better check on Molly before we go. See if she was hurt."

"And pay for the chair," Yukio said with a grin.

"Don't laugh yet. We still have another fine diplomat to deal with. An equally craven knave."

Twenty minutes later, they found the German minister about to leave for a dinner party at the Russian legation. He was waiting impatiently in the entrance hall as his wife adjusted her ermine cape so her ruby necklace and fine bosom were suitably displayed.

As the men walked in, Elsa's eyes lit up. "How nice to see you again, Captain Drummond," she cooed. Walking across the marble foyer, she offered her hand to Hugh, gazing up at him from under her lashes in open invitation. "It's been such a *long time* since we've seen you. You must join us for dinner. Frederick, tell Captain Drummond how much the Russian minister will enjoy his company."

"Yes, yes, of course, join us Drummond, by all

means." Frederick von Gunther was a man of the world. He knew of his wife's liaisons as she did his. But then, faithfulness had never been a requirement in the haut monde, the leisured class inured to such bourgeois concepts.

"If I might have a word with you first, Mr. Minister," Hugh remarked politely. He smiled at Elsa. "It won't take a minute."

"I'm so pleased you're back, Hugh, darling; I'll be free later tonight," she whispered, ignoring Yukio who was obviously a bodyguard and by definition invisible. Turning to her husband, she said in a carrying tone, "Why don't you men adjourn to the library for your business." Much addicted to pre-dinner champagne and gossip, she offered the men a charming smile. "I'll go on without you. Betsy's recital is first—something I'm sure you won't mind missing." She waved her jeweled hand. "Dinner's at nine sharp, though—you know Sergei—so don't be long."

The German minister was young for his post, only recently forty, but his family had influence and Hong Kong was a profitable posting. Business was still done with a handshake and a bribe or two—and nothing was accomplished without a percentage to everyone involved. Frederick von Gunther could make his fortune in five years if the climate didn't kill him, and return to Berlin to live like a prince.

"A brandy?" he offered pleasantly as the men entered the library, moving to the liquor table. "It's a rather good year if I do say so myself."

"Thank you, no. We won't be long."

Something in Hugh's voice made the minister

turn around. "What can I do for you?" he asked carefully, his gaze going from one man to the other.

"I understand you're acquainted with Nitta Tadashi," Hugh said.

"Yes, we're working on a project together. As you know, we're building a number of shipyards for the Japanese."

"And you're dealing with a railroad now."

The minister's brows rose. "Where did you hear that?"

"Jesus, Freddy, everywhere. This is a small town. But you needn't worry. I don't give a damn about your railroads. What I care about is Nitta's reward for the Princess of Otari. She happens to be a friend."

"I don't know what you're talking about," the minister blustered, understanding he'd just been threatened, no matter the captain's soft voice and bland statements. Moving to his desk, he used it as buffer between himself and his guests. The captain's reputation for violence was well known and the Japanese looked as though he'd cut your throat and eat his breakfast while you bled to death. Resting his hand near the drawer that held his loaded pistol, he offered Hugh a fraudulent smile. "I think someone gave you some erroneous information."

"Don't think about shooting anyone, Freddy," Hugh said gruffly. "You wouldn't stand a chance. As for my information, we have it from a reliable source." Sitting down to ease the minister's alarm, Hugh waved Yukio to a chair. "The reason I'm here," he said gently, "is to warn you off. If you

need the reward money, you'll have to find it elsewhere. The Princess is going to Europe with me
and if anyone decides to interfere with my trip,
they'll have to answer to me. In the event you or
any of your colleagues are unsure about my interest in this affair, let me tell you what I told the
Japanese minister. Do not persist in your search
for the princess or I will kill you and everyone in
your family. Oh, hell, now I've frightened you."

The German minister had gone as pale as his
ash-blonde hair.

Reaching out, Hugh picked up the brandy bottle from the liquor table and shoved it across the
minister's desk. "Relax, Freddy. Have a brandy.
And consider, you have so many other options out
here for making money. Did Nitta tell you about
the munitions plant they want to build in
Hokkaido? He must not have. There. You see. A
percentage of that will do you nicely." Coming to
his feet, Hugh nodded at the white-faced minister.
"Give my regrets to Elsa. I won't have time to dine
with you tonight. And congratulations on your
new estate near Potsdam. I hear it's very nice."

The minister sat down heavily, his face ashen.

Yukio pointed at a portrait of young, towheaded
children on the wall. "And say hello to your children."

"You wouldn't," Freddy gasped.

"We won't have any need, will we?" Hugh
replied mildly. "Good night, Freddy. We'll let ourselves out."

Chapter
27

The following day the *Southern Belle* was heavily guarded, every seaman armed and on alert, the canon primed, guards posted at the gangway. In addition, a cadre of Yukio's friends kept watch on the docks and in nearby boats. When Tama inquired about the added security, Hugh dismissed any need for alarm. "I have a few more enemies than I thought," he remarked casually. "It's nothing serious. We're just taking precautions until we sail tonight. And then we're on holiday—did I mention that?"

She smiled. "Not more than a dozen times since breakfast."

"Because I'm a man of restraint," he said, grinning.

"Which is what I find most fascinating about you."

His dark brows flickered in amusement. "The fact that you can come ten times to my one, you mean?"

Blushing, she glanced around to see if anyone had heard.

"Even if they had heard, darling, do you think anyone will say a word? Now come here and give me a pre-holiday kiss."

She ran, but he caught her.

Or maybe she caught him.

Yukio and Sunskoku were already on holiday, the couple not having come on deck that morning. Yukio's message to Hugh had been brief and succinct. "You'll have to get along without me until Le Havre." He wasn't completely serious, of course, but he was temporarily indisposed. With his yakuza friends taking care of his share of the security today, he could enjoy what he was—well—enjoying. . . .

The dresses arrived from James Delaroche early in the afternoon.

And the moment the delivery man departed, the engines fired and the *Southern Belle* put to sea.

While Hugh hadn't been precisely worried, he found himself relaxing as the colony disappeared from view. And by the time they made open sea, he decided a small celebration was in order. An invitation from the captain was delivered to Yukio, Sunskoku, Noguchi and Paddy. Dinner at the captain's table at eight, it said. White tie.

Tama would have an opportunity to wear one of her new dresses.

He would have an opportunity to watch her dress.

And mostly, he felt like celebrating.

He didn't question his motivation. Nor give a thought to the fact that he'd not felt this good in years. He particularly didn't dwell on the reason he was feeling so good. It was easier not to. It was safer.

Delaroche had selected rich brocades and damasks as a tribute to Tama's heritage and beauty and Tama picked out a glorious crimson with a plum underweave to wear that night. It reminded her of her father's study where crimson silk adorned the pillows and screens, the silk produced and woven on their estates.

Pushing aside painful memory, she pulled the dress from the armoire Hugh had given over to her. "Do you like this one?" she inquired lightly.

"I like what you're wearing more." Lounging in a chair near the fire, he raised his brandy glass to her, contented, maybe even half in love if he'd allow such sentiments to enter his consciousness.

She wore only a filmy white chemise and ruffle-frilled pantalettes so sheer, he could practically count the hairs on her pubis. Definitely a lure to the eyes. The French were the only nation that truly understood seduction, he thought pleasantly. "Turn around for me," he said softly.

Tossing the gown on the bed, she pirouetted with the grace of an expert swordsman before coming to rest. "I'm *not* wearing the corset, however," she said with a sunny smile. "It's absolute torture."

"You don't need it." Her breasts were delectably plump and so much more available when not laced into a corset. "Throw it away."

"I already have. All of them. And the man sent dozens of petticoats, too. Really, Hugh-san, one's sufficient."

That much less to take off, Hugh reflected cheerfully, but said instead, diplomatic and tactful, "Suit yourself, darling. Be comfortable by all means."

She made a small moue. "How would I do that in these gowns with pinched waists and tight boning? I don't know how western women can move."

"Indulge me, sweetheart. Delaroche outdid himself."

"Very well, but in Paris," she said pointedly, "I'll have some better kimonos made to wear."

"If you wish to go out in Parisian society, you'd do well to dress as the French do."

"Then, maybe I'll choose not to go out."

"You'll need to be introduced, at least. Your brother will agree, I'm sure. Is he not in Paris precisely for that reason—so his wife is accepted into society?"

"You needn't sound so reasonable, Hugh-san. It's very annoying," she said with a pout.

"Don't forget, you might like some diplomatic support for your cause. It might be worth wearing a gown or two."

She wrinkled her nose and then sighed softly. "If I can train for Bushido, I suppose I can wear these confining gowns," she muttered, picking up the gown from the bed.

"Or you could choose not to go out much." His tone was softly suggestive. "At least for a time—you could say you're indisposed from the long sea voyage. . . ."

He'd piqued her interest. "And you would keep me company?"

"I *could*," he drawled, the promise of pleasure implicit. "Once my cargo is sold, I'd have some leisure. . . ."

"We could find something to do," she purred. "All alone . . . just the two of us . . ."

His smile was unabashedly sensual. "That's what I was thinking."

"And I'd just have to wear these clothes that pinch and squeeze and choke the air from me on occasion."

"Only if someone very important sends you an invitation."

She studied him for a moment. "How important?"

He shrugged. "You'll have to ask your brother. Your important and my important are different, I suspect."

"Why?"

Because Hugh's invitations to dinner weren't really about dinner, but more about *after* dinner. "Society can be so dull, I prefer not going out unless the, er, guests amuse me."

"And I must go even if the guests don't amuse me?"

"You'll have to consider the diplomatic advantages. No one's going to talk business with me over dinner. Your brother, on the other hand, must know partisans who are receptive to the future development of your country. The French are even more interested in finding new patronage in Japan since the shogun was deposed. Who knows—you may not only find champions but discover you like society as well."

"You're right, of course. I must look beyond my selfish interests." She smiled. "And I do like their champagne."

He grinned. "There. You see?"

"I would like some now so I won't feel the pain when you hook me into this torture gown. And I will worry about society when we reach France, Hugh-san, and not a moment sooner."

"Fair enough," Hugh replied, rising from his chair to open the bottle of champagne he had chilling for her. A moment later, he took the gown from her and handed her a glass. "Drink that down and I'll lace you into this dress."

She poured the champagne down her throat as though anticipating her need for the liquor to dull her pain.

"Arms up, sweetheart," Hugh said, lifting the voluminous skirts over her head.

"Don't muss my hair."

Her mundane comment, the casual tone in which it was uttered, jarred his sensibilities, and for a shocked second he stood arrested. She sounded like a wife; he was acting like a husband. It was a most disconcerting sensation. And then telling himself that she wasn't a wife, she was his paramour and he'd helped a lover or twenty into a dress on occasion before, he dropped the gown over her head.

"This short hair is very nice," she murmured,

pulling a few errant tresses behind her ears before slipping her arms into the sleeves of the gown. "It's not heavy."

He liked her clipped hair. She looked different from all the other women he'd known or maybe he would have liked her hair no matter the length. For in truth, there was nothing about her he didn't like. Another disconcerting thought.

"Would you like more champagne?" he asked. "I'm going to have some."

"Why not?—defense, as it were, against my discomfort."

He poured them both a glass, drank his down—discomfort could take many forms—and poured himself another before handing Tama's glass to her.

"This décolletage is very revealing," Tama murmured a short time later, glancing at herself in the cheval glass as Hugh began hooking the back of her gown. "Are you sure this is acceptable?"

He looked up. The distraction was welcome; his body took immediate note of her low décolletage. And thoughts on being chained and fettered by marriage were overwhelmed by a sudden wave of lust. "It's the fashion, darling."

"But my nipples almost show."

"You're not allowed to bend over. Or at least not for another man."

"But I may for you?" And with a smile, she put action to her words, her plump breasts swelling above her chemise and falling out of the low neckline as she bent over.

"Now, that's an enticing picture," he drawled,

wrapping his arms around her to cup her breasts in his palms. "I may have to follow you around tonight—just in case."

She gazed at him in the mirror. "You may follow me around and hold my breasts anytime at all, Hugh-san. It sends little tingles down between my legs."

His erection was at full mast and only inches away from her lush bottom. "Do the tingles get better if I squeeze them like this?" His fingers closed on the soft, luscious flesh. "Your nipples are looking very hard, darling. Do you think they'd like to be kissed?"

"Without a doubt, they're telling me."

"Then we need them a little closer," he murmured, lifting her, turning her around so she was facing him, taking her nipples gently between his thumbs and forefingers.

"Maybe we shouldn't," she whispered, pressing her thighs together as the heated ache shimmered and swelled, rippled up her vagina. "We'll be late for dinner."

"You're not telling me I can't have sex with you?" His fingers tightened.

She moaned softly. "I would never be so stupid," she whispered.

He didn't say, "Let our guests wait," but clearly that was his intent because he dipped his head to take a nipple in his mouth.

"This dress is uncomfortable," she murmured.

Their eyes were at a level, his mouth half open, framing one taut crest. "I'm not unhooking it and rehooking it again." And then his mouth closed, he sucked hard and she forgot everything but the rush of heat spiking through her body, the tremulous pathway in a direct line from Hugh's mouth to her vagina. And by the time he'd shifted his attentions to her other nipple she was beyond thought, whimpering softly, her hips writhing, the dewy essence of arousal readying her body to receive him. "Please, please, please," she begged, addicted to his touch, her senses on fire, every receptor throbbing.

"Bend over," he whispered, unbuttoning his trousers.

She quickly obeyed as though he might rescind his offer if she didn't comply swiftly enough. And she saw him behind her in the mirror looking at her as he drew out his towering penis, his gaze fevered.

But his voice was gentle as he said, "Hold your breasts up for me. And spread your legs."

She couldn't know that it took enormous self-control to strip the rampant, frenzied need from his voice. She didn't know he coveted her as much as she did him.

Lifting the skirt over her bottom, he slid his hand between the divided legs of her pantalettes and touched her drenched, swollen cleft. He slid one finger in as though testing her readiness and she trembled at the glorious sensation. "Tell me you want me," he whispered.

"Yes, yes, always, always . . ." she panted, moving her hips and bottom as though to entice him.

He didn't need enticement. If anything, he needed a curb on his rapaciousness. "And you'll do anything I want?" He was possessed by an overwhelming need to own her, keep her.

"Yes, anything—please . . . I'll do anything . . ." she panted.

He didn't know what had overcome him to make such a demand, but her answer satisfied the unbridled lechery impelling him. "Good girl," he breathed, as though she were his now—body and soul. And he drove into her succulent passage with a savage violence that both salved and incited his brutishness, plunging in again and again with a mindless fury, only half hearing her wild, frenzied screams. Finally recognizing her shrill, climactic cry, he instantly released his own orgasmic explosion as though he must mark his territory with his come.

He lifted her into his arms afterward or she would have fallen and he carried her to his bed and laid her down and kissed her gently in apology. "I'm sorry. I don't know what came over me." Dropping into a sprawl beside her, he took her hand in his. "I'll cancel dinner if you wish; I'll apologize all night."

Her blissful sigh and subsequent chuckle brought him up on one elbow.

"You didn't hurt me." Her smile was angelic, no bruised ego evident. "You needn't cancel dinner and you're lying on my skirt. I can't move."

He grinned and rolled away. "I suppose someone who can take on Hiroaki's assassins has a certain grit and vigor. You're not hurt?"

"I'm feeling extremely fine. I have no complaints."

"Then I needn't be forgiven?"

"Not so long as you promise to make yourself available after dinner."

"I'm always available to you," he said simply, his need for her no longer daunting.

She smiled. "Thank you very much, Captain Drummond. I am reassured."

"And I'm the happiest of men. But your dress is ruined. You'll have to change it after all."

"Do we have time?" she inquired playfully.

He gave her a jaundiced look. "Don't start."

"Yes, sir."

He laughed. "We do make a good pair."

Her eyes twinkled with amusement. "Indeed."

Everyone was arrayed in their finest that evening, Paddy in evening rig that looked largely unused, Yukio and Noguchi in rich garments of silk, Sunskoku in a western gown that Yukio had procured for her in haste when the invitation was delivered. Adept with a needle and thread, Sunskoku had altered the evening dress to fit and she looked resplendent in cloth of gold and lace.

The two women accepted their compliments with graceful bows.

Champagne was poured.

And Hugh's celebratory dinner began.

The cooks had devised a menu that offered western and Japanese cuisine in great variety and greater abundance, the table in Hugh's dining room groaning under the weight of their expertise. Conversation was easy, everyone feeling a comradeship of shared purpose and intent.

Noguchi and Paddy had formed their own friendship of shared interests, both sworn to bachelorhood and the pleasures of drink. They teased their dinner partners mercilessly that evening about the dangers and pitfalls of love. But the recipients of their mockery only smiled and exchanged tolerant glances and instead considered themselves the most fortunate of beings.

So no matter their disparate sympathies, everyone was pleased with their current condition, the food was superb, the liquor freely flowing, and much later over port and pipes—for tobacco was a genderless indulgence in Japan—they all raised their glasses in toast to the joys of the future.

That first evening at sea set the genial pattern for their passage to Europe, the voyage a time of enormous well-being and indulgence. Perhaps they all needed a time of rest and repose, perhaps the two young couples enjoying the pleasures of love deserved their blissful, carefree days. They had all endured emotional hardships and suffering. They'd earned a reprieve.

And for those weeks at sea, they deliberately chose not to acknowledge the uncertainties that lay ahead.

Chapter
28

The *Southern Belle* entered the harbor of Le Havre beleaguered by heavy rains and high seas, the engines laboring against the offshore winds, their approach hampered by the many ships lying at anchor in the storm.

Hugh was on the bridge, piloting the ship through the narrow channels between heaving vessels, fighting to hold his course in the high waves, finally reaching landfall with an appreciative oath and an odd mix of emotions.

On one hand, he was gratified to have reached France where his cargo could be sold—a change in plans he'd made en route for reasons he didn't choose to dwell on. On the other hand, staying with the princess set into play some rather sizeable changes in conduct and presumptions of independence that he also chose not to examine too closely. He swore again, as though the expletives could ease the tumult in his brain. With an indefinable unease that had to do with his visible presence as escort to the Princess of Otari, and what that public exposure might affirm, he handed over command to Paddy.

But his voice gave away none of his uncertainty when he spoke, his tone urbane. "If you'll deal with the customs and off-loading, we'll go on ahead. You can reach us at the Grand."

"Settin' up housekeepin', are ya'?"

"No." A crisp, clear, faintly defiant utterance because that was exactly what he did *not* wish the world to infer.

"More like you're still on holiday?"

"More like it's none of your business," Hugh retorted brusquely.

"I jes' don't want you doin' anythin' foolish," Paddy noted.

"I don't recall doing anything foolish lately."

Unless one counted his near-death experiences on the way to Osaka for a woman he barely knew. "That may be, but livin' with the princess at the Grand's gonna go around town in about half a day. Depends how her brother looks on an arrangement like that." He shrugged. "Jes' a warnin', Boss."

"Thank you for your concern," Hugh said drily. "This from a man who married a woman he met in a pub."

"Don't forget, I lived to regret it."

Hugh stared at him for an uncomfortable moment, the truth in Paddy's statement disquieting. "Fine. I'm warned. You've done your duty. Now," he went on briskly, "I'll talk to the silk merchants tomorrow. Those bolts Kusawa gave us are prime and well worth the wait. Yukio's contacting some friend of a friend here in Le Havre and then meeting us in Paris. We'll celebrate our profits when you reach the city." Moving toward the door, he half turned and smiled. "And I heard you loud and clear—okay?"

"As if it'll do any good," Paddy muttered as the door clanged shut on Hugh.

"He likes the ladies, he do," the bos'n said with a grin. "You ain't gonna talk him out of fucking that princess he ain't left for goin' on three months. Not with *no* words of advice."

"Then we'll jes' have to watch him drink himself into oblivion when he gives her up like he sure as hell will before long. He's gun shy, that one, make no mistake."

"Can't exactly blame him, what with his marriage troubles and all."

"Ain't that the truth."

"I'll give you three to one he gets out before a fortnight."

"Nah. You'll just lose your money."

"I seen him in action almost as long as you, and I say a fortnight, not a day longer. I'll make it five to one, jes' to make it interestin'."

"You make it hard for a man to refuse," Paddy declared.

""If'n you're afraid . . ."

"You're on, Bo, jes' don't come cryin' to me when you lose."

Tama had spent the afternoon packing her new gowns in the trunks Hugh had carried in and when he returned to the cabin, he found her seated on the edge of a chair, dressed, even to her hat and coat.

"You look anxious."

"I'm shaking." She held up her hands, gloved in lavender leather. "Look."

"So you're not exactly ready for combat," he teased.

She smiled. "Maybe that's what I need. Something familiar—my swords in my hands."

"Did you pack your swords?"

"Of course. First. My father had them made for me when I was ten."

She looked about ten right now, he thought, her daintiness accented by the narrow-waisted gown and form-fitting jacket, by her little pert hat with feathers and bows. "Give me a minute to throw some things in a trunk and I'll give you your first train ride."

She sat very still as he packed, her hands clasped in her lap, her bottom lip caught in her teeth, her thoughts in turmoil. Now that she was actually here in France, it didn't seem quite as easy to simply walk into her brother's house and tell him he had to go back to Japan and face possible death. He might refuse. Perhaps any sane man would. Was she irresponsible to even think she could take on the might of the new government and win?

Chapter
29

It was the middle of the night when they reached the hotel, but apparently Hugh had stayed there before because the manager greeted him by name, said, "Your suite is ready, Captain," and escorted them to a second floor apartment overlooking the Seine.

Tama took no notice of the manager's surreptitious glances, immune to the censure of the world, her status in Japan assuring her she could do no wrong.

Hugh ignored the manager's behavior as well, familiar with doing as he pleased. But he knew what the man meant when he said slyly, "Enjoy your stay with us, Captain. You won't be disturbed."

Not about to respond, Hugh said, "I'll be needing a carriage soon."

"It's ready, sir. The instructions you telegraphed were specific."

"And the driver? He is cognizant of events in Paris?"

"He's the very best, sir. He knows everyone of consequence in the city."

"Send him up."

"Now, sir?" The manager shot a glance at Tama, who had taken off her jacket and was standing before a mirror, lifting the confection of a hat from her head. "Ah . . . a Delaroche, no doubt," the Frenchman murmured. "The feathers are his signature. The lady certainly does the hat justice, sir, if you don't mind my saying. She's very lovely."

Hugh looked at him for a three count. "Yes, is she not? The driver, if you please."

Meeting that hard stare, the manager understood he'd overstepped his bounds and with a low bow, apologized. "I beg your pardon. I'll send the driver up directly, and if you require anything more—"

"I'll ring," Hugh said crisply.

"Yes, indeed. It's a pleasure to have you with us again." And bowing again, the manager backed from the room, mystified by the captain's sudden prudishness. The ladies he'd brought to the Grand before had been clearly on a pleasure junket. This one must be different.

Placing her hat and gloves on a console table, Tama turned to Hugh. "I suppose we must wait until morning to see my brother."

"I'd think that reasonable."

Her brows rose faintly. "And you're always reasonable."

"I wish I were." If he were, he wouldn't be standing in a hotel room in Paris with a woman whom he should have walked away from—say at Osaka or Hong Kong, perhaps at some port on their way to France. Certainly at Le Havre he could have bid her good-bye without jeopardizing her safety. "What we could do in the interim," he said, ignoring all the reasons he should have left, "is take a carriage ride through Paris. It's only a few hours until dawn. Then, at a more respectable hour, we could call on your brother."

"What's respectable?"

Her directness always amazed him—unlike other women he'd known who dealt with the world in more oblique terms. "Nine, at the earliest."

"Nine! I would have been up four hours at home, finished with my morning practice in the dojo and well into my daily tasks."

"In Paris, only those virtuous souls who attend morning matins are up by nine. The vast bulk of society rarely open their eyes until noon. But we can at least *call* at nine and leave our address."

"If my brother isn't up at nine, I'll wake him. He won't mind."

"You know best."

She slanted a look at him. "You don't usually defer so readily."

He shrugged. "I'm not putting myself between you and your brother. It's not my place."

"Exactly. It's not."

With that tone she was baiting him—perhaps as unnerved as he about his place and her place and what it all meant. "That's right, Princess," he said calmly, not rising to the bait. He had too much to lose. Although, not quite certain losing was the right term, he added softly, "Look, we're both tired. Let's take that carriage ride and not think about morning till morning."

"Good idea." She smiled faintly, reminded of Zen Master Dogen's counsel to set aside all involvements and let the myriad things rest.

Hugh rang to change his instructions and a short time later they came out of the hotel to find their carriage waiting. The driver was a small, wiry Provencale who had lived in Paris long enough to know the Parisian underworld, the haut monde and the location of every avenue, street and medieval lane.

The moment he saw Tama, he said with Gallic presumption, "There's a small colony of your countrymen in Enghien."

"We're looking for the Prince of Otari," Hugh remarked as he handed Tama into the barouche. "He's recently moved." Tama's brother's last letter before the war had said he was buying a new house.

"From the Marais to Enghien," the driver noted. "He keeps one of the better stables."

Tama smiled, feeling as though she were close to home. Her brother had always been enamored of horses.

"We'll call on the prince at nine. In the meantime, take us on a tour of the city." Climbing into the carriage, Hugh shut the door and slid into a comfortable sprawl. As the carriage began moving he was struck by a curious sense of déjà vu as though he'd been riding like this with Tama before. Christ, he *must* be tired.

Even at that late hour the streets were busy with the well-born and fashionable on the move between dinners and receptions and soirees—society's amusements often lasting until dawn.

Tama seemed not to notice the congestion and bustle, her mood introspective, her gaze unfocused on the world outside.

Choosing not to quiz her on her thoughts, their morning visit having all the possibility of disaster on several levels, Hugh spoke instead in a casual way of the sights they passed, offering a historical footnote from time to time, letting the silence lengthen at intervals as his own ruminations came to the fore.

Their visit could be uneventful if they were lucky and acrimonious if they weren't—the outcome dependent on the Prince of Otari's current views on etiquette. While sexual liaisons in Japan didn't impugn a woman's honor, the double standard prevailed in the West. Women were not allowed the same freedoms as men. If the prince were to take issue with their relationship, Hugh wasn't sure what he'd do . . . or not do. He'd not been in this position before.

Liaisons, sexual and otherwise, weren't a priority in the muddle of emotions tumbling through Tama's brain. What was most troubling to her was her brother's constancy—or more pertinently, his lack of said element. After his first trip to France, he'd come home fascinated with all things European. After his second visit, he'd become even more disinterested in the political struggles that had eventually led to Japan's civil war. He'd never been a warrior, always more interested in poetry and painting, in his books.

How would he react to her demand that he take on his role as head of the house of Otari and all that meant in terms of risk?

She wasn't sure.

Chapter
30

The Prince of Otari was *not* at home, a butler haughtily informed them when they called at his country house shortly after nine.

"Tell my brother, the *Princess* of Otari wishes to speak to him. And if he's still abed, wake him," Tama commanded.

Taken aback by her sudden peremptoriness, Hugh glanced at the small figure at his side who was presently outstaring the butler. "I'd suggest you get a move on," he said. "She's mighty good with a sword."

Hugh's words apparently nudged the startled majordomo into action, for he motioned a footman over. As he turned to speak to his underling, Tama began moving away.

"We'll wait for the prince in the drawing room," she said. "And tell my brother to hurry."

At her sharp imperious tone, the majordomo's head swiveled around so quickly you could hear his starched neckcloth snap.

Suppressing a grin, Hugh winked at the man.

"She's used to having her own way. Maybe you should go tell the prince yourself."

The drawing room had no mementoes of Japan, the decor exclusively French in the contemporary mode—heavily fringed and ornate, the fabrics brilliant in pattern and color, the furniture in the florid style much beloved in Louis Napoleon's Third Empire.

"Your brother has transformed himself into a Frenchman, from the look of things," Hugh observed, surveying the room with an appraising glance. *And no expense was spared,* he thought, recognizing the Third Empire's most expensive furniture maker.

"I'm not sure I wish to hear that," Tama retorted, trying to suppress the tension creeping up her neck, as aware as Hugh of the overt evidence of that transmutation. Walking to the windows overlooking the garden, denuded now of color save for the trimmed yews, she forced herself to a modicum of calm. Komei was her brother, she told herself. He would come to her aid.

Standing apart from the modishly attired young woman at the window, Hugh was overcome by a sense of constraint. He had no particular right to be here in the bosom of her family, and assailed by the sudden thought, he said abruptly, "Would you rather I leave?"

She swung around. "Do you want to?"

"I just thought I might be in the way."

"You're not in the way," she said tartly.

"Calm down, sweetheart.

"I'm perfectly calm."

* * *

"Who are you to be calling my sister sweetheart?" a chill voice inquired.

They both turned to the doorway.

"Komei!" Tama cried, quickly moving toward her brother.

"Who is this man?" the Prince of Otari demanded, standing motionless on the threshold.

"Captain Drummond, and he saved my life so you may thank him instead of sounding like the chief executioner." Tama smiled as she reached her brother. "Komei, Hugh Drummond, Hugh, my brother." And then she embraced her brother.

"My apologies, Captain Drummond." Komei offered Hugh a reserved smile over Tama's shoulder. "My sister has always been—impulsive."

That small pause before the word impulsive triggered a surge of jealousy to which Hugh had long thought himself immune. The princess wasn't afraid to ask for what she wanted—particularly in terms of sex. "In combat, her impulsiveness saved my life," he said, choosing a less indelicate example of her boldness. "I'm indebted to your sister."

"We narrowly escaped any number of times, thanks to Hugh," Tama pointed out as she stepped away from her brother. "He gave me passage on his ship as well, so I could come to you. They've taken everything, Komei," she said quietly. "Father and his army were massacred. Our home is gone, our enemies determined to crush us. You *must* come back and help."

Two servants came in bearing tea trays.

"Come, sit," the prince proposed, waving the servants toward a small tea table.

Tama curbed her impulse to send the footmen away, their appearance unpropitious. Instead, she said, mildly, "I see you still like sugar cakes." The confections their cook had always made for them as children were on the tea tray.

"Some of our servants came with me."

"I'd forgotten. Of course." At the time Komei left, the loss of a dozen servants was incidental. Although none of their old retainers were in evidence, the only visible staff French.

As the servants arranged the tea service, the conversation focused on the weather and their sea voyage. But once the footmen departed, a sudden tension filled the air.

"I don't see any of our retainers," Tama remarked casually, helping herself to a sugar cake.

"They're belowstairs." Komei looked up from pouring himself a cup of tea. "You understand."

She did. Perfectly. Her brother wished no evidence of his heritage to mar the image of French country gentleman to which he aspired. His short hair, his tailored clothes, his cravat and diamond tie pin, the rings on his fingers were all comme il faut. "Father died at Wakamatsu," she pronounced unceremoniously, wanting to jar his beau ideal impersonation. "I didn't know if you'd heard the details. It was a long siege, a bloody battle and ultimately a massacre. Shosho lived long enough to bring me father's last message."

"I grieve for father," Komei said, his voice without emotion. "We heard of the battle and the end of the civil war, of course. Disastrous news comes quickly. But it all seemed so senseless—the terror and killing, the loss of so many fiefdoms."

"It's not senseless to try to stop tyrants, Komei. Father was fighting for a less repressive government, for a just cause. We must carry on for him. The emperor *needs* the powerful families on his side. Come back with me to plead our case—help me fight for what's best for our country."

Komei set down his teacup. "This is my country now. And the emperor won't pardon us. You know how Satsuma and Choshu have always worked to secure our downfall. They're in power now. It's over. Don't you understand?"

"It doesn't have to be like that," Tama exclaimed, setting her cake down, leaning forward in her excitement, convinced she was right. "Don't you see! There were a dozen clans at Wakamatsu who have already been pardoned—some age-old enemies of Satsuma and Choshu. Yoshinobu, the shogun himself, is living in retirement, his estates barely touched. We can go back. We *can*, Komei!"

"We're not going back."

The voice was soft and low, but uncompromising. "Tell her, Komei."

Komei's wife stood in the doorway, their small son in her arms. "You knew this was going to happen if she survived." Miyo remained unmoving in the doorway as though she might be contaminated by the noxious past if she came in. "You knew your sister would come for you." Tears shone in her eyes. "You knew what she would say."

Rising from his chair, Komei went to his wife and gently drew her forward, the small boy in her arms surveying the strangers with a hesitant gaze. "Tama, this is Miyo and our son Taro. Miyo, meet my sister and Captain Drummond."

Miyo greeted Tama and Hugh, although her reluctance was evident, her expression somber.

"Sit," Komei coaxed his wife, offering her a chair. "Have tea with us."

The prince's wife was indeed beautiful, Hugh thought, dazzling enough to turn Komei's head. Or perhaps they were soul mates—a less likely possibility with the great differences in their status. But whatever the reason, the prince wouldn't be returning to Japan. That was crystal clear.

Before they'd finished tea, Tama understood as much. With an enthusiasm she'd never seen before, her brother spoke of his new home and country, of his railroad stock that was enormously profitable, of the salons where he and other poets read their poetry to an appreciative audience. One of his racers had taken a first at Longchamps, he said, his delight unmistakable. But perhaps what made her certain he wouldn't change his mind was his announcement that he and his wife were expecting another child. "And consider," he went on, "when Hori Kura no Kami urged Yoshinobu to commit *seppuku* after his defeat at Toba, the shogun laughed at him and said that such barbarous customs were out of date. He was right— the feudal way of life is but a memory. Stay here with us," he offered. "Don't even think of going back and risking your life."

Tama glanced at Hugh.

He'd spoken little, unwilling to express his opinions in what was clearly a family matter. "Your brother's right about the risk." He shrugged faintly. "But then, you could be run over by a bad driver on the Champs Élysées."

Her sudden smile reminded him of the unfettered, spirited woman he'd fought beside to Osaka.

"Or die of boredom."

He grinned. "You wouldn't want that to happen."

Folding her napkin, Tama placed it on the table. "You must come to see us at the Grand Hotel," she said, smiling politely as she rose from her chair, her disappointment in her brother's decision not entirely unexpected. "Come for lunch some day and then little Taro can join us."

"Us?" The prince's mouth set in a firm straight line, his expression turned obstinate.

"The captain and I have an apartment at the Grand."

"Together?" Miyo said in alarm, glancing at her husband as though for moral succor.

"Yes, together."

"Such situations are not accepted here," the prince announced, a distinct chill to his voice.

"No one at the hotel seemed to mind." Tama wasn't likely to yield to her brother's authority when she never had before. "Would you rather meet us at some other—"

"Why don't you come and visit us whenever you like, Tama," her brother suggested. "It would be less disruptive to everyone."

His deliberate omission of Hugh in his invitation was a blatant snub.

This time it was Tama's mouth that set in a firm line. "The captain saved my life, Komei. He deserves your respect."

"And you deserve his."

"I have it," she replied crisply.

"I have no wish to offend you," Hugh interposed in an attempt to forestall sibling warfare. Having risen when Tama did, he gestured toward the door. "I'll wait outside."

"You certainly will not!" She shot a glance at Hugh. "Don't you dare move. Komei, you apologize this instant!"

The prince scowled.

While Komei apparently approved of certain rules of etiquette, standing when a woman did was not one of them, Hugh reflected. The prince's canons of protocol were flexible, it seemed. "No apology is necessary," Hugh murmured. "I understand your brother's wish to protect you."

"Ha," Tama grunted. "Protect me from what? Some French rules of decorum? He would do better to stand at my side against our enemies."

"The sword solves nothing," Komei declared angrily. "Something our father should have realized long ago. If he had, our lands would still be intact."

"Those who marched against us were sworn enemies," Tama retorted hotly. "Would not anyone defend their lands against such men?"

"I came to France to avoid such decisions."

"He's not like you!" Miyo exclaimed. "Can't you see! He's a poet and a man of peace!"

"And he has an opportunity to pursue those interests because our father defended what was ours and his father before him back through the centuries. The freedom to choose one's way isn't without a price."

"He's happy here! Can't you see that!" Miyo

cried, clutching her son so tightly he was beginning to squirm. "Everyone's not like—"

"Hush, Miyo." Komei placed his hand on his wife's arm and then met his sister's gaze. "I can't fight like you," he said softly, the anger draining from his voice. "I never could. I'm sorry."

"I know." Perhaps she'd always known. "I shouldn't have come."

"Stay here with us," her brother pleaded. "Don't go back. Talk to others in our refugee community. You'll see—everyone will agree with me. Your life is at stake if you return."

"Why don't I think about it?"

"I know what that tone means. Come to Hattori's salon on Wednesday," the prince beseeched. "Talk to him. He has contacts in the new government. He'll tell you how unforgiving the court is to those who opposed them."

"Thank you, I will. And now, if you'll excuse us, I'm going back to the hotel and sleep."

"Sleep here," her brother offered, standing, holding out his hand.

"Maybe later, Komei, but thank you."

"I'll send you a note with Hattori's address," he said quickly. "Promise you'll come."

She nodded. "I will." Glancing at Hugh, she smiled. "Are you ready?"

"Yes, ma'am."

The smoldering heat in those two simple words shocked the westernized, newly prudish souls of the prince and his wife and, mouths agape, they watched as their guests strolled away hand in hand.

Chapter
31

"Are you disappointed?" Hugh asked as their carriage bowled down the drive through perfectly manicured grounds.

Tama turned from the window. "Yes, of course. But I'm not really surprised."

It had been apparent to Hugh on first sight that Komei was no warrior. But he asked politely, "Might your brother change his mind?"

"If I wished to harangue him, perhaps." She smiled faintly. "But his wife would change his mind back the moment I left."

"You could always stay with them and protect your, er, investment in the future, as it were."

She glanced up at him. "Are you wishing to rid yourself of me?"

But she asked the question with a brash assurance, he thought, as though no man would be so stupid. Nor was he. "I'm not wishing any such thing," he murmured. "In fact, I thought we might take in some of the entertainments as long as we're in Paris. We could go to the Variétés tonight, if you'd like.

"Are you trying to distract me?"

He gave her high points for perspicacity. "Distract us both, I thought. Why think of enemies and warfare all the time?"

"Surely our weeks at sea were a holiday from conflict."

"But not long enough. I've been at war in one form or another for nearly eight years." He looked out the window, his breath warming the glass. "Maybe I'm getting old," he said with a sigh.

"How old are you?" She'd never thought to ask.

"Thirty-four." He turned back to her. "And you're—" He'd forgotten.

"Twenty-two."

"You're too young for me."

Her eyes twinkled. "When I wasn't yesterday or last week?"

"You're *probably* too young for me." He grinned. "Ask your brother. I'm sure he'd say you were."

"No, I'm not—and my brother has nothing to say about my life."

"Fine." He smiled. "I'm not going to argue."

"Good. So tell me, will I like this *comedie*?"

"Yes. You'll laugh."

"Perfect. And will you laugh as well?"

"Without a doubt. I'm more than ready to laugh." After years of war he was not only ready but eager to yield to more cheerful diversions.

The performance that night featured an heiress and a rogue and a chorus of dancers who broke into song at the least provocation. There was also a calculating uncle and a lovesick swain, and by the end of the first act Tama and Hugh had truly and unreservedly laughed at all the outlandish machinations in the farcical operetta.

At intermission they joined the throngs in the lobby who were waiting for an ice or a glass of champagne, or perhaps to hear the latest gossip. For some, the desire to see and be seen impelled them to brave the jostling crowd.

Having forced his way through the mob, Hugh had returned and was handing a glass of champagne to Tama when a voice in the crowd trilled, "Hugh! Hugh Drummond! Is that you?"

It was a softly modulated cry—the southern drawl buttery smooth—the sorcery in the voice from his past triggering a rush of emotions.

He didn't turn around at first, certain he'd been mistaken.

But the second time his name was called, the voice was closer and unmistakable. "Excuse me," he murmured, and swiveling around he saw his ex-wife bearing down on him, the crowd parting before her as though yielding to her opulent femaleness.

She was tall and blonde and as voluptuous as ever.

She was also fully aware of the impact she made in black lace with a décolletage so low her nipples were barely concealed.

On reaching him, she held out her hand. "What a pleasure to see you again, Hugh darling," she murmured, sultry and low, as though she'd not walked out on him for a Yankee, as though her leaving hadn't been critical in the loss of his plantation, as though she hadn't fucked him over royally.

"Hello, Lucinda. Small world."

"I hope you're not still angry with me, darling," she said with a pretty little pout and eyes innocent as a babe's. "Everything was such terrible anarchy and tumult during the war. You understand, don't you, why I had to do what I did?"

"Perfectly."

She smiled, ignoring his sarcasm. "I knew you'd understand. You always were such a darling," she cooed. "But then, we always got along so very, *very* well, didn't we?" The sexual invitation in her tone was honey sweet, her heated gaze highly inappropriate for a married woman.

Not sure whether the invitation in her eyes was unnerving or intriguing, Hugh said, "Where's your husband?"

"He has other amusements," she replied airily. "Banker's amusements."

He didn't know what the hell that meant, but it didn't really matter when she was obviously offering more than friendship. And for a fleeting second, he almost asked, *Are you happy?* But he'd spent too many days drinking away his resentment over her marriage to be so callow. "You haven't met the Princess of Otari," he said, instead, taking Tama by the hand and drawing her forward. "Princess, I'd like to introduce you to Lucinda—I don't recall your husband's name. . . ."

"Burke-Todman."

"Ah . . . Lucinda Burke-Todman, meet the Princess of Otari."

"Does she speak English?" Directing her question to Hugh as though Tama were deaf, Lucinda turned to survey the princess with a supercilious gaze.

"I do. It's a pleasure to meet you."

"My goodness!" Lucinda's blue eyes widened in dramatic surprise at Tama's clipped English. "Where in the world did *you* learn English?"

"From my English tutor."

"How charming." Lucinda turned a dazzling smile on Hugh. "How clever she is, Hugh. A protégée of yours?" she inquired archly, implicit in the word protégée a distinct insinuation.

"We're good friends," he said. "The princess is not in need of mentors. She's quite self-sufficient. Lucinda's my ex-wife," he said, and in so saying making it plain to Tama that Lucinda was from his past. "I haven't seen her in years," he added, driving the point home.

"But we had a *lovely* marriage all those years ago, didn't we, Hugh, darling. We were *inseparable.*" Even to the most obtuse, it was unmistakable what she meant by the word inseparable. "Do you remember what they used to call us in Peachtree County, darling? I'll bet you do . . ." she murmured, moving a step closer so her huge breasts were practically brushing his chest. "The sweethearts of Peachtree County . . ."

"That was a long time ago," he replied gruffly. But the memories came flooding back, of young love and hot sex, of always knowing they'd be married someday. Of everyone knowing they'd be married someday.

"I still think of 'us' a lot," she whispered.

"I don't suppose your husband would appreciate that."

"Oh, pooh—what do I care . . . the Yankees are a different breed, Hugh. They're not like us."

"Maybe you should have thought of that before you married him."

She made a small moue. "Don't scold me, darling, for doing what a lady had to do to survive. You don't understand how terrible it was—with no food or money, with the war coming closer every day. It was horrible." She lifted her face so he could see the tears welling in her eyes. "I had no idea where you were, whether you were dead or alive—what was I to do?" A single tear spilled over and trailed down her cheek. "Forgive me," she whispered. "I'm not looking for sympathy. I don't deserve it from you."

If she was acting, she'd gotten better; if she wasn't—he felt the years roll away and he was back home with the scent of jasmine on the air, the summer heat a mist in the twilight. Lucinda was running toward him as the first stars twinkled in the sky, meeting him in the summerhouse by the river. Too young to marry in those days, they'd met secretly and made love with the eager, hot urgency of youth.

The intermission bell rang, intruding on his brief reverie, returning him to the bustle and boisterous crowd. "There's nothing to forgive," he said with a calmness he wasn't feeling. "The war changed us all." Offering Tama his arm, he smiled at Lucinda. "The second act is about to begin. It was pleasant to see you again." With a bow, he moved toward the stairway.

"You may sit with your wife if you wish," Tama offered.

"Ex-wife, and no thank you."

"She seemed willing to make amends. Is she not pleased with her new husband?"

"I don't know and I don't care." He smiled at her. "With Lucinda, one never knows what's real or not."

"I see," she said politely in lieu of saying—*so your ex-wife's a liar.*

"And the past is the past. It's not coming back."

"Would you like it to?"

He paused for the merest second. "No. Not really."

"I like your distraction tonight, Hugh-san," she offered, politely segueing to the banal, well aware that he had to decide himself whether his ex-wife would stay in the past or not, while her mission to continue her father's work allowed for no detours. "I find it wonderful to laugh again," she said pleasantly.

He grinned. "And think of nothing save the absurdity of the characters on the stage."

"It is quite nice to think of nothing. I find it—relaxing."

"Amen, darling." He felt better, more sure, the endearment easy to his ears, his darling no longer in question.

Chapter
32

But he found himself lying awake that night after Tama fell asleep, wondering what Lucinda was doing. Was she in bed with her husband? Was she in bed with someone else? Was she thinking of him?

Quietly rising, he poured himself a drink and sat by the dying fire. It sounded as though her marriage was far from perfect. Did he care? Or how much did he care? After so many years of thinking *what might have been,* here she was—as alluring as ever . . . and obviously available unless he'd misinterpreted her sexual cues. And that was unlikely, knowing her as well as he did.

So—was he going to do anything?

Was he going to respond to her invitation?

Or was it too late, too self-destructive to go back?

Or was it—irresistible?

"Can't you sleep?"

Tama's groggy voice reminded him of his current obligations or amour—or however he wished to designate their relationship: that defining something neither of them had been willing to do. "I'm just having a drink."

"Don't stay up too late. . . ."

"I won't," he said politely, amused at her maternal tone, but she'd dozed off again and his reply fell on deaf ears. Tama offered an agreeable, gratifying pleasure he'd not known in other relationships, her only demands sexual. And he wasn't likely to complain about that. But in all else she had no expectations or requirements of him. Self-sufficient, confident, sure of herself, she was unique among his female acquaintances.

Someday soon, he supposed he was going to have to make a decision about leaving. Tama was returning to Japan. There was no equivocation on that point, particularly after her visit with her brother. They'd spoken of her plans on their return to the hotel that morning, but it wasn't a long discussion. She'd said she was going back as soon as she could and thanked him for all he'd done for her.

Clearly, he was expendable. *An irony,* he thought with a smile, when he'd so often treated women in the same casual way. Not that he was ready for anything more. Nor was he sure he ever would be.

The knock at the door was more of a muffled tap, and glancing at the clock, he wondered if Paddy was drunk and paying calls. Throwing on his robe, he walked to the door, opened it and found the night porter holding out an envelope.

"A message, sir," he whispered. "From a lady."

Hugh felt his pulse quicken as he took the offered missive. There was no question of the lady's identity. "Wait," he murmured, ripping open the envelope, pulling out the card, quickly scanning the contents. Looking up, he said quietly, "Tell her I'll be right down," and shoving the note into his robe pocket, he shut the door and strode into his dressing room. Quickly pulling on some clothes, he exited the suite through the dressing room door.

Tama had come awake at the knock. When she heard the dressing room door click shut, she knew where he was going.

After meeting his ex-wife tonight, she'd understood it was only a matter of time before the woman would approach him.

The tall blonde with the chill gaze hadn't waited long.

Not that she blamed her. If her own life held even the remotest possibility of planning for a future, the captain would have made a most delightful companion. And she would have considered plying whatever womanly wiles she possessed to entice him to stay. But unfortunately, her world was in apocalyptic flux, the events facing her on her return to Japan unknown. She couldn't ask him to risk his life for her again.

So it hadn't been a difficult decision to return alone. It was a rational one.

And yet . . . She forced the wistful thoughts from her mind, relegating hopeless whimsy to the fantasy world where it belonged.

The captain wasn't available, in any event.

He never had been.

* * *

Unconcerned with appearances, Lucinda was waiting in the lobby. Let people look. She didn't care if she was alone in a public place at this late hour. They could think what they wished. She'd realized very young that her beauty insulated her from much of society's censure. And she was well dressed and obviously wealthy. No one would dare take issue with her presence.

As Hugh came into sight on the grand staircase, she rose from her chair and ran to meet him.

Midway down the flight of stairs he saw her, her cheeks rosy, her blonde curls in disarray, her beauty dazzling. And it seemed like yesterday that she'd been his. Her pinked cheeks and disordered curls called to mind the familiar image of his wife tousled, heated from lovemaking, coming back from the torpor of orgasm. How often had he seen her like that, how often had he heard her beg for more only seconds after climax? How often had he obliged her?

Feeling himself quicken at the memories, he cautioned himself to restraint. He wasn't about to forget the misery of the last four years for some transient sex. Although apparently his erection had a mind of its own, surging upward without regard for logic and constraint. He swore softly.

They met at the base of the stairs as though some hand of fate had arranged the perfect trajectory, he stepping off the last step just as she flung herself at him like an impassioned fury.

Fortunately his reflexes were superb. Taking the full impact with ease, he caught her in his arms, the familiar warmth of her body melting against his. The feel and scent of her filled his senses and his erection swelled—his carnal reflexes immune to issues of sensibility and reason.

"You don't know how much I've missed you," she whispered, clinging to him, pressing into his hard, rigid arousal. "Leaving you was the biggest mistake I ever made." Choking back a small sob, her eyes wet with tears, she looked up at him.

"It's been a long time," he replied neutrally, trying to separate lust from intellect, finding it difficult with her hips moving in a slow, languorous rhythm against his throbbing erection.

"Tell me you missed me—maybe just a little?" Her voice was imploring, a provocative invitation in her gaze.

It was obvious he was responding to her; he couldn't affect disinterest with his rock-hard penis leaving an imprint in her belly. "There were times you were on my mind." He chose not to mention he'd spent tortured weeks drinking away her memory.

"Could we go somewhere?" Her voice was low, breathy. "Away from here?"

He hesitated, but she was rubbing against his cock, and the longing in her eyes was a damnable distraction.

"Please . . ." she whispered.

Tama was sleeping upstairs. He couldn't completely ignore that fact.

Aware of his indecision, Lucinda offered him an artless smile. "I just want to talk, darling—tell you how sorry I am for everything that happened. It's been so long since we've been together. I have a cottage nearby, if you have time."

He could have said no. Perhaps he *should* have said no, considering the hour and the princess in his bed. "Where is it?" he said instead.

"Near St. Cloud—thirty minutes . . . no more. It's very private; we'd be completely alone."

She was telling him he could be fucking her in half an hour—that after all the bitterness and torment he could have what he'd been wanting for so long. For a moment more he debated what allegiance he owed Tama, although he wasn't sure he owed her anything. They'd both been careful to make no promises, conscious of the fleeting nature of their arrangement. There. Problem solved. "Is your carriage here?"

She smiled, recognizing capitulation when she saw it. "It's outside."

"Wait for me there." Easing her arms from his waist, he stepped away. "I'll be right out."

"Are you going to tell her?" Lucinda suppressed a smile. She'd won. But didn't she always?

He nodded. "Give me five minutes."

"I don't want to stay with him anymore," she declared, raising the ante in the event Hugh might be thinking about changing his mind.

"I don't care about him."

"I just wanted you to know," she said.

He nodded, but his heart had done a quick lurch when she'd spoken of leaving her husband. He held up his hand, fingers spread. "Five minutes and I'll be back."

"I'll be waiting," she purred, wiggling her fingers at him in a little wave before turning in a swish of black velvet and lace and walking away.

He stood for a moment watching her, his plans

for St. Cloud equivocal. Sex aside, his physical response aside, after so many years, he wanted some questions answered first. He wanted to know why she'd done what she'd done, what had gone wrong and why. After that, he'd decide whether he wanted sex or not. He half smiled. Or at least he'd try to make a thoughtful decision.

As the doorman waved Lucinda through into the night, Hugh walked to the small library off the lobby. Writing a short note to Tama, he explained that he was going to St. Cloud and would be back the next day. He debated apologizing for leaving with Lucinda, but in the end chose not to. Exclusivity had never been an option in his life since his divorce. In closing, he offered to escort her to Hattori's reception on Wednesday.

Giving the note to a footman as he left, he instructed him to slip it under the door.

There was no point in waking Tama.

He might be back before she woke.

Chapter

33

Lucinda's carriage was luxurious, the seats padded with down, the interior panels inlaid tulipwood, the carriage lights crystal and gilt, the carpet Aubusson. Such splendor was rare—an indication of her husband's wealth or perhaps his nouveau riche status.

"You'd have to give up all this luxury," he drawled as he slid into a sprawl opposite his ex-wife. "This is quite a carriage, not to mention the liveried driver and post boys. You haven't been suffering."

"I never said I was suffering *materially*." Smiling, she patted the seat beside her. "Come a little closer, darling. I like the feel of you."

"Give me a minute," he said, bracing himself as the carriage picked up speed. "Tell me, do you have children?" He didn't know why it mattered, but it did.

Her brows rose fractionally. "Why would I want children?"

"Does your husband share your sentiments?"

She made a small moue. "Hugh, for heaven's sake. Must we talk about Calvin?"

"Calvin?" Hugh fought to restrain his smile and didn't quite succeed.

"You needn't laugh," she said with a little pout. "It's some family name—handed down from some grandfather or great-grandfather who left him a very sizeable fortune, I'll have you know."

"That you're now enjoying."

"It's not a sin to like nice things," she said airily, adjusting her diamond bracelet on her wrist. "As I recall, you're not exactly the economical type. Even when you were young, you bought the most outrageously expensive racehorses. And don't say you didn't," she added with an arch smile.

"I wasn't debating frugality. I was questioning the practice of selling yourself to the highest bidder," he said softly.

"How very rude you are, Hugh Drummond! I hope you don't intend to be tiresome and scold me the entire way to St. Cloud. You don't know how hard it was not to have new gowns or nice parties once the war started. And our slaves all ran away and Mama just cried and cried . . . it was a complete, utter horror. Don't think I didn't try to adjust and make do, but it was awful, Hugh! Do you know I didn't see Paris for four whole years!"

While he was trying to stay alive on the North Atlantic and do his share to bring in enough weapons to keep the Confederate Army on the battlefield, his wife was bemoaning her lack of new gowns and servants. It certainly put things into perspective. "Calvin must have promised you new gowns."

"Really, Hugh, if you're going to be hateful," she said with a petulant toss of her curls, "we might just as well turn the carriage around and go back to Paris."

"I thought you were leaving your husband."

"I'd certainly *like* to. Come, darling, could we please, *please* talk of more pleasant things or," she added softly, "perhaps not talk at all. Do you remember the time we made love in our carriage on the drive in front of my parents' house and the houseboys came running out wondering why we weren't moving?" She winked. "When we were moving very nicely indeed, weren't we?" She squirmed a little, the pulsing between her legs a hard, steady rhythm. "For heaven's sake, Hugh, when are you going to make love to me? I don't want to answer any more senseless questions. I just want to feel your wonderful, great big, beautiful truncheon deep inside—"

"Your hot little cunt?"

"Hugh!" she exclaimed in mock horror. "How terribly vulgar you are"—she smiled—"and deliciously arousing," she finished in a purr. "No one is as big as you, although I suppose you hear that all the time. Bless my soul, I'm getting all frenzied and wet just thinking about you cramming your way in. We fit together so nicely, didn't we? Tight as can be and yet so, so perfect. You've always been my gold standard for lovers, you know."

He didn't care to hear about her lovers, although there was no question her talk of fitting tightly was doing predictable things to his cock.

"Do you remember the first time we made love down by the creek, while our families were having their picnic just around the bend?" she went on, wetting her lips with the tip of her tongue.

"I remember." His voice had dropped half an octave.

"I'm getting hot just thinking about it," she whispered, unclasping her cape, letting it slip from her shoulders, the soft velvet and silky fox puddling on the seat. Fanning herself with her fingers in a flirtatious little gesture, she lounged back and smiled at him—a temptress in black lace.

Her breasts rose above her décolletage in great huge mounds, her tightly corseted waist a handsbreadth wide and lure to the touch, her heated gaze offering him everything. Maybe he should just mount her and fuck her all the way to St. Cloud and screw the questions. He could ask them after he'd come a few dozen times. After all, a fuck was a fuck was a fuck and she was ready and willing, no mistake.

But a curious speculation sprang into his mind as though some small voice of reason still existed in the fevered lust coursing through his brain. "If I stay with you in St. Cloud," he said, "will your husband divorce you?"

"Of course he won't divorce me. But I might divorce him," she murmured, beckoning Hugh with a crooked finger. "If you give me reason to?"

It suddenly struck him with such clarity, he wondered why he'd never thought of it before. Lucinda was for sale. As she'd always been, if he'd allowed himself to face the truth. He'd been the richest young man in Peachtree County, so she'd set her sights on him. But when the war took him away, she'd simply found herself another rich man. That he happened to be a Yankee was incidental.

And unless his bank account was sufficient to lure her away, she would stay right where she was—playing at love while her husband payed the bills.

It wasn't a pretty picture.

"Hugh, really, have you changed so much that I have to come over there and attack you?" she pouted, not familiar with being slighted by a man. "Don't you like what you see?" She posed prettily, her breasts thrust out, her arms open wide. "You always used to—"

"Maybe I'm more discriminating now."

"You're angry with poor little old me, aren't you?" she whispered. "I understand. Maybe I could find someway to apologize. . . ." Her voice was a little girl sweet drawl that had always served her well when men were angry with her. "Would it help if I did this?" Drawing her lace skirt upward, she revealed her shapely legs and a moment later her bare thighs, smooth and pink above her stockings and garters. "Is that better?" she purred, pushing aside her skirts so he could see not even a scrap of lace covering the golden hair on her mount of Venus. "I've really missed you, darling. . . ."

He was trying to decide when he'd crossed that line between unbridled lust and indifference. He was also trying to understand what had overcome him that the hot, wet cunt within reach held no appeal. Even the heady scent of arousal failed to move him when in the past he would have plunged headlong into that aromatic cunt.

Was it possible to become monkish in split seconds? Had he suddenly matured enough to discriminate between sex and desire? Was Lucinda's self-assurance annoying?

Or was it something else?

Someone else.

"I think I'm going to pass," he murmured.

Her eyes flared wide and an instant later an ugly expression distorted her face. "Apparently you've been unmanned since last we met," she spat. "Or after being at sea so long do you prefer men?"

"Neither, actually," he replied mildly. "This just wasn't a good idea. It's not you, Lucinda," he added politely, feeling benevolent in his newly revealed maturity. "Too many years have gone by." He shrugged. "We're different now." Or perhaps, more aptly, he was and she wasn't.

"I still don't think it's very nice of you," she pouted, partially mollified by his explanation, pushing her skirt back down with a flick of her wrist. "I don't see why we couldn't make love just for old time's sake . . . especially since you've always been my favorite."

The implication in being her favorite wouldn't have bothered him a short time ago—even an hour ago. In fact, he'd always preferred the anonymity of being one of a crowd. "Why don't we just shake hands for old time's sake instead," he suggested with a smile.

"Pooh on you, Hugh Drummond. A little healthy sex would be fun."

A little healthy sex with the lady in his bed back in Paris would be more fun, he decided. "Sorry, Lucinda. You'll have to get healthy with someone else."

His calm withdrawal was so confounding she found herself affected by a rare need for candor. "Tell me the truth, Hugh. What happened? And don't worry about hurting my feelings. I doubt I have many left."

"If you don't like your husband, why don't you divorce him?" Hugh inquired pointedly.

"I like his money, sweetheart. He's very, very rich."

"Ah."

"So what stopped you?" she quizzed, in quest of an explanation.

"The princess, I suppose."

"You suppose?"

"I'm not sure. I'm as unattuned to my emotions as you. Perhaps we're both out of practice." He glanced out the window, uncertain of most of his feelings save one. He didn't care to go to St. Cloud. "Let's have this carriage turned around."

"So she won't be angry?"

"I doubt she will. I miss her, that's all."

"Did you ever miss me?"

"Of course," he said in bland reply to his months of unremitting remorse. "This is different, though." *Good different,* he thought, but he wasn't so rude as to verbalize his recent judgment. Reaching up, he banged on the carriage ceiling to get the driver's attention before opening the door enough to lean out and shout, "Go back to Paris!"

On the return trip he learned more about Lucinda's marriage than he cared to know, her conversation exclusively of the petty difficulties of wedded bliss—such as trying to keep up with the numerous social events she was forced to attend with her husband, who simply didn't understand that bankers and bankers' wives were the most boring people on the face of the earth. And then there were the staff problems she disliked and Calvin insisted she attend to when everyone knew that southern women weren't raised to oversee a household; there were perfectly capable servants to do such menial work.

"Yankees are really so much more industrious," she said petulantly. "Work, work, work. I can't imagine spending your entire life making money."

He was feeling too benign to point out that her entire life was devoted to spending it. "It must be hard on you," he said mildly.

"You see why I need diversions—even though you weren't willing to oblige me tonight," she murmured coyly.

"I understand."

"No, you don't, but then, what man does understand a woman," she noted with a dismissive wave. "And by the way, you're the first ever," she added, "in case you wanted to know. . . ."

His brows rose.

"To turn me down."

"I won't tell anyone. Your secret's safe with me." And he seriously began to review the events in his life he'd previously perceived as disastrous—his divorce, the loss of his plantation and home—as perhaps mere prelude to a more satisfying existence.

How would he have survived a lifetime married to someone as shallow as Lucinda?

And worse, he wouldn't have met Tama, he thought, a sudden sense of elation infusing his soul at the revelation of his superb good luck. "So tell me, Lucinda, what do you do when you're not in Paris?" he asked, in expectation of a lengthy monologue. All he'd have to do was nod on occasion or commiserate from time to time—allowing him a considerable interval to reflect on the bright, beautiful, infinitely enchanting woman waiting for him at the Grand.

And curiously, the concept of exclusivity no longer struck him with dread.

Chapter

34

Hugh bid Lucinda adieu with politesse and good wishes for her future and then literally bounded up the stairs to his suite.

Striding through the parlor into the bedroom, he came to an abrupt standstill.

The bed was empty.

After a swift perusal of the suite, there was no question Tama had decamped. So much for his misconceptions about her getting angry. Apparently she'd taken issue with his note—discarded on the table. All the gowns he'd bought for her in Hong Kong were still in the armoire, all the slippers and undergarments left behind. Only her swords were gone and one or two of the kimonos.

He almost smiled, reminded of the first time he'd met her in Edo when she'd been traveling light then, as well. If he hadn't been frustrated by her absence he would have found humor in her ability to move residence with such ease. But Paris was a big city, it was the middle of the night and he was damned tired. If she'd gone to her brother's, he didn't relish the confrontation. It was the obvious destination though, he decided with a sigh. He rang for his carriage.

He knew better than to wake the Prince of Otari at four in the morning. Having the carriage wait by the kitchen garden, he entered by the servants' entrance and found two sleepy maids lighting the kitchen fires. If Tama had arrived in the dead of night, the house would have been wakened, the servants would have been aware of her presence. Neither maid knew of any recent guests in the house. He thanked them with a profound sense of relief and made a quick exit. Fortunately, he wouldn't have to deal with Tama's martinet of a brother. He never knew what to say to people with uncompromising moral codes.

Shortly after dawn he boarded the train to Le Havre.

Hopefully, Tama wouldn't secure passage to Japan before he could locate her. But the hours to Le Havre seemed endless, his mood disquieted. She was a woman of zeal and enterprise. Who knew how intent she was on leaving by the first tide. Exhausted, but unable to sleep, he spent the entire journey in a state of trepidation.

What if he missed her?

How could he possibly find her on the vast Atlantic?

And more pertinently, did he know what he'd do if he did?

* * *

More distressed than she would have thought possible, Tama lay abed in a small inn near the harbor. She could have contacted someone on the *Southern Belle* if she'd been so inclined—talked to Sunskoku or Yukio or Paddy perhaps if they were still in the city. But she'd not been in the mood to discuss her leaving or the reason for her leaving . . . or anything having to do with Hugh. Primarily because she didn't understand in the chaotic tumult of her thoughts what she felt or didn't feel, why it mattered that Hugh had gone to his ex-wife, why she wasn't able to accept the fact that he might still have feelings for Lucinda. And until the actual moment she'd read his note, she considered herself completely rational about the state of their relationship.

It was transient; they'd both agreed.

Their lives were currently so irregular there was scarcely any point in making plans more than a day at a time.

But as she'd perused the few lines he'd written, she'd found herself convulsed with pain and displeasure and a maddening sense of outrage. She immediately knew she didn't wish to be there when he returned. She couldn't bear to hear his lies or see his happiness.

There was no longer room for her in his life.

So here she was in Le Havre, morose, ill-tempered in regard to tall, blonde ex-wives, and completely unable to gather her energy to any good purpose. She felt so out of character she began to wonder if the French air could actually sap the strength from a person.

She sighed, knowing better, of course, knowing

what and who had sapped her energy. And she would return home because she must.

But not today. She didn't have the strength.

Pulling her silk-wrapped swords closer, she hugged them to her body, pulled the quilt over her head and shut her eyes.

Maybe sleep would restore her vitality.

Chapter

35

He woke Paddy when he came aboard the *Southern Belle* and explained his needs.

"We'll send out runners to all the hotels and inns. She's bound to be in one of them."

"Is Yukio still here?"

"I saw him last night. He's in and out at all hours."

"Have Harry see if he's on board. Yukio has contacts we don't."

"It's amazing, but he does. In every port."

"The brotherhood's reach is long. He could help locate Tama."

"Are you sure the princess is in town?"

Yukio asked the same question when he appeared pulling on his jacket a few minutes later.

After apologizing for waking him, Hugh gave his reasons for thinking Tama was in Le Havre. Her brother was briefly discussed as well. "I can't imagine where else she'd go. She's on her way back to Japan."

Yukio's brows rose in query. "Are you taking her?"

"Yes."

Paddy's head swivelled around at Hugh's answer. "The silk's not all unloaded yet."

"Put more men on it. We sail as soon as I find the princess." Hugh turned to Yukio. "Do you have any wish to return to Japan?"

The young yakuza grimaced faintly. "If I had my way, I would. But Sunskoku won't go back. She's deathly afraid of returning. So we stay."

"Here?"

"I'm thinking of buying a business in Paris. Some friends have made me a good offer."

"A legitimate business?"

"It has to be; I can't ask Sunskoku to marry me otherwise. There's no certainty of living a long life in my current profession," he added with a grin. "My mother would be proud." While he spoke lightly, it would have pleased him had his mother lived to see his success. She was his fondest memory of childhood.

"Count me in for the return trip," Paddy offered. "I can see Paris anytime. And there's somethin' to be said for Cecil's hospitality," he cheerfully noted.

"If you return to Japan at some later date when Sunskoku is less frightened, I may go with you. My friends are in the railroad business and Japan's going to need railroads."

"You're welcome anytime on any of my ships." Hugh glanced at the clock. "How long do you think it might be before I have word of the princess?"

"Give me an hour," Yukio said. "This isn't a very big town." And compared to the million souls in Edo, it wasn't.

* * *

When Yukio left, Paddy looked at Hugh with skepticism. "I didn't want to say nothin' with Yukio here, but are you serious? About her, I mean. This ain't no regular trip to Japan, is it?"

"Probably not—provided I get what I want—not always a sure thing with the princess."

"So what the hell do you want—besides her, obviously."

"That's it."

"And she calls the shots?"

"In some things, yes."

"But not in everythin', I hope," Paddy said grimly.

"No," Hugh replied softly. "Not in everything."

Paddy exhaled loudly. "You had me worried there for a minute, Boss. Jesus, I think I need a drink. I don't know what I would have done if'n you were gonna turn into some hen-pecked husband."

Surprise registered on Hugh's face. "I didn't say anything about marriage."

"You didn't have to, Boss. I could tell the minute you come in."

Chapter

36

Tama woke up at the sound of a key turning in the lock. Swiftly unwrapping her swords, she jumped from the bed as the key on the inside of the door fell to the floor.

The door slowly opened and a deep familiar voice said, "Don't slice me up before you listen to my apology."

A moment later, the smile that always brought her joy came into view.

Stepping into the small room, Hugh shut the door and held up both his hands. "I'm unarmed."

"Maybe I don't care." Dressed in trousers and a short jacket, she still held her swords poised.

"I missed you."

"Did she send you on your way?" Tama asked tartly.

"Not exactly."

"Will you be seeing her again?"

He smiled, pleased with her jealousy. "I will never be seeing her again."

"So certain, Hugh-san?"

He liked that she'd referred to him in her native tongue; perhaps they were both tired of France. "I'd like to take you back to Japan if you'd allow me."

"I'm going home to stay—one way or another."

She'd spoken in a firm, live-or-die sort of way. "I understand. I have a small present for you—by way of an apology," he added, pulling an envelope from his jacket pocket. He'd made a short detour via Hattori's, who apparently was about as well connected as one could get.

Hugh wore his sailing clothes, the navy blue wool jacket and dark trousers she'd come to recognize as his uniform. "Did you wear that with her?" It was a woman's question.

"Should I change?"

"I meant wouldn't she have preferred you in evening dress? I'm sure my brother's wife would."

He shrugged. He'd only thought about swiftness and comfort when he'd dressed. "It wasn't high on my list of priorities."

"Did you make love to her?" That would have been on his list, she knew.

"Does it matter?"

"Very much."

"Good." He wanted her to care as much as he. "I didn't touch her, not even a handshake." He disregarded Lucinda's throwing herself into his arms as unavoidable. "I won't be seeing her again—ever. Here, take this. I wanted to give you something you'd like."

"No jewels?" she noted archly, setting one of her swords down to take the envelope from him.

"If you want jewels, we'll get jewels."

"Would you give me diamonds like hers?"

He grinned. "You can have a whole store full of diamonds if you wish."

"I don't."

"I know. Open that. It's better than jewels."

Slicing the envelope open with her short sword, she dropped the envelope to the floor and read the letter written in Japanese characters. It was lengthy and so increasingly astonishing as she continued to read it that she had to sit down on the nearest chair before her knees gave way. At the end, she looked up. "Now why would the emperor's nephew give me carte blanche to return?"

"Why don't we say he was in a benevolent mood."

"You threatened him."

"What good would that do you in Japan? I didn't threaten him. And the letter's only a carte blanche for your return. Once you're home, you'll have to petition the courts like anyone else to reclaim your properties."

"Except he's sending a letter to the high court to expedite my petition."

"Well, he wanted something I had—a couple of things, actually," Hugh said with a smile. "We were able to come to an agreement advantageous to us both."

"What things?"

"Two of my racing yachts. He wants to compete in the Cowes Regatta next year. I promised to teach him how to sail . . . or his crew, more precisely. I doubt any of the royal family are likely to be found hauling canvas."

"You did this for me?"

"For us."

"How exactly is it about us?"

"If you'll marry me, it will be about us. And you'll make me very happy in the bargain."

Her gaze narrowed even as her heart filled with joy. "When did you decide on marriage? I thought we were both too busy for marriage."

"I changed my mind."

"Just like that?"

"My choices were limited when I found you gone."

"Do you think you have but to propose and I will accept?"

He smiled. "Let's say I'm hopeful."

"Even if that hope might be confirmed, I'm not sure I wish my husband to be on board his ship more than he's at home."

"I won't be. Just say yes. We'll figure out the rest."

"We have to talk about—"

"Anything you want—later. Say yes."

"I can't make such a serious decision just like—"

"Jesus, Tama," he growled, advancing on her.

"Very well, yes, but—"

Swiftly closing the distance between them, he pulled her from her chair and curtailed any further reservations she might have with a deep, heated kiss. When his mouth finally lifted from hers, he said, "If you don't want me to sail, I won't."

"You won't?" Still half breathless, the words were a whisper of sound.

"It's been eight very long years at sea. Even Ulysses eventually came home. I want to be married here, though, before we sail."

"In case you change your mind, you mean." She'd been suspicious of his abrupt *volte face*.

He shook his head. "In case you do. I found what I want and need and I'm selfish enough to want to make sure you stay. My motives are not benign."

"Would your motives include love in any way, shape or form?"

He smiled. "I'm sure they would in some ardent, amatory way, shape or form, at least. How about you?"

"I'm of a similar opinion—ardently speaking." Her smile was rueful. "Are we so lacking in the tender sensibilities or simply cynical?"

"I don't have the perfect words to describe how I feel, but I'm keeping you, that I know."

"Why don't we keep each other," she amended carefully. "That does not include you keeping another wife or concubines," she firmly added.

He grinned. "As if I'd have the time, with you to satisfy."

"Good, because I don't share well," she noted, understanding what her father had tried to tell her so long ago. *When you know, you know,* he'd said, refusing to consider another marriage after her mother died. Now she knew why.

"Amen to that. And I'll build you a new home," he murmured, holding her close. "We've both been adrift too long. Although, the *Princess* will be our home for the next few weeks." His smile was boyish. "They're repainting the name as we speak."

"I'm honored, so long as you don't paint over my name if you become angry with me."

"If I become angry with you, I know a much better way to have my revenge."

She loved that tone. "Such as?"

"Such as spanking your sweet little bottom."

"What if I run?"

"You won't get far."

"Is that a promise?" she purred.

He quickly surveyed the room. "Guaranteed . . . that's a mighty small bed over there."

"Were you thinking about sleeping?"

He laughed. "Not likely with you."

"Oh, good."

"No kidding. But we only have an hour. The ship's being refueled; we sail on the tide."

"I'll have to settle for an hour, then."

"A half hour. There's a preacher waiting downstairs."

"And when we reach Japan, we'll have a priest marry us."

"Whatever you want, darling." But he wanted it legal in the West because the emperor's nephew aside, if something should happen to him, he wanted her to inherit his shipping company. Or their children, he thought, with a small lurch of his heart.

"Twenty-nine minutes," she whispered.

"Sorry. Where were we?"

"On the bed . . . almost."

"At your service, ma'am," he drawled, sweeping her up in his arms and moving toward the bed. "With twenty-nine minutes you can only come ten times," he said, grinning.

"That's what I love about you," she said cheerfully.

His brows rose in query.

"Your generosity."

Placing her on the bed, he followed her down, resting lightly above her, his smile only inches away. "It's not generosity, sweetheart, it's mad, irrepressible lust. I can't get enough of you."

"Starting now?" she suggested, wiggling out of her trousers.

"Starting now," he murmured, an old hand at swiftly unbuttoning his clothes. "And always and ever," he whispered, slowly entering her a moment later.

But she was no longer listening.

She was enjoying the hot tidal wave of pleasure beginning to inundate her senses.

He shut his eyes against the fierce, riveting shock to his brain, took a measured breath and plunged deeper.

Her soft whimper intensified in little breathy resonances as he thrust and withdrew in perfect harmony with her urgent desire, her soft cries ascending in frenzied degrees as his rhythm tumultuously matched hers, until her orgasm exploded and she screamed in wild, irrepressible ecstasy.

He smiled.

It was going to be a very good life.

For the next twenty-some minutes.

And for the foreseeable future.

Epilogue

The castle of Otari was rebuilt in the cloud-covered northern mountains, the roses that had been planted by a long ago prince bloomed once again, and a son was born one day to inherit his mother's titled property and his father's fortune. He was a much beloved child, an only child for many years until the miracle of a sister came into his life when he was almost grown.

It was a time of rapid change in Japan and around the world, the mechanized forces of commerce and war overwhelming the ancient ways. But the Otari heir learned the art of Bushido as had each Otari prince since feudal times and took up the brush to write a fine hand as was expected of a man of his lineage. But he was a world traveler before he was three, his family dividing their time between Japan, Europe and America. He spoke more languages than a well-traveled diplomat, was schooled at the Sorbonne and was as much at ease in the fashionable set as he was with the Tendai monks at home.

His beauty cast a spell over any woman who met him, but why wouldn't it, anyone who knew his father would say. There was a certain fascination in a handsome, virile young man with money.

He became friends at a young age with a yakuza's son who'd been born in France and the two boys were inseparable whenever their paths crossed. The yakuza's son lived primarily in Paris, but he joined his father on his frequent trips to Japan and he too bore his father's stamp with a prideful swagger.

When the two young bloods were on the town, there was no telling what might happen. They were wild and willful and unutterably charming.

It was a volatile mix.

They made plans to meet in Paris for their twenty-fifth birthdays.

Those who knew them well prayed the city was ready.

Here's a peek at UNDONE,
the historical romance anthology featuring
Susan Johnson, Terri Brisbin, and Mary Wine.
Turn the page for a preview of Susan's story,
"As You Wish."

Fortunately for the earl's pressing schedule, the night was overcast. Not a hint of moonlight broke through to expose his athletic form as he scaled the old, fist-thick wisteria vines wrapped around the pillars of the terrace pergola. The house to which the pergola was attached was quiet, the ground floor dark save for the porter's light in the entrance hall. Either the Belvoirs were out or already in bed. More likely the latter with only a single flambeau outside the door.

He'd best take care.

Kit had described the position of Miss Belvoir's bedchamber—hence Albion's ascent of the wisteria. Once he gained the roof joists of the Chinoiserie pergola, he would have access to the windows of the main floor corridor. From there he could make his way to the second floor bedchambers, the eastern most that of Miss Belvoir, where, according to Kit, she'd been cloistered for the last month, being polished by her stepmother into a state of refined elegance for her bow into society a few weeks hence.

Which refinements, in his estimation, only served to make every young lady into the same boring martinet without an original thought in her head or a jot of conversation worth listening to.

Hopefully, there wouldn't be much conversation tonight. If he had his way there wouldn't be any. He hoped as well that she wouldn't prove stubborn, but should she, he'd stuff his handkerchief in her mouth to muffle her screams, tie her up if necessary, and carry her down the back stairs and out the servants' entrance. It was more likely, though—with all due modesty—that his much practiced charm would win the day.

Pulling himself over the fretwork balustrade embellishing the pergola, he stood for a moment balanced on a joist contemplating which window would best offer him ingress. His mind made up, he brushed himself off, navigated the vine-draped timbers, and reached the window. Taking a knife from his coat pocket, he snapped open the blade, slipped it under the lower sash, and pried it up enough to gain a finger hold.

Moments later, he stood motionless in the dark corridor. The stairs were to the right if Kit's description was correct. After listening for a few moments and hearing nothing, he quietly made his way down the plush carpet and up the stairs. A single candle on a console table dimly illuminated the hallway onto which the bedrooms opened. Pausing to listen once again and distinguishing no undue sounds, he silently traversed the carpeted passageway to the last door on his right.

It shouldn't be locked. Servants required access if the bell pull by the bed was rung. For a brief moment he stood utterly still, wondering what in blazes he was doing here about to abduct some untried maid in order to seduce her. As if there weren't women enough in London who would welcome him to their beds with open arms. Considerable brandy was to blame, he supposed, along with the rackety company of his friends who had too much idle time on their hands in which to conjure up wild wagers like this.

Bloody hell. He felt the complete absence of any desire to be where he was.

On the other hand, he decided with a short exhalation, he'd bet twenty thousand on this foolishness.

Now it was play or pay.

He reached for the latch, pressed down, and quietly opened the door.

As he stepped over the threshold he was greeted by a ripple of scent and a cheerful female voice. "I thought you'd changed your mind."

The hairs on the back of his neck rose.

He was unarmed was his first thought.

It was a trap was his second.

But when the same genial voice said, "Don't worry, no one's at home but me. Do come in and shut the door," his pulse rate lessened and he scanned the candlelit interior for the source of the invitation.

"Miss Belvoir, I presume," he murmured, taking note of a young woman with hair more gold than red standing across the room near the foot of the bed. *She was quite beautiful. How nice. And if no one was home, nicer still.* Shutting the door behind him, he offered her a graceful bow.

"A pleasant good evening, Albion. Gossip preceded you." *He was breathtakingly handsome at close range. Now to convince him to take her away.* "I have a proposition for you."

He smiled. "A coincidence. I have one for you." This was going to be easier than he thought. Then he saw her luggage. "You first," he said guardedly.

"I understand you have twenty thousand to lose."

"Or not."

"Such arrogance, Albion. You forget, the decision is mine."

"Not entirely," he replied softly.

"Because you've done this before."

"Not this. But something enough like it to know."

"I see," she murmured. "But then *I'm* not inclined to be instantly infatuated with your handsome self or your prodigal repute. I have more important matters on my mind."

"More important than twenty thousand?" he asked with a small smile.

"I like to think so."

He recognized the seriousness of her tone. "Then we must come to some agreement. What do you want?"

"To strike a bargain."

"Consider me agreeable to most anything," he smoothly replied.

"My luggage caused you a certain apprehension, I noticed," she said, amusement in her gaze. "Let me allay your fears. I have no plans to elope with you. Did you think I did?"

"The thought crossed my mind." He wasn't entirely sure yet that some trap wasn't about to be sprung. She was the picture of innocence in white muslin—all the rage thanks to Marie Antoinette's penchant for the faux rustic life.

"I understand that women stand in line for your amorous skills, but rest assured—you're not my type. Licentiousness is your raison d'être I hear: a very superficial existence I should think."

His brows rose. He wondered if she'd heard about Sally's when she mentioned women standing in line. She also had the distinction of being the first woman to find him lacking. "You mistake my raison d'être. Perhaps if you knew me better you'd change your mind," he pleasantly suggested.

"I very much doubt it," she replied with equal amiability. "You're quite beautiful, I'll give you that, and I understand you're unrivaled in the boudoir. But my interests, unlike yours, aren't focused on sex. What I do need from you, however, is an escort to my aunt's house in Edinburgh."

"And for that my twenty thousand is won?" His voice was velvet soft.

"Such tact, my lord."

"I can be blunt if you prefer."

"Please do. I've heard so much about your ready charm. I'm wondering how you're going to ask."

"I hadn't planned on asking."

"Because you never have to."

He smiled. "To date at least."

"So I may be the exception."

"If you didn't need an escort to Edinburgh," he mildly observed. "Your move."

"You see this as a game?"

"In a manner of speaking."

"And I'm the trophy or reward or how do young bucks describe a sportive venture like this?"

"How do young ladies describe the snaring of a husband?"

She laughed. "Touché. I have no need of a husband, though. Does that calm your fears?"

"I have none in that regard. Nothing could induce me to marry."

"Then we are in complete agreement. Now tell me, how precisely does a libertine persuade a young lady to succumb to his blandishments?"

"Not like this," he drily said. "Come with me and I'll show you."

"We strike our bargain first. Like you, I have much at stake."

"Then, Miss Belvoir," he said with well-bred grace, "if you would be willing to relinquish your virginity tonight, I'd be delighted to escort you to Edinburgh."

"In the morning. Or later tonight if we can deal with this denouement expeditiously."

"At week's end," he countered. "After the Spring Meet in Newmarket."

"I'm sorry. That's not acceptable."

He didn't answer for so long she thought he might be willing to lose twenty thousand. He was rich enough.

"We can talk about it at my place."

"No."

Another protracted silence ensued, only the crackle of the fire on the hearth audible.

"Would you be willing to accompany me to Newmarket?" he finally said. "I can assure you anonymity at my race box. Once the Spring Meet is over, I'll take you to Edinburgh." He blew out a small breath. "I've a fortune wagered on my horses. I don't suppose you'd understand."

This time she was the one who didn't respond immediately, and when she did, her voice held a hint of melancholy. "I do understand. My mother owned the Langley stud."

"That was your mother's? By God—the Langley stud was legendary. Tattersalls was mobbed when it was sold. You *do* know how I feel about my racers, then." He grinned. "They're all going to win at Newmarket. I'll give you a share if you like—to help set you up in Edinburgh."

Her expression brightened and her voice took on a teasing intonation. "Are you trying to buy my acquiescence?"

"Why not? You only need give me a few days of your time. Come with me. You'll enjoy the races."

"I mustn't be seen."

Ah—capitulation. "Then we'll see that you aren't. Good Lord—the Langley stud. I'm bloody impressed. Let me get your luggage."